ALSO BY KEVIN ROBERT ALDRICH

Mysteries & Thrillers

Cameron Hauk Mysteries

Eyes in the Dark

Key Witness

Scale of Justice

Tête A Tête

Romance

Flames of Freedom

Bare Trap

Spellbound

Racing Hearts

Alli & Ollie

TÊTE-A-TÊTE

KEVIN ROBERT ALDRICH

ALDYS BOOKS

Tête-a-Tête

TÊTE-A-TÊTE

For Holly, Jayda, and Taegon

1

Even though the high-tech mansion had been built to be impressive, Cameron Hauk wasn't impressed. When he slipped undetected through the delivery entrance to the kitchen, he wasn't surprised, either, by what he saw.

The mansion was as cold and tasteless on the inside as it seemed from the outside. A drone's-eye view of the property looked like a series of concrete boxes stacked on top of each other by a careless two-year-old. According to Celina, Pete Dufresne, the tech bro mega-millionaire who owned the house, fit that description perfectly.

Inside, the concrete theme continued. The walls were a dark grey textured variety. They were offset by polished light grey floors. Even the ceilings high above looked like they were made of the stuff. There were windows twenty feet high and thirty feet wide, with gentle yellow lighting throughout the space to soften the feel, but all that concrete made the home seem cold, sterile, and imposing. Very trendy in Silicon Valley circles. Definitely not to Cam's taste.

Cam carried a thin wooden crate slung over his shoulder, one leather-gloved hand holding on to the wide, padded nylon strap. As he crept quietly through the house, careful not to let the crate drag on the ground or bang against anything, he took note of the furnishings and the appointments. Everything was designer-chic and high-quality, redolent with the reek of wealth in the stylish lines of the furniture, the sleek interior design, the brushed aluminum accents on the sconces, the table edges, the light fixtures. It was beautiful. And sterile. It was the kind of home that seemed like no one lived in it.

Befitting its owner, the house was tricked out with all of the latest smart home and smart security equipment. Infrared and heat-detecting cameras covered every inch of the property, inside and out. There were no door handles or light switches visible. If they weren't automated, the lights were voice-controlled, and every door had NFC proximity sensors that would automatically unlock and swing open the door when an authorized user came near. The floors had radiant heating throughout to keep that concrete from freezing the owner's bare feet. And, of course, every imaginable gadget, dial, and gauge in the house was connected to wi-fi so it could be controlled by a smartphone or a tablet from anywhere in the world.

Not that Dufresne ever used any of those gadgets or checked any of those dials or gauges. He just liked to say he could. Beyond the tech and the ostentatious price of the home, his favorite thing to crow about was the cantilevered design of the house. "Pushing the envelope," he would say. "Frank Lloyd Wright on pure bio-available creatine. Designed it myself in AutoCAD, with a little help from a custom AI, of course."

To Cam, like so much else that passed for innovation in Silicon Valley, it seemed to him like a massive waste of money.

A lot of money. Aside from the cost of the technology, the house itself was enormous. It had to be at least fifteen thousand square feet. From the inside, all the space and concrete made Cam feel like he was walking through a very clean, very large shipping container. He wore soft-soled, non-marking sneakers and stepped quickly, carefully, and soundlessly through the cavernous space, careful to keep the crate he carried close by his side, one arm steadying it to keep it from swinging around his hip as he moved.

The crate wasn't overly heavy, nor was it overly huge, only about four feet by six feet. The shoulder strap and the handles set into the side made it straightforward to carry, but the crate was still awkward to maneuver. The last thing Cam wanted was to knock down a vase or a lamp and alert the homeowner.

Dufresne was in his late-forties, divorced, with two resentful teenage daughters who lived with their mom on the East coast. He had thinning blonde hair cut into a quoiff he could not pull off, thick stylish black glasses too large for his face, and a round, chonky dad-bod that did not fit into the skinny jeans and t-shirts he wore every day.

He'd risen to SVP level in a social media company, then hit the jackpot when it IPO'd. Instantly, Dufresne's net worth shot to nine digits, which only seemed to encourage his already puerile and insecure nature. Divorce followed soon after.

Cam could hear Dufresne, now the sole inhabitant of the massive home, playing some kind of immersive VR first-person shooter while cranking death metal through ten-foot speakers five rooms over. From the volume of the echoes careering through the cavernous house, there was little chance Dufresne would be hearing anything but ringing in his ears for the rest of the night.

Even so, Cam didn't work sloppy. His parents had taught him better than that. He stepped softly and took care with the wooden crate.

"The gallery is the next door on your right."

Celina's voice in Cam's earpiece was low and sultry. After nine months together, including the last five where they had been living together in Celina's beach house in San Francisco,

Cam still felt a thrill roll through him at the sound of her voice. He smiled to himself, then pushed aside the thoughts that instantly came into his mind.

He would think about those things later. Definitely.

But not until the job was done.

From years of training and an abundance of caution, he checked his augmented-reality glasses for signs of anyone nearby. Seeing no one, he angled from the shadows toward the door Celina had mentioned. It glowed with a soft blue highlight in the view through his glasses.

Cam had obtained the prototype glasses in a job almost two years earlier from the home lab of the tech genius Christopher Nestrom. While Cam was there at the house, Dr. Nestrom had met an unfortunate end at the hands of his own family. Cam had managed to escape without being implicated in the death, but only barely. Despite the murder and the mess, he'd still managed to lift the tech on his way out. All in all, it had been a rewarding few days of work.

Since then, Celina had made some modifications to the glasses. Turns out she had a prototype of her own, one she had invented and built herself, similar in design and function to the Nestech glasses. Comparing the two, she found a few new features to add to her prototype, and tweaked Cam's hardware to add several new features to his, including eye tracking, sub-vocal amplification and transmission, and auto-sync with the glasses she and Cam's mother, Paulie, wore. Now, with a simple command, Cam could switch his view to show him what Paulie or Celina were seeing and hearing.

The glasses also showed Cam any people in the area for miles around. If they were near an internet-connected camera, he could see them, along with whatever personal information facial recognition and data mining could provide. Cam could see Celina around the corner in the windowless panel van, working on her laptop and waiting for Cam to return.

Cam smiled a little. Even her avatar in the glasses made him smile. He was over the edge and off the deep end, for sure.

At the moment, though, Cam was mainly concerned with Dufresne. Celina had hacked the home security system. Dufresne thought he had military-grade home security, and maybe he did. But that hadn't stopped Celina from hacking it in less than ten minutes.

She had tapped into a camera view of the game room. From a window inset in the lower-right corner of Cam's screen, he could see that Dufresne was standing on a thick carpet in the center of a huge room, leather couches and large-screen TVs lining the walls. He wore grey skinny jeans, no shoes or socks, and no shirt. His rotund belly swelled over his waistband like bread dough that had risen for too long. Sweat glistened on his hairless chest under the soft recessed lighting from above. He wore a massive VR headset that covered the top half of his head. Though Cam couldn't hear what Dufresne was saying over the din of the metal music, he could see that Dufresne was shouting like a testosterone-flooded teenager, spinning in circles, shooting computer-generated enemies and generally acting like the infantile asshole he was.

With that idiot safely distracted, Cam approached the door.

"Notifications disabled," said Celina in his earpiece.

Cam held up his smartwatch to trigger the door to unlock and open. The action would have popped an alert into Dufresne's VR headset. With notifications disabled, the tech bro would have no idea.

Cam slipped inside, careful not to scrape the crate against the doorjamb. The door closed automatically behind him. "I'm in."

He spoke in a hushed whisper, a sub-vocalization barely loud enough to hear himself. Because of the amplification technology Celina had added to the glasses, when the message transmitted to Paulie and Celina, it would be loud and clear, and in Cam's natural voice.

"Notifications re-enabled," said Celina. If notifications were disabled for too long, Dufresne would see a different kind of alert. The security really wasn't that hard to bypass, but there were enough checks and balances that Cam and the others had to stay on their toes.

Cam took a moment to assess the room. They'd spent hours studying floor plans and camera feeds for the last two weeks, but being physically inside a space was a completely different experience. He closed his eyes and pulled in several long, slow breaths, let his heart rate slow and settle, then took the time to extend his senses into the room, to feel the volume of it, the weight and quality of the air, the smells and the sounds.

The air felt still and heavy and old. That meant there was little circulation. But it didn't feel stale. There must be a ventilation and purification system somewhere, perhaps one that worked very slowly, or only at long intervals.

Cam pulled in another slow breath. He could smell leather and old cigar smoke and a slight chemical smell, the kind that came from new carpet that hadn't been aired out.

Sounds were muffled, leaving the room deathly silent. Cam could no longer hear the heavy metal music at all. He cleared his throat softly. The room seemed to swallow the sound, as if sound was not allowed to exist in that space.

And when Cam opened his eyes, he could see why. Thick pile carpet lined the floor from wall to wall. A brown leather couch and two leather armchairs were situated around a long coffee table in the center of the space, angled toward the far wall. The lighting was dim, emerging from an LED strip hidden behind a large square coffer set into the ceiling.

The room had no windows. Oak bookcases stained dark brown covered two opposing walls from floor to ceiling, filled with leather-bound volumes—the kind you would buy in a set from a book dealer—and large-format books with huge letters on their spines, showing titles like *Picasso*, *Dali*, and *The Impressionist Masters*. Coffee table art books, shelved as if they were ancient scholarly tomes.

On the wall beside Cam was a long, well-stocked bar, with expensive, artisanal liquors lining several shelves above a small sink, stylish crystal glasses in all shapes and sizes stacked and hung to one side, and a wine rack, a wine cooler, and a small refrigerator underneath.

But the focal point of the room, the focal point of Cam's attention, was directly opposite the door. The only thing hung on the wide wall, under a soft spotlight in the center, was a painting. A modest thing, only about three feet by five feet, held in a simple black wood frame, hand-carved and sturdy, but unadorned. The image showed a nude woman, reclined, with her hands crossed behind her head, oriented vertically on the canvas. The colors were muted, simple tans and reds and blacks against a green and red and black background.

There was nothing garish in the colors. But the painting itself was stunning. Cam's breath hitched in his chest when he laid eyes on it. This was no ordinary painting.

This was *femme nue*, the naked woman. Also known as *La Danseuse d'Avignon*, the dancer of Avignon.

This was an original Picasso from 1907.

This was the painting Cam had come to steal.

2

CAM DOUBLE-CHECKED the camera view in his AR glasses to make sure Dufresne was still occupied with his video game. He had the sound turned off, so he couldn't hear the feed, but he saw Dufresne standing spread-legged, holding both arms out straight and shaking them violently like he was loosing a barrage of bullets from an automatic rifle in each hand, Rambo-style. Then, he threw his head back, arched his spine, and opened his mouth wide in what appeared to be a victorious laugh.

The man was an imbecile.

Cam padded across the thick, soundless carpet to stand before the Picasso. His heart pumped heavy in his ears. Up close, the painting was even more stunning. The colors that had seemed muted from a distance leapt off the canvas up close. The cubist style, the juxtaposition of hues, the design that was simultaneously both completely benign and incredibly suggestive in Picasso's inimitable style. It all hit Cam at once.

That, plus the fact that he was standing in front of one of the most expensive privately-held paintings in the world. No public sale of this painting had ever been recorded, but esti-

8

mates put its value upwards of $250 million. If it fetched even half that much, the painting was still worth a fortune.

And here it was hanging in the mansion of some tech bro prick who didn't even know what he had. He'd just bought it so he could brag to his cronies. The fact that Cam could smell cigar smoke in the room, that Dufresne would hang a painting that was more than one hundred years old in the open air in a room where he smoked fucking cigars was a criminal act, in Cam's opinion.

Didn't matter. After tonight, the painting would be in better hands.

Cam slipped the nylon strap off his shoulder and set the crate on the ground. The sides were wide enough that the crate stood on its own, its height just above Cam's waist. He pressed a button on the side and the top of the crate popped up about one inch on one side. The top was hinged on the opposite side.

Cam swung it open and drew out a roll of translucent glassine paper and a roll of beige cotton muslin that had been tucked against the inside corners of the crate. He set the rolls on the ground beside the coffee table behind him and pushed the crate until it was parallel to the Picasso and just underneath it.

A sculpted glass vase stood in the center of the coffee table, half-full with glass beads colored pale blue and sea green. A single stem with a cluster of purple orchid flowers at the end rose up from among the beads.

Cam gave the petals a quick sniff. Fake. Naturally.

He set the vase on one of the leather armchairs beside the table. With the table now clear, Cam unrolled a layer of muslin across the surface, leaving the remainder rolled at the edge, then did the same with the glassine paper, layering it on top of the muslin.

He turned back to the Picasso. They'd scouted the room as

best they could ahead of time through the camera feeds and Celina's inspection of the home security system once she'd hacked into it. They hadn't found any evidence of a security system specific to the Picasso, but now that he was in the room Cam wanted to check again, just to be sure. Again, from an abundance of caution.

Cam inspected the wall around the painting and the ceiling above, looking for sensors or wires or any evidence of a security system. Finding none, he pulled a scanner from his pocket and waved it slowly around the painting, looking for evidence of radio signals, bluetooth signals, or any other kind of signal that might indicate an alarm trigger of some kind.

He found nothing.

Dufresne was truly an idiot. One of the most valuable paintings in the world, made by one of the greatest painters in history, and Dufresne just hung it on his wall with no protection and no security, like it was nothing more than a cheap reproduction.

In a few minutes, that's exactly what Dufresne would have.

Celina had told him the story of how she'd first learned about Dufresne and the painting. She'd met Dufresne years earlier at a party he'd hosted for the tech elite in Silicon Valley, just a few months after his divorce had been finalized. He'd slicked his hair back for the evening, worn too-tight leather pants and a matching jacket, and gotten far too drunk, then bounced around the house, yelling about his new-found freedom, slobbering over all the women that were there and generally making everyone uncomfortable.

Celina had come in, the blaring music deafening as it echoed throughout the house. She spent three minutes getting the vibe of the place, then was on her way back out the door when Dufresne swept her into a tour he was giving to a handful of bemused guests. He threw his arm around her shoulders and manhandled her into walking along with him.

His breath reeked of bourbon and Altoids, and the way he walked, Celina was carrying him more than he was steering her. He held a full tumbler of whiskey in his other hand. It sloshed over the lip with each step and splashed onto the floor.

Celina was about to drop him right there on the concrete and walk out when he steered her and the rest of the group into the room with the Picasso.

And then she did drop him. She slid his arm off her shoulder, turned him toward the other guests, and propped him against a wall while he gave them his spiel about the painting.

Celina approached the canvas alone. She examined the work closely. It wasn't a print. The paint wasn't new and the colors didn't look to Celina like modern paint colors. The brush strokes seemed to match other Picassos she'd seen in museums and display collections. If it was a reproduction, it was an old one, and a very good one.

She lifted the frame away from the wall to examine the backing. The canvas was gallery-wrapped, with the excess tucked safely and carefully inside a second wooden stretcher. But what she could see of the canvas looked like linen, not a more modern cotton material. She turned on the flashlight on her phone and held it up to the back of the canvas, then looked at it from the front. She could see light coming through from the back, and couldn't see any grid lines or other marks that might suggest a forgery.

Celina was no art appraiser, but the painting seemed like a real Picasso to her.

She was no Picasso expert, either, but the painting looked like *La Danseuse d'Avignon*, a preparatory study Picasso had made before painting the famous *Les Demoiselles d'Avignon*, which was part of the permanent collection of the Museum of Modern Art in New York City.

"Cost me a pretty penny, believe me," slurred Dufresne to

the crowd still waiting by the door. Celina turned to look at them. Not one of the six guests seemed remotely interested in the painting, or in Dufresne, for that matter. They were all checking their phones, nodding blankly at Dufresne, looking like they were waiting for the tour to end.

"Where did you get this?" called Celina from across the room.

Dufresne turned his bleary-eyed attention to her. Gratitude washed over the faces of the other guests. They all made their exit while Dufresne weaved around the furniture toward Celina.

She moved several steps to the side of the Picasso. She didn't want the fumes from Dufresne's breath to damage the painting.

"You like this?" he said. He gestured toward the painting, sending a large drop of whiskey hurtling toward the canvas. Celina held her breath as she watched it arc through the air, then let out a grim sigh of relief as it curved downward and landed harmlessly on the carpet. She pulled Dufresne several feet further back and angled him in a safer direction.

"Where did you get it?" she repeated.

"Cost me a pretty penny," he slurred, repeating his line from a moment earlier.

"I'm sure it did," Celina said. "Where. Did. You. Get it."

Dufresne shrugged in an attempt at casualness. As drunk as he was, he just sloshed more whiskey onto the carpet— with no risk to the Picasso—and stumbled back onto his heels, swaying backward as he struggled to regain his balance.

"A friend of a friend." He swayed forward again and leaned toward Celina, eyes opening wide. "In Rome," he said, then nodded slowly as he swayed away again. "Italy," he added. He took another sip from his drink, his wide eyes staring meaningfully at Celina.

The man was too drunk to be of much use, but she might be able to get a few more details.

"Bet it cost you a pretty penny," said Celina, leading the horse to familiar water.

Dufresne leaned in, eyes even wider, and pointed at Celina.

"Ninety," he said, then looked unsteadily over his shoulder before looking back at Celina. "Million."

Celina was actually impressed. "That is a lot," she said.

Dufresne leaned back and squeezed his eyes shut, frowning and nodding slowly and solemnly. "Hell of a lot more than that prick Suckerbird paid for his shitty fucking Care Vag... Car Bag..."

"Caravaggio."

"Carve Edge..."

"Caravaggio."

Dufresne pointed at Celina and nodded. "Care Vagina," he said, then heard what he'd said, squinted his eyes shut again and snickered, a soundless wheeze. When he opened his eyes again, he looked at Celina in a different way, as if the word "vagina" had triggered an instinctive response in him. He scanned her from head to toe and back again.

That was Celina's cue to leave.

She turned and walked halfway to the door without a word of goodbye, then thought better of it. She returned to the wobbling Dufresne. His confused frown brightened to a knowing leer when he saw her come back, then into a frown again when she pulled the tumbler from his hand, dumped its contents onto the carpet, then dropped the empty glass onto the floor and walked out.

A legitimate Picasso, in the possession of a legitimate idiot.

Now, years later, Cam was about to correct that particular glitch in the universe.

He pulled off his leather gloves and stuffed them in his

back pants pocket, then took a pair of nitrile gloves from his front pocket and worked his hands into them. He reached into the crate and carefully drew a rectangular fiberboard frame from it. The fiberboard was thin, but about six inches deep. Halfway down the side was a narrow shelf that ran the perimeter of the rectangle. Clipped onto that shelf was a painting. Cam unclipped the painting and held it up beside the Picasso.

Nearly identical.

The composition was exact. The reference images they'd found online were good. Color reproduction in photos is always a problem, but the colors and the paint strokes were very close. An expert appraiser would see it as a fake from a mile away, but to the average viewer the two paintings would be indistinguishable from each other.

And there was no way in hell Pete Dufresne would ever notice the change.

Cam and Celina had done good work.

Cam leaned the reproduction against the crate, then set the fiberboard frame on the coffee table on top of the glassine and muslin. He turned back to the wall and ran his gloved hands over the frame of the Picasso, checking once more for any sign of a trip wire or a sensor. Finding nothing, he gently grasped either side of the wood frame and lifted, slowly and carefully. After a moment of resistance, the frame slid easily up and off the wall, leaving behind two picture hooks and a gaping, empty space.

Cam turned and stood the picture frame upright on the thick carpet. He pulled a multi-tool from his back pocket, unfolded it to a set of pliers, and pried up the retainer clips holding the canvas in the frame. He eased the canvas out, letting the now-empty frame tilt forward and thunk softly against the carpet.

In that moment, the thought struck Cam that not only was he holding $250 million dollars worth of art in his hand, not only was he holding a priceless piece of history, he was holding the very same canvas that Pablo Picasso, the master himself, had held over a hundred years earlier.

Cam felt a bead of sweat drip across his left temple. He balanced the canvas in his right hand and wiped the sweat away with his left shoulder. The last thing he wanted was for his own perspiration to soil Picasso's canvas.

He held the canvas with both hands on the inside of the canvas stretcher, stood slowly, and turned toward the coffee table. He set the Picasso face-up in the fiberboard frame, letting it rest against the narrow shelf, supported as if floating in the center of the fiberboard. Carefully, Cam reached underneath and clicked the retaining clips against the back of the canvas stretcher, then stood back and breathed a long, slow sigh, careful to turn his head away from the Picasso. Sweat was no good. Neither was spit.

Step one, the hard part, was done. The Picasso was safely in the holder.

Holding the glassine roll and the muslin roll together, Cam quickly wrapped fiberboard frame several times. He used the knife on his multi-tool to cut the glassine and muslin, then rotated the frame ninety degrees and wrapped it again.

He didn't have tape to secure the wrappings, but he cut the last wrap so that the edge fell on a corner of the fiberboard. He held the edge tight as he lifted the frame and slid it carefully into the crate. Cam had built the crate himself, including a slot that was perfectly fitted to the fiberboard frame, holding it suspended in the middle of the crate. The loose edge of the wrapping slid tight against the slot. It wasn't going to go anywhere.

The crate held the wrapped fiberboard frame suspended

in the center. The fiberboard frame held the canvas suspended in the center. All engineered to protect the Picasso as well as possible.

Cam snapped the hinged lid shut on the crate. Step two, done. The Picasso was packed for transit.

He put his leather gloves back on and made short work of setting the reproduction in the old frame and hanging it on the wall. There was no need for special care anymore. So long as there were no finger marks or other blemishes on the painting or the frame, it would be fine. Cam finished the hanging, replaced the fake flower, gathered his tools, and slipped the strap of the crate over one shoulder. He moved to the back of the room to admire his handiwork.

It looked perfect. To a inexpert eye, everything looked exactly like it had when Cam walked into the room.

"All done," he whispered into the headset as he moved toward the door. "Ready to leave."

Celina had been quiet, no doubt giving him space to concentrate. Cam checked his watch. The whole process had taken less than four minutes.

He heard no reply from Celina.

"Ready to leave," Cam whispered, again eyeing the far wall, the floor, and the coffee table, looking for anything he might have missed. "Disable notifications."

Again, no response.

He felt his pulse thump in his ears, then closed his eyes and took a long, deep calming breath. Everything was fine. Dufresne was oblivious, playing his VR game and listening to heavy metal.

Calmly, he said, "Celina, acknowledge."

"I'm here," she said. "Sorry about that, Cam."

Cam released a long breath and opened his eyes.

"We have a problem."

Cam's eyes darted to the window in the corner of his viewscreen, the camera feed of the room Dufresne was in.

The room was empty.

Dufresne was gone.

3

CAM'S PULSE thumped in his ears again. He ignored it, relying on his years of training to focus on what was happening around him, not on his emotional reaction to it. Don't ignore the emotions, but don't let them control you, either. That's what his parents had always taught him.

Dufresne had stopped playing his video game and left the room. No problem. He could have just gone to the bathroom or to the kitchen for a beer. Cam checked the screen in his AR glasses for Dufresne's current position.

Instinctively, his eye was drawn first to Celina's avatar, still outside in the van. And then he could see Dufresne.

Right behind him, on the other side of the door.

Cam spun and checked the hinges. They were on the inside of the room and on the opposite side of the door. The door would swing inward, with the opening toward him.

Just as it swung open, Cam darted across the face of the door. The door itself would hide him, for a little while.

Cam peeked through the crack between the doorjamb and the open door. Dufresne was there, a step from the doorway. If it were possible for Cam to reach through the crack, he could have tapped Dufresne on the shoulder.

And Dufresne was coming in.

The doorbell rang, a deep *bong-bong*, like the sound of church bells on a Sunday morning. Not the doorbell Cam would have expected. He would have guessed more of a trumpet fanfare or the 8-bit music from the end of a Super Mario level.

"Fucking hell," Dufresne muttered, stopping short in the doorway. He spoke under his breath, but he was close enough that Cam could hear it clearly even without the sound amplification his glasses provided.

Dufresne pulled his phone from his pocket and tapped on the screen. Through the crack, Cam could see that he was pulling up a camera view of the front porch.

There was no one there.

"Piece of shit," Dufresne said, then shoved his phone back in his pocket.

And came into the room.

Cam was still hidden by the open door, but it was automated. If no one shut it manually or stood in the doorway to keep it open, it would shut itself after a certain amount of time.

Leaving Cam totally exposed.

"Keep the door open," he said under his breath. He knew Celina would hear it clearly.

"Working on it," came her reply. Cam could hear keys clacking furiously on her laptop keyboard in the background.

In the meantime, he needed a plan.

In his glasses, he could see Dufresne's avatar standing at the bar. He heard ice dropping into a glass, bottles clinking against one another, the snick and thump of the refrigerator door opening and closing, the brief splatter of water in the sink.

Dufresne's attention was occupied. Cam couldn't see him,

but there was a good chance his back was toward the room while he fixed his drink.

Cam had only seconds before either the door closed or Dufresne turned from the bar. Or both.

If he was going to do something, he had to do it now.

With a soft click, the door began to swing shut.

Cam slid the nylon strap off his shoulder, leaving the crate standing against the wall beside the door. He crouched and darted along the bookcase and across the room, hiding behind the nearest leather armchair.

"What the fuck?" he heard Dufresne say.

Cam took a moment to switch the camera feed in the lower corner of his glasses to show the room he was in. He could see himself crouching, the angle from above and behind him. He held his breath, half expecting to see Dufresne creeping up on him, holding a gun or a baseball bat he'd stashed by the bar.

Instead, he saw Dufresne, drink in one hand, shambling over to look at the crate.

Cam had bought some time.

If Dufresne turned when he got to the crate, Cam would be in full view. Cam kept his crouch and darted across the front of the room, under the fake Picasso, and hid behind the leather armchair on the other side, away from the door and Dufresne.

He watched the feed. Dufresne didn't seem to have heard Cam's movements. He was still staring down at the crate, his drink in one hand, his posture slouched.

That was good for Cam.

But now he had to keep Dufresne from opening the crate. He looked around him for something, anything he could use to distract Dufresne. All he saw was carpet and the back of the armchair.

He glanced at the wall. He could knock the painting down,

but that might cause Dufresne to think about it. Cam was confident Dufresne wouldn't spot the fake, but he didn't want to call any attention to the painting if he didn't have to.

But he might have to.

Then he remembered the fake orchids on the coffee table. He turned to look, pressing his face close to the chair. The leather was cool against his cheek, and the scent of it filled his nose.

The coffee table was a step or two away, too far to reach from behind the armchair. He would have to move to get to it. If Dufresne turned around, he'd see Cam plainly.

But if Cam could get the glass vase, he could throw it into the corner and shatter it. Then, when Dufresne went to investigate, Cam could sneak out with the crate.

Cam sighed softly. It wasn't a good plan. In fact, it was a terrible plan. But it was a plan.

Still crouching, Cam crept around the armchair toward the coffee table. If Dufresne turned now, Cam would be fucked.

He didn't need the camera feed to see Dufresne take a long pull from his drink, then reach out toward the crate with his free hand.

Cam's hand closed around the vase.

The doorbell rang. Then it rang again. Then a third time.

Dufresne turned, frowning as he pulled out his phone.

Cam froze. His pulse flared, pounding in his ears.

Dufresne was facing Cam. If he looked up, he'd see Cam squatting beside his coffee table, his hand clutching a glass vase with a fake flower, like he was trying to steal it. Cam couldn't move, unwilling to risk Dufresne seeing the movement in his peripheral vision.

Dufresne peered down at his phone, his attention completely consumed, inspecting the screen closely as he stepped away from the crate and toward the door. Dutifully, the door swung open when Dufresne got close. He turned into the doorway, still staring down at the phone screen.

With Dufresne's back turned, Cam took the vase and swung behind the leather armchair again, ignoring the spike in his pulse. He switched his video feed to the front porch so he could see what Dufresne was seeing.

The front porch was still empty.

It had to be Celina. She'd hacked into his system. She must be triggering the doorbell.

Cam flipped back to the view of the room he was in. Dufresne swore and shoved his phone in his pocket, muttering and shaking his head as he turned back toward the room.

Then all hell broke loose.

The doorbell rang again and again and again. The lights in the room flickered wildly, like an old horror movie when a poltergeist appears. Through the door in the camera feed, Cam could see lights going on and off throughout the house.

The door opened, then closed, then opened again, banging against Dufresne each time. Heavy metal music from the other room was blaring again, this time over the house-wide speaker system. Even in the hushed room they were in, the sound was deafening.

An endless series of buzzes and alert noises came from Dufresne's pocket. He pulled out his phone, nearly dropped it when he looked at it. Cam poked his head around the armchair to see the phone screen over Dufresne's shoulder. It was blowing up with notifications and alerts, scrolling across his lock screen like a roulette wheel.

"Jesus H fucking Christ!" Dufresne shouted. He stormed out of the room, down the hallway, and out of Cam's view.

Cam was up and headed for the crate before Dufresne's had rounded the corner. He kept one eye on Dufresne's avatar in his glasses as he slung the strap of the wooden crate over his shoulder and slipped out the door, timing his movements to exit while the door was on an opening swing.

Dufresne had gone to the left, toward the kitchen where Cam had come in, so Cam went the other way. He'd scouted and memorized half a dozen ingress and egress routes, so he knew which way to go. Dufresne was still moving in the opposite direction as Cam slipped out the front door, knowing that Celina would have disabled any recordings that might have captured his movements.

As Cam darted left over the damp lawn, away from the front lights and into the shadows, the heavy metal music blared from the house. He could still hear it in the background when he came around the corner to the back of the dark grey van parked a quarter-mile down the dark private street.

The back doors of the van swung open as Cam approached. Celina squatted there, a wry smile on his face.

"That was exciting," she said.

"Every good plan will eventually fail," Cam muttered as he lifted the crate into the van. "Nice trick with the whole..." He waved his hands in the air.

"The whole making the entire house freak out? That was my Plan Z." She smirked as she slid the crate further inside. "He's gonna be working all night to untangle the mess I made for him."

Cam hopped into the van with her. Together, they lifted the crate against a padded blanket they'd fastened to the wall. Cam held the crate while Celina set another padded blanket over it, then they secured it to the wall with bungee cords, making sure it was held tight.

Cam shut the doors, first peering into the gloom of the night, then checking his glasses to make sure no one had followed them. The heavy metal music had stopped, but Dufresne was still in the house.

He slouched forward into the passenger seat as Celina pulled the van away.

"Plan Z?" he said.

Celina glanced at him, then back at the road, a smile twisting the corner of her mouth.

"Okay, fine. I was gonna do it no matter what." She glanced back at Cam. "What? That fucker deserved it. A little going away present." She grinned. "Something to remember me by."

"And the stolen Picasso wouldn't be enough?" Cam said.

Celina blew a raspberry. "If I thought that asshole would notice, it might have been."

It hit Cam then, all at once. The adrenaline drained from him and his hands began to shake. They felt cold. He rubbed them together in his lap. It happened at the end of every job. After all the planning and the focus, after the execution and the inevitable improvisation, his body could finally relax and release all that tension.

They'd done it. Cam had done jobs a lot harder, but few that were as meaningful as this one. They'd liberated a rare work of art from an owner who would undoubtedly have done it irreparable harm one day.

And now, Cam and Celina could find it a good home. They hadn't stolen it for the money. They didn't need the money, and had no intention of selling the work, even though Cam knew of several buyers who would pay a premium for it. No, they'd agreed to enjoy it themselves for a week or two, then donate it to the MOMA. Celina had a contact there that would ask no questions.

After a few minutes, Cam's hands warmed and stopped shaking. He looked over at Celina. They were on a real road now, out of Dufresne's neighborhood. The passing streetlights lit Celina's face with an ethereal white glow, enhancing her already overwhelming beauty.

She glanced at Cam, saw him looking at her, then raised

one eyebrow suggestively. Her favorite expression. All those thoughts Cam had pushed aside earlier in the evening came rushing back, along with the usual physical response.

Celina reached over as she drove and ran one hand slowly up Cam's thigh. He groaned softly as he stiffened even more, then took her warm hand in his, held it in his lap, and settled in for the ride home.

4

THE PICASSO JOB was a fucking great score. Celina Maxwell had pulled van duty, which sucked, but she was a better hacker than Cam, and they hadn't wanted to bring in any other players on the job. Anyone else would want them to sell the painting and split the money.

Which was actually what Celina wanted to do. But Cam had appealed to better angels Celina didn't even know she had. She'd agreed to make the painting an anonymous donation to the MOMA.

Her friend at the museum would shit a gold fucking brick when she saw what the donation actually was.

Celina sipped her espresso as she opened the door to the viewing room where they'd decided to hang the painting before they donated it. No windows, good ventilation, controlled temperature and humidity. It was where Celina hung the most prized items in her art collection. She'd taken down an original Monet to put the Picasso in its place. She could almost hear Pablo cackling and old Claude rolling in his grave at the swap.

But the Picasso was an absolute stunner. Like the first time she'd seen the David in the Accademia gallery in Florence, when she'd come around the corner during a private viewing on a Monday, when the museum was closed to the public. The statue stood in a rotunda at the far end of a long hallway. Natural light poured down from a massive skylight, shadows setting the angles and curves of the sculpture in sharp relief. In that light, the marble took on a white hue so pure it looked almost silver.

The sight had taken Celina's breath away and instantly brought tears to her eyes. Not something that usually happened to her. But the beauty, the majesty, the sheer incongruity of seeing such a famous work right there in front of her was sublimely moving. It was a feeling she would never forget. She'd stood there for a full hour in complete silence, just soaking up Michelangelo's masterpiece.

The Picasso was just as mesmerizing. She'd been staring at it almost non-stop for two weeks and it still knocked her out every time she set eyes on it. Cam and Paulie must have felt the same way. Instead of spending their time on the deck, at the beach, or lounging in the library, like they'd done for months, they had both been hanging out in the viewing room almost as much as Celina.

They were there when Celina stepped in, sitting quietly on opposite ends of the couch in the center of the space, staring in rapt silence at the Picasso.

Celina nestled into an overstuffed armchair beside Cam and tucked her bare feet under her, taking another sip of the hot, rich espresso before setting it on a side table to her right. Her chair was close enough to the couch that she could reach her arm lazily across and stroke Cam's tousled brown hair. It had gotten long since the end of school, nearly down to his shoulders. Celina didn't usually like long hair on men, but it gave Cam a roguish look that creamed her panties every time he looked at her.

She wound his soft locks around her fingers and stroked

the contours of his head. Cam pressed back against her hand, then turned to gaze at her. The dreaminess in his eyes and the faint smile on his lips stoked a flame deep inside her.

"Shouldn't you be looking over there?" Celina nodded toward the Picasso.

"Why?" Cam replied with a lazy smile that made Celina almost growl with desire. "I'm already looking at the most beautiful thing in the room."

Celina barked a short laugh. "Wow, art gallery pickup lines? Never thought I'd taste that kind of cheese."

"Only the best for you."

Celina wound more of Cam's hair around her fingers, then grabbed a tight handful as she rose up on her knees and leaned across the arm of the couch, her lips hovering above his. She stared into his clear brown eyes, her heart stuttering as usual at the sight of their depths, at the flecks of orange and yellow that swam in them.

Her voice was low and soft. "I'm gonna overlook the implication that my beauty is my most important aspect," she murmured, "and that you just referred to me as a thing."

She let her gaze fall to Cam's lips, full and inviting amid three days of stubble, then brought it back to his eyes again. She licked her bottom lip slowly.

Cam gulped, and the dreaminess in his eyes turned to a smoky heat, a look that fanned the flames building in Celina.

"I'll have to make it up to you somehow," Cam whispered.

"Yeah," Celina replied. "You will."

Celina held Cam's gaze for a long, delicious moment, letting the heat between them blaze hotter and hotter.

"Damn, you guys are even making me hot."

Cam and Celina stopped cold, then turned to look across the couch at Paulie. She was leaning with one elbow on the couch back, her head propped on her hand, watching and smiling at them.

"Forgot I was here, didn't you?" Paulie smiled. "Love'll do that to ya."

Cam started to shift away, but Celina grabbed his head in both of her hands, turned it back to her, and kissed him, long, deep, and slow. That fire in her wasn't going to die down so easily. She needed to vent some of the heat first.

"Atta girl," said Paulie after Celina finally released Cam, both of them breathing heavy.

Cam rubbed his hands on his knees and cleared his throat, then stood and walked toward the Picasso, clearly embarrassed. Celina looked across at Paulie, who winked and grinned back at her.

Celina loved that woman, almost as much as she loved her son.

"Okay," said Cam, clapping both hands together and turning back toward Celina and Paulie. "It's moving day."

Celina sighed heavily and drained the rest of her espresso. A part of her had been hoping Cam would change his mind about donating the painting, even though she knew that would never happen.

"Did you contact your friend at the museum?" asked Cam.

Celina nodded. "She'll be ready. Tomorrow night at nine at the loading dock."

"And no one else will be around?"

Celina shrugged. "There might be some others, but it doesn't matter. It's an anonymous donation, and I've already told her the painting came to me through a tangle of channels and that I don't know where it originated."

"What if that guy..." Paulie snapped her fingers, trying to remember the name. "The tech guy, the one we stole it from."

"Dufresne."

"Yeah," Paulie said. "I knew it sounded like a suburb of Pittsburgh."

"That's Duquesne," said Cam.

"Exactly," Paulie replied. "What if he makes a stink about it being stolen?"

"He won't," Celina said. "He can't. First off, the artwork was probably stolen by the Nazis in the first place. Second, Dufresne wouldn't want to admit someone broke into his place—while he was in the house, no less—and stole the painting from under his nose. And third, he probably won't even notice it's missing." She shrugged. "Worst case is that he gets tagged as the anonymous donor. Big fucking deal. That'll make him feel important. He can brag about anonymously donating a painting he paid ninety millions dollars for."

"If he wanted to be anonymous," Paulie frowned, "why would he brag about it?"

"Subtlety and irony are not in the skill set for these kinds of people," said Celina.

"Okay, fine," said Cam. "We still taking the jet to New York?"

Celina nodded. "The flight plan is already filed. We're scheduled to take off at six tonight, but we can leave any time. We'll have dinner on the plane."

"Leave at six. That'll put us on the ground at what, three AM Eastern?"

"Closer to two, but there are beds on the jet and I've booked the penthouse suites at the Plaza. Coming from LaGuardia at that hour, we should be snug in our hotel rooms by three."

Cam nodded. "Okay," he said. "That's that." He turned toward the painting. "We just need to pack it up."

"Say goodbye to the dancer of Avignon," said Paulie.

Slowly, Cam backed up to sit on the couch again.

Celina sighed.

They sat in silence, soaking up the beauty of the Picasso until it was time to leave.

5

THE FOOD on the plane was delicious, naturally. Celina's private chef had earned two Michelin stars before looking for a change of pace.

And the sex on the plane was even better. Joining the mile-high club isn't hard when your jet has a private bedroom. Celina finally got to release the heat that had been simmering since that morning.

They got to their hotel on time. Celina and Cam had spent a lot of time in the bedroom on the plane, but had gotten very little sleep, so they crashed until after noon. Paulie was in her suite enjoying lunch when Cam and Celina knocked, bleary-eyed and hungry for breakfast.

The painting in its travel crate had been loaded from the plane into a windowless black van and taken to a secure private storage facility a block from the MOMA. They would meet it at the loading dock that evening. Celina had complete faith in her staff, both for their skill in handling the Picasso safely and for their discretion in keeping it secret.

With nothing else to do until nine o'clock that evening, the three of them ate slowly and leisurely. Paulie had a turkey club with potato chips wedging a paperback romance open with her thumb. Cam and Celina devoured Western omelettes and copious amounts of coffee. After, they took their time getting ready for the day, including steamy, slippery sex in the huge shower in their penthouse suite.

When they were finally dried and dressed and ready, it was still only five-thirty PM. Cam suggested a sunset walk through Central Park, just across the street from the hotel. Celina put on an overcoat and a scarf, and the three of them wandered in the park, leaving the city behind for a moment.

The sky was a dusky early-evening blue and the sun was full and low after a sunny day, but the late-October air had that delicious crisp bite to it. They didn't write songs about autumn in New York because it was miserable and ugly. Fall was Celina's favorite season, and New York City was her favorite place to spend it.

The leaves on the trees had already started to change, exploding in oranges and yellows and reds so vibrant and saturated they seemed like a painting. Ducks splashed in the pond. Kids in sweaters and beanies screeched and laughed on the playground. Celina could hear the distant bark of a sea lion in the Central Park Zoo. She and Cam and Paulie strolled along the paved walkways, enjoying it all. It was a perfect evening.

But Celina didn't feel perfect. She was happy enough. Happy to be there with Cam and Paulie. Happy that Paulie was free and she and Cam were together, with no more deceptions between them.

But she was restless. She had hoped that getting closure with Jenkins and Stratham and getting together with Cam would quiet the feeling deep inside that nagged at her constantly. The feeling that woke her at dawn or kept her staring at the ceiling in the small hours of the night. That fucking needling feeling that something wasn't right, that some task needed doing or some score needed settling. But she could never figure out what that task or score actually was.

Attorney General William Jenkins had agreed to deal with his campaign finance chair, Vernon Stratham, a wolf in accountant's clothing who had the blood of dozens of people on his hands, including Celina's late father. Celina had taken a risk in trusting Jenkins, her father's old protégé. She had Stratham right there in Jenkins' office. She could have killed him with her bare hands. But at Cam's urging—and maybe the urging of those better angels of hers—Celina had agreed to let Jenkins handle it.

But since then she hadn't seen any news in the paper about Stratham.

Jenkins' campaign for the presidency was cruising along. The primaries hadn't even started and Jenkins was already not only the presumptive Democratic nominee, but the presumptive winner of the general election. The Republicans weren't even putting their A-list people in the race, leaving it to the perennial also-rans to take the loss next November.

With that kind of success, even if Jenkins didn't pursue prosecution, a shake-up with the campaign finance chairperson would be big enough news to warrant at least a mention on the front page of the newspapers. Yet Celina hadn't heard a peep about it.

Of course, she hadn't seen any news about Stratham on the campaign trail, either, but that wasn't unusual. Stratham avoided the spotlight, preferring to work quietly through cocktail party conversations, private meetings, and murmured discussions at the tables of fundraising dinners. He had never been in the papers, so his absence now was no indicator that Jenkins had held up his end of the deal.

Celina would have to do some digging of her own. Jenkins owed her, and she intended to make sure he made good on his debt.

Beside the walkway in the park, a red-tailed hawk flapped to a landing on the wide bulb of a black lamp post. It turned its head to the side, fixing one stern, dark eye down on Celina, then screeched once, loud and piercing. It turned the other eye toward Celina, as if to make sure she'd heard, then flared its wings wide for a moment, looking like an eagle atop a flagpole, and flew off into the blue sky.

Celina scowled.

"Jesus, that was loud," said Cam, rubbing his right ear. He touched Celina on the shoulder. "You ok? You look like someone just insulted your mother."

Celina turned toward him and snorted. "If anyone's going to insult my mother, it'll be me."

"Okay," he said.

He fell quiet, but watched Celina carefully.

"What?" Celina said, her voice sharper than she intended.

Cam shrugged. "You don't talk about her much."

Celina drew in a long breath, but stopped herself before she let out a heavy sigh, then gave Cam a tight smile and shook her head.

"She's not that important."

He nodded thoughtfully.

Celina didn't like the half-puzzled, half-pitying look on Cam's face. She looked away, up at the sky where the hawk had been. That nagging feeling tugged at her, but there was an idea forming deep in her mind. It was still amorphous and swirling, but it felt like the kind of idea that might help quiet that nagging feeling. For a little while, at least.

She turned back to Cam. He was watching her, concern in his eyes. Celina slid her arm through his and pulled him tight against her, tight enough to feel his heat through two overcoats.

Beside them in Sheep Meadow, a man tossed a frisbee for his German Shepherd. The dog sprinted, tongue lolling, then leapt shockingly high in the air to catch the frisbee before racing back to its owner, pure joy in every movement.

Celina smiled, a full, bright smile this time. "You guys hungry yet?" She pointed across the meadow. "We can eat at the Tavern."

"It's Saturday," said Cam. "I doubt we'll get a table without a reservation."

Celina gave his arm a squeeze and steered him across toward the restaurant. "Come on," she said. "I know a guy."

"Of course you do."

They chose a table outside on the patio. By the time coffee and dessert arrived, the propane heaters were at full blast, the sky was dark, and the strands of lights overhead made a soft-glowing big top tent above them. Through the strands, they could even see the few stars bright enough to overcome the glare of the city.

Happily stuffed from the meal, they decided to walk to the museum to help their food settle. They arrived just as Celina's team was pulling the black van through the gates and into the museum's loading area.

Celina's contact was waiting for them. When they got the crate inside and she opened it and saw the Picasso, she sucked in her breath sharply and put one hand to her mouth. Celina smiled quietly. Her contact was not easily impressed. She watched the woman's face work through the gamut of surprise, shock, doubt, then skepticism, followed by the return of the veil of stoic professionalism that her contact usually wore.

Celina would have been disappointed by anything else. Her contact was a pro, but the painting was a Picasso. If Uncle Pablo hadn't broken through that professional stoicism, Celina would have checked the woman for a pulse.

They filled out all the paperwork, officially transferring ownership of the painting to the museum trust. Technically,

Celina didn't have the legal right to do that, but with the ownership of the painting shrouded in the shadows of history, the legality was flexible enough that the museum could make it work. It wouldn't be the first time a high-profile museum had come to possess a work of questionable provenance, and it wouldn't be the last.

She felt a stab of loss as she signed the final piece of paper, but Cam and Paulie stood right beside her. Celina wasn't accustomed to leaning on others for emotional support. Since her father died, she'd supported herself. But she'd been surprised at how easily she'd come to trust Cam and Paulie in the last few months.

Celina's contact gave them a few minutes in silence to take one last long look at the Picasso before she showed them out of the receiving room, leaving the painting in the hands of her own staff. As a thank you for the donation, she offered them a private tour. Celina had been on several in the past after prior donations she'd made, but she never turned down an opportunity to stroll through the MOMA at her own pace, without the crowds and the guards in the way.

Celina's contact was not just a professional curator. She was a knowledgeable and entertaining tour guide, as well. Three hours in the museum flew by. They spent the cab ride home in silence, each of them lost in their thoughts about the incredible artwork they'd just seen, and the incredible artwork they'd given up. When Celina suggested a nightcap in the suite, Cam and Paulie were quick to agree.

The view from the sitting room in Celina's and Cam's penthouse suite was breathtaking. A huge picture window offered an unobstructed view of the park, its darkened canvas framed by the lights of the traffic along 5th Avenue and Central Park West. The lines of the lamplight along the walkways turned and twined and lit the trees and the lake with a dim yellow glow. A full moon had risen, casting a faint silver sheen over the view. From their height, the sounds of the traffic and unceasing car horns were a faint murmur far below.

They sat in overstuffed leather armchairs in front of the window and drank small-batch maple bourbon from a distillery upstate, neat. With each mouthful, the hint of sweetness on Celina's tongue was followed by a warm burn down her throat. They sipped languidly, soaking in the view, superimposed by the dazzling memory of the artwork they'd just seen.

When they'd all reached the bottom of their glasses, a comforting fuzziness in their heads, Celina set her glass on the table and stood at the window facing Cam and Paulie. They raised their eyebrows and watched her expectantly.

"So," said Celina, clasping her hands in front of her chest.

She looked at Cam. His mouth twisted up in a slight smile and his eyes narrowed in mild suspicion. She shifted her eyes to Paulie, who looked relaxed and amused. While Celina held her gaze, a smile slowly crept across Paulie's face and her eyes grew bright and sharp.

"Now that this job is done," Celina began, shifting her eyes back to Cam, "I have an idea for what we can do next."

Cam glanced at Paulie, then back at Celina.

"Is that right?" he drawled. "Okay. What's your idea?"

Celina held both hands straight out, glancing back and forth between Cam and Paulie, letting the anticipation build.

Then, breezily, she dropped her arms and said, "You guys ever been to Washington in the winter?"

6

Fifteen years was a very long time to spend in prison.

Paulie Hauk had made the best she could of it. She'd made a lot of friends, among both her fellow cons and among the COs. She'd stayed out of trouble, even helped ease some of the tensions that occasionally flared around her. But prison is a passionate place and criminals are passionate people. When the passions of those around her became too strong, Paulie got out of the way and let life do its thing.

She'd made the best of it, but it was still prison, and prison was not Paulie's style. That's why she and her husband, Sam, had worked so hard to stay out of it.

The food wasn't good, but she could deal with that. The orange prison jumpsuits were itchy and ill-fitting, but she adjusted to it. It was no fun being in a cramped cage with another person, only seeing the sky for an hour each day in rain, snow, or sunshine. She and Sam—and, later, Cam—had reveled in the unspoiled spaces in the world, the forests and coastlines and lakes where life was natural and authentic. Being removed from that authenticity was torture, but Paulie even found a way to cope with that over time, finding authenticity in other places.

What really killed her, though, was the boredom. Endless hours in that tiny cell. She'd read all the books, played all the games they were allowed to play, asked her cellie all the questions she could think of and more. She took to meditation, not for spiritual enlightenment, but just for a way to pass the time. She focused on being completely present in each moment so that she didn't go insane from the endless monotony. She didn't tell him until she'd gotten out, but Cam and his weekly visits were about the only things that kept her from losing her mind completely.

But now that she was out, the world felt brand new again. She sat on Celina's deck and noted all the shades of blue the sky went through during the day. She ate every meal at a snail's pace, tasting each forkful, identifying every ingredient. Every subtle flavor was a firework of sensation for her starved tastebuds. Walking on the beach, she nearly wept at the feel of the moist sand piling over her feet, grinding against the soft webs between her toes, the salt breeze stinging her face, the icy cold of the Pacific Ocean swirling around her numb ankles.

And most of all, she loved watching Cam and Celina. When she watched them hold each other, tease each other, or even just exchange meaningful looks with each other, she thought of herself and Sam. They'd done all the same things. Seeing Cam and Celina brought bittersweet feelings for Paulie. She was happy that those two had found each other, had found that love. She was sad that Sam was gone. And she was grateful that they'd experienced that kind of love for themselves before he died. She knew how rare that was. She knew that she was one of the lucky ones.

Watching Cam and Celina also made Paulie laugh, though she did her best to keep the laughter inside. They thought they were being sneaky. Maybe they thought Paulie would be offended by their affection, or maybe Cam just felt weird squeezing his girlfriend's butt in front of his mother.

They thought they were sly and hid their shenanigans well, but Paulie could see it all. Every stolen kiss, every butt slap, every thigh caress. Every meaningful look.

And thank God she could. After fifteen years, Sam's death was as fresh in her mind as the day she'd held him in her arms, bloody and bleeding, on a curb a hundred miles south of Celina's San Francisco home and watched the blazing, indefatigable life force in those heart-stopping hazel eyes fade to a dull, glassy nothing. She craved the feeling of his strong arms around her, his coarse beard against her skin, his soft lips against hers. She would give her life just to see him throw his head back one more time and laugh that barrel-chested laugh of his, the one that rolled like thunder around the room until everyone in it was laughing with him.

All she had of Sam now were her memories and her undiminished love. But she could see the same love sparking between Cam and Celina. Paulie would pretend to read or feign sleep, just to put them at their ease. Cam might not want to kiss Celina in front of her, but Paulie wanted him to. She wanted to see it, the way they teased each other, the way their hands found each other subconsciously, just for a touch, whenever they stood or sat near each other.

Cam had always said he wanted what Paulie and Sam had had, and now the opportunity was right in front of him, with Celina. Paulie wanted to see Cam take it, seize it, recognize their burgeoning love for the rarity it was and nurture it until it was invulnerable and unwavering.

She wanted to know that her son would feel what Paulie had once felt. What she still felt.

Cam and Celina had found love. But just because you find it doesn't mean it comes easily. Cam and Celina were both stubborn people, and stubborn people can push away even the strongest love if their pride or their fears get in the way. To love someone is to be vulnerable to them. Love is an act of courage, and sometimes people are too afraid of being hurt to muster that courage. They would rather hurt themselves, the devil they know, than risk being hurt by the other.

Sitting in front of the window of the penthouse suite in New York City, Central Park laid out far below, the lights of the city like a muted sun beneath them, Paulie watched Cam debate Celina's latest plan with her. These were the moments that defined a relationship. Not the vibrant days filled with beautiful weather and exciting activities. Not the quiet nights snuggled by the fire with a movie or a good book. A relationship is defined by moments of disagreement, moments of debate. That's where the couple learns to put their love for the other above their love for their own ideas. That's where the couple strips away the fat of their egos and digs down to the muscle of their ideals. Only then can they see whether they can pull together or are destined to push each other apart.

Paulie knew that Cam and Celina would pull together, if they could ever get through their own egos, through the tight-woven nest of fears and dreams and self-recriminations they'd built throughout their lives, one broken branch at a time.

She didn't care what Celina's plan was. Paulie was all in for anything. Not only had she been stuck in prison for fifteen years, but she loved her son fiercely. She would stay by his side as long as he would let her.

And she loved Celina, too. She could see the passion Celina ignited in Cam, and that was enough to make Paulie love her. But she could see the passion in Celina, too. The intelligence, the resourcefulness, the beauty.

And the pain.

Something about Celina's mother. Celina tried to dismiss the topic whenever it came up. She tried to pretend it wasn't important. And sometimes mothers aren't important. But when that's the case, the children don't have a problem talking about them.

Celina wouldn't talk about her mother. Ever.

Someday, Paulie hoped she could meet Celina's mother. She wanted to let Celina's mother know what she'd lost, and she wanted to know what pain in Celina's mother would have caused her to walk away from her daughter. There was always a reason. All humans want love, yes, in some capacity. But even more, humans want to avoid pain. Some pain in Celina's mother must have made her walk away from her daughter. Paulie wanted to know what it was.

Celina's mother had chosen to avoid pain instead of finding love. As she watched Celina explain and argue and passionately debate her plan with Cam, Paulie desperately wanted to help her avoid the same mistake.

7

CAM STARED out the window of Celina's jet as they made their final approach to Reagan National airport in Washington D.C. The afternoon was clear, and the setting sun cast a gold sheen over the city. Reflections of the sky rippled orange and red on the surface of the Potomac River, as if there were a fire burning beneath the water. Across the river, Cam could see the spire of the Washington Monument straining for the heavens and the marble pate of the Jefferson Memorial hunkered among the cherry trees surrounding the tidal basin, their leaves an artist's palette of amber and orange and crimson.

He hadn't expected to be back in the capitol so soon, and he was a little pissed off to discover that the sight of his old stomping grounds made him feel guilty. Not triumphant, not nostalgic. His thoughts were focused on the friends he'd made during three years of graduate school in criminology. Friends he'd eaten with, studied with, laughed and commiserated with.

Friends he'd lied to.

They still didn't know the truth, but they knew that their friend Sam Davis—Cam's false identity for the three years he'd spent in school—had disappeared without a trace. Sam had given them a story to keep them from being worried enough to mount a search party or make a missing persons report to the police, but he'd ghosted them ever since. Cam had deleted all of his Sam Davis accounts. Any emails to the old address would bounce. Any texts to the old number would be undeliverable. Any calls would get three piercing beeps and a recording of a lady's voice cheerfully informing them that they must be an idiot because that number is no longer in service.

He was sure his friends would be worried. He was sure they'd be hurt.

And he was quite sure they would be angry.

And he couldn't blame them for it. Cam felt terrible about the deception.

And he felt terrible about feeling so terrible. He hadn't gone through three years of grad school to make friends. He'd worked his ass off to be top of his class for the sole purpose of freeing his mother from prison.

Celina still gave him no end of grief over that plan, seeing as she'd managed to swoop into the same school halfway through the final year and achieve the same result. She'd hacked her way to the top of the class, easily penetrating the school's computer system and manipulating her GPA to get to the top of the class rankings. Once she'd learned of Cam's plan to free his mother, she'd intentionally created a tie with him so they could both get what they wanted: an audience with Attorney General William Jenkins, now the presumptive successor for the Presidency of the United States, even though the election itself was more than a year away.

But Cam's hacking skills weren't as good as Celina's, so he'd done it the hard way. He'd faked his identity and his credentials to gain admission to the school, but the work he did to earn the top spot was real.

As real as the friendships he'd made along the way. Jem, Sarah, Annie, and Motsu were real people, good people, and good friends. They didn't deserve to be treated the way Cam had treated them.

He could seek them out to apologize, but he would have to tell them everything in order to make them understand. Going up to four recent criminology graduates to admit that you were a lifelong criminal who had blackmailed the Attorney General of the United States in order to free your criminal mother from prison was not exactly what Cam would consider to be a smart plan.

And even if he did it, how would he expect them to respond? If they didn't turn him in, they'd be aiding and abetting. These were people who had worked hard their whole lives so they could become the next rising stars of the criminal justice system. They wanted to be Attorneys General or Supreme Court justices or congresspeople. Maybe even President of the United States one day. They were among the best and the brightest. Who knew what their future would bring them?

But if Cam told them the truth, their future wouldn't include any of those achievements. The world had always been competitive, but these days it was lethal. If they knew the truth, Cam would become a blemish on their pasts that would show up in someone's oppo research down the line. No matter how bad he felt about the lying and the ghosting, Cam wouldn't do that to his friends.

Cam barely felt the jet touch the tarmac when they landed. Celina knew how to find and hire good people. From her chefs to her art handlers to her jet pilots, she surrounded herself with the best. It made sense. Celina, herself, was the best at just about everything she did.

Sometimes Cam wondered what the hell she saw in him.

A private car was waiting when they stepped off the plane.

Twenty minutes later, it stopped in front of a gorgeous renovated three-story brownstone that Celina owned in the Capitol Hill neighborhood, just a few steps from Stanton Park and a few blocks from the Capitol building.

The exterior of the brownstone was stunning, a gorgeous Victorian that had clearly been either very well maintained or recently renovated. The brick was a bright carmine, the gabled roofs a rich espresso black. The windows were arched with ornate brickwork. The rails and newels and stair risers leading to the front door were all of wrought iron. From the curb, the home exuded an imposing elegance that dominated the more modern row houses around it.

The inside was just as elegant, and even more imposing.

The entry was long and narrow. A staircase went upward on the right-hand side. On the left, a sitting area with a couch, two chairs, and a small, marble coffee table were arranged in front of a gas fireplace. Beyond the sitting area, the room wrapped behind the stairs to more of the house.

What made it imposing was the color, or the lack thereof. The interior of the home was composed entirely of spotless, gleaming white. White ceilings and raised panel walls, white couches and chairs, white rugs and tables, and white stair risers, all set against white oak flooring so pale it was nearly colorless. The effect was a visual wash of unspoiled purity, elegant, intimidating, and ice cold.

The only variation on the endless sea of white was the occasional bit of espresso black, the same espresso black as the exterior of the house. The espresso hearth around the fireplace, espresso window frames, and espresso balusters, leading up the stairs like a row of servants waiting for orders, gave Cam's eyes a place to catch their breath amidst all the white. Even the artwork on the walls was desaturated or monochromatic, all whites and blacks and greys and gunmetal blues.

Adding to the imposing effect was the fact that the home itself was absolutely stunning. Even standing in the entryway, Cam could see that everything in it was of the highest quality and of the most refined taste in design and decor. Cam would call it impressive, but the word was so weak he felt like he shouldn't be allowed to stay there until he found a word more suitable.

Cam and his mother stood in the entryway, gawking.

"Why didn't you live here while you were in school?" Cam asked.

"That wouldn't have been much of a cover story, would it?" Celina replied. "A poor grad student living in a four million dollar brownstone in downtown DC?"

"Fair point," said Cam.

He and Paulie wandered through the sitting area and past a table and chairs with room for four, Celina trailing behind. Once past the stairs, the room opened up to an elegant kitchen. Cam goggled at the professional range and hood and the huge marble center island with an inset sink and three tall stools set under an overhang that served as a breakfast bar. The marble was pure white, as was all the cabinetry. Even the silver metal of the range and the faucet and sink somehow seemed paler than usual, as if they, too, were cowed colorless by the white all around them.

To Cam, the decor was uncharacteristic, but it made sense that the kitchen would be professional-grade. Celina was an amazing chef.

Beside the kitchen was another sitting area with yet another gas fireplace, this one built into the wall in front of another couch, two armchairs, and a coffee table. Again, all brilliant white.

A wide double door opened onto a spacious outdoor patio with a large grill, a table for six, and two cushioned wicker patio chairs. The patio abutted another home directly behind.

"Guest house," said Celina, following Cam and Paulie into the early-evening chill. "Two bedrooms."

She sighed, as if the guest house irritated her somehow.

They turned back to tour the rest of the main house. Two more floors, filled with white marble bathrooms, white bedrooms with white bedcovers, a white-walled workout room with black dumbbells, two theater rooms with long white couches resting on shaggy white rugs, two huge offices with desks and high-end computers and wall-mounted televisions, and countless fireplaces.

Each floor had a deck extending out the back. The entire roof was another deck, with a retractable cover controlled by a switch on the wall, and a gazebo with a television and yet another fireplace. A full outdoor kitchen stood to one side, with a large grill, several separate burners, and various drawers for warming, cooling, and storage.

Everything was elegant. Everything was stunning.

Everything was starkly black and white.

"Did you... decorate this place?" asked Cam as they went back downstairs to the kitchen.

"Why do you ask?" said Celina. She sounded defensive.

"It's gorgeous," said Cam, quickly, trying to sound conciliatory.

"Stunning," Paulie agreed.

"It just... doesn't really seem like you."

Celina grunted in reply. Cam couldn't tell whether it was a good grunt or a bad grunt. He wasn't used to Celina grunting. Teasing him, yes. Occasionally chewing him out, sure. Moaning in pleasure, oh yeah. Grunting, not so much.

"What seems like me?" Celina asked.

"A lot more color, for starters," Cam said as they found their way down two flights of stairs and back to the first-floor kitchen. "When I met you, your apartment looked like a

Pantone truck had crashed into a Jelly Belly factory. In a good way."

This time, Celina snorted. A snort was better than a grunt. Cam figured she couldn't be too offended by his first comment.

"And the furniture," he continued. "It's all beautiful. Impeccable taste, gorgeous interior design, all of that. But it looks like the photo shoot for a Restoration Hardware catalog."

He squeezed the back of the couch in the sitting area beside the kitchen. It looked cushy, but it was rock hard.

"Has anyone actually sat in any of this stuff?" he asked.

Celina opened the refrigerator. It was fully stocked with an array of fruits and vegetables that were so colorful the view practically blinded Cam in relation to the rest of the house. The food in the fridge was neatly and perfectly arranged on the shelves, as if someone had delivered groceries that morning to what had been a completely empty refrigerator.

Celina pulled items from the fridge and stacked them on the center island.

"It's my mother's house," she said casually, dropping one stack and going back for another. "She rarely uses it."

She filled her arms with a last batch of food and kicked the fridge door shut behind her. She dumped the armful on the marble island, then leaned against the counter with both hands spread wide and stared at Cam and Paulie for a moment.

"The decor is her doing," she said. Again, her voice had that casual air, but Cam could see the muscles in her jaw flexing. "And it definitely seems like her."

Cam did his best to keep his shock from showing on his face. The best he could manage was to stop his jaw from falling open. Those few sentences were the most he'd ever heard Celina say about her mother without being prompted.

He had so many questions. A glance at his mother, standing beside him, told him that she had questions, too.

Celina leaned down and pulled a wooden cutting board, a block of knives, and several pots and pans from cabinets built into the underside of the island. She set them down with a clang and a clatter, then leaned on the counter again.

"You two just gonna stand there ogling me," she said, "or are you gonna help with dinner?"

Cam had never seen Celina that way before. Her face was calm and poised, her voice light and casual. But her movements were tight, choppy. When she moved a pot, it screeched over the burner grate. When she sliced a red onion, the knife banged against the cutting board like she was firing a machine gun.

He and Celina had been seeing each other for less than a year, but they'd been together for ninety percent of that time. Over time, Cam had attuned himself to the subtle ebbs and flows of Celina's emotions.

But he didn't need months of attunement to feel the tension coming off of her. He glanced again at his mother. She could feel it, too.

Without another word, they both hustled around the island and set to work helping with dinner.

8

THEY COOKED and ate dinner largely in silence. Celina had hacked into the security system from the jet and disabled all the sensors and cameras, so they had the run of the house without worrying about detection. After dinner, they watched a movie in the theater room on the second floor and then went early to their bedrooms. Paulie stayed on the second floor while Cam and Celina took the master suite upstairs.

Celina had been quiet all night. Her responses weren't clipped or rude; when Cam or Paulie spoke to her, she replied easily. But she wasn't her usual self. Cam could tell something was still off with her, and he could see that Paulie sensed it, too. In everything Celina said and did, there was an underlying current of agitation, even low-simmering anger.

It came out even more that night in bed.

Celina was an adventurous lover, passionate and experimental. But no matter what was happening, she was always sensitive to Cam's experience, making sure that he was enjoying himself as much as she was.

But that night, there was a self-centered ferocity to her that Cam hadn't experienced with Celina before.

The sex was intense, feral, and Celina was insatiable. On

51

the soft shaggy rug in the bedroom, on the cold marble tile in the bathroom, in the chill night air on the balcony. In the shower, on the bed, up against the wall. She bit and clawed and threw Cam around like a sack of flour. She ordered him from position to position, barking orders. When her head wasn't thrown back in orgasm, her face was pressed into a focused glower.

It was definitely odd, but Cam didn't mind it. It was a new experience for him, a new facet of their sexuality together. If she were like that all the time, it might be an issue, but Cam could see that something was bothering Celina at a deep level, and this was one way she was trying to exorcise those demons, to bring them into the light and rid herself of them. If this was how she needed his help, he was more than happy to give it to her.

Though they'd gone to the bedroom early after the movie, the sky was already starting to lighten when they finally stopped, both of them dripping with sweat despite the coolness of the air in the room. At the end, Cam had his feet on the bed and his hands on the floor, holding himself in push-up position. Celina had wrapped her legs around his hips from underneath, her arms twined behind his neck. She'd been pulling herself up and down along his sweat-slicked body, faster and faster until they'd both tensed and arched into each other and screamed together before sliding slowly down to the floor as their muscles relaxed and gave out at last.

They slept like that, in a naked heap, half on the shaggy white rug, half on the hard marble tile, so tired they weren't even bothered by the sunshine that brightened in the window.

When Cam woke, hours later, the sun was blinding. Celina was still entwined in his arms. He didn't want to disturb her, so he just watched her sleep.

She was dreaming. From the scowl on her face, it didn't seem to be a good dream. Her legs twitched, then her arms.

Her mouth worked as her scowl deepened. She gave one last twitch, straightening her arms hard against Cam's chest, pushing herself against his encircling arms.

"No!" she shouted.

Her eyes opened. Cam stared into those mysterious emerald green eyes he'd come to love like the air he breathed. He watched a storm in them slowly clear, watched the scowl on Celina's face slowly ease, felt her arms slowly soften as she came out of her nightmare. A troubled look still on her beautiful face, she tucked herself into Cam's chest. He wrapped his arms around her again and held her in the streaming sunlight until she was ready to move again.

When they went down, Paulie was sitting on a stool at the marble island in the kitchen, sipping tea and reading an ebook on her cell phone. An empty plate sat before her, littered with the crumbs of what looked to have been a sandwich. Cam's stomach grumbled at the sight. He was famished.

Celina sat on a stool beside Paulie while Cam went to fetch them both coffee and something to eat.

"Good morning," was all Paulie said, but Cam could see in her eyes the questions she had, the answers she found in Celina's movements, her expressions, her attitude.

"Morning," replied Celina, her voice sounding much more normal than it had last night. Cam could tell that her demons were still there, gnawing at her, but that last night had helped Celina to push them back into the darkness once more.

For the time being, at least.

He set a double espresso in front of Celina. She gave him a grateful glance before draining half of it in one sip. When she finished it a few moments later, Cam was ready with a second cup. He set that down before her and whisked away the empty.

The omelettes took a while longer, but by the time they'd

both eaten and had their fill of coffee, the three of them were chatting and laughing as usual.

"So, we're casing the Capitol building today?" said Paulie.

Celina nodded, checking her watch.

"Our tour starts in an hour, but we should get going. I want to look around the grounds first."

"Wouldn't security be pretty tight?" asked Cam. "It's the US Capitol, after all."

"You'd think so, but it's not like the White House." Celina stood as Cam took the dishes to the sink to rinse. "Security at the Capitol is shockingly weak."

"Even after January sixth?" asked Paulie.

"That's what I want to find out," said Celina. "I know they beefed things up, but that doesn't mean much. Security at the Capitol has always been mainly physical. Just metal detectors and Capitol police."

"No alarms or sensors?" said Cam

"There's nothing much there to steal. You can't slip the Rotunda ceiling under your shirt."

"So what are we trying to steal, then?" Cam asked.

Celina smiled. "Not everything valuable is on display."

It was late October, and the lines at the Capitol weren't as long as they were in the summer. Kids were back at school, and parents were more focused on Halloween costumes than family vacations. The air was cool, but the sky was a cloudless blue and the afternoon sun was bright. As they approached the long, broad steps of the Capitol building from the back, the historic dome towering over them, Cam couldn't help feeling a swell of patriotic pride.

He was a criminal. He'd spend his entire life breaking laws. He was good at it, and he'd made a good living from it. But he was still proud to be an American. He lived in a country where people like him were free to choose to be criminals, where laws existed that could be broken. Sure, he would go to prison if he were ever caught, but that was part of the game. He wouldn't have it any other way.

In another kind of country, he'd be killed if he were caught. In a dictatorship, or in a feudal system, the lords and leaders would be criminals, too. In America, the rich were usually corrupt and crooked, but they at least paid lip service to the law. And if their money ran out or the public caught wind of the truth, there was always the chance that the rich could be taken down. It rarely happened, but it was possible.

Cam was proud to live in America, and standing before one of the world-famous symbols of American democracy was inspiring. He'd spent three years in Washington D.C. while he finished grad school, and every time he looked at the White House or the Lincoln Memorial or the Capitol or any of the other famous monuments and buildings, he still felt a swell of pride and amazement at what America had built over its rich history.

"They've added more crowd-containment fencing," said Celina

She pointed at rows of portable waist-high steel fences arrayed in a circle around the Capitol building. Like ten-foot-long bike racks, the fences were linked arm in arm by metal hooks and loops. It was a weak deterrent, at best. It would keep tourists from wandering into places they shouldn't be, but as the whole world had discovered on January 6, 2021, when an armed and angry mob had stormed the Capitol, they didn't do much to stop anyone who was determined to get in.

"And they've beefed up the police force," she said, nodding at two uniformed cops, one wearing a bike helmet, his bicycle leaning against his thigh as he chatted with the colleague standing beside him. "But that's about the extent of it."

"Cameras?" asked Cam.

"Yes, everywhere, and Capitol police monitoring the feeds

from a control room inside, but no alarms or triggers or electronic surveillance of any kind."

"Any lockdown mechanisms?" asked Paulie.

"Nope." Celina shook her head, amazed. "Too expensive, I guess. Or they can't get Congress to approve the appropriations bill. Even the most basic, simple tech-based deterrents. They don't even bother."

"Like you said," said Cam, "nothing to steal."

"And no one to target," Paulie added. "Most people in America couldn't even name a senator or a representative, let alone take the trouble to attack them."

Cam snorted. "Tell that to Nancy Pelosi."

"Makes our job easier, that's all," said Celina.

"You still haven't told us what we're stealing," Cam said.

Again, Celina just smiled. "Let's head inside."

9

CAM WORE GREY SLACKS, black loafers, a white button-down shirt, and a dark-blue wool blazer. The outfit was casual enough to seem like a wealthy businessman on vacation, one who couldn't quite let go of the business suit he was used to wearing every day, but formal enough to pass for a congressional staffer who was working on a day off.

He patted his chest over the inner pocket of the blazer, where he was keeping the House staff credentials Celina had forged for herself and for Cam. He felt the stiff lamination of the credential card and the jutting edge of the fastener for the lanyard, safely tucked away.

But the staffer routine was Phase Two of today's plan. Phase One was to act like a tourist.

Like every other tourist, Cam and the others entered the Capitol building itself through the underground entrance to the Visitor Center. The metal detectors were standard-issue, as were the Capitol police officers standing watch. The lines were short and moved quickly. Within minutes, the three of them were making their way down the sandstone steps into the expansive Emancipation Hall.

Despite the short lines at the entrance, the hall itself was relatively crowded. Several hundred tourists wearing cross-body fanny packs, L.L. Bean jackets, and unfashionable shoes with well-cushioned soles milled around, looking at the various statues arrayed around the room or waiting in line at desks and ticket booths on both sides of the room. In their hands were Capitol visitor guides, already rolled into tight tubes in their hands. All those curious tourists filled the cavernous space with a murmuring hum that Cam found soothing.

Two large skylights set into the ceiling high above let the afternoon light cascade into the room, adding to the serenity Cam felt. If he could somehow block out all the marble and the statues and the people and just see the light, just hear the murmur, he could have easily been sitting by a stream in a sun-dappled forest as standing in the Capitol Visitor Center.

As they weaved around the lines of people and crossed the hall, Cam looked up through the skylights. High above, the Capitol dome angled into the sky, filling the view through the window. He felt another flush of patriotic pride. The architects knew what they were doing when they built these places. The Visitor Center had only been built in 2005 or so, yet they borrowed from the playbook of the late 1800s, with huge spaces and dramatic viewing angles meant to inspire awe and remind us all of how small a role we play in the arc of history.

If only they'd built those same kinds of views into the House and Senate chambers, so the people who worked there wouldn't act like such selfish idiots all the time.

They made their way across the hall and climbed the stairs to the balcony above a twenty-foot-tall plaster mold of the Statue of Freedom, the same mold used to cast the bronze statue atop the Capitol dome. They took a moment to look across the hall they'd just traversed. Ostensibly admiring the room, all three of them were searching for security details. Camera locations, security guards, sensors. There weren't many. Aside from the capitol docents, only two officers guarded the room, one on each side. Cam and the others watched where the guards watched, noticed what they noticed, and noticed what they didn't notice.

Some of the statues in the room, including the mold right in front of them, had real historic value. Yet they were completely unguarded. True, it would be a feat to steal a statue weighing several tons of bronze or marble, but it could be done. Yet there seemed to be almost no security at all beyond the scant manpower on the floor. And there were no visible countermeasures in place.

The best security systems were invisible, except to trained professionals. The invisible features were the ones to prevent theft or alert authorities of an attempt in progress. But most systems also had more obvious measures in place to deter more casual would-be thieves before they even tried a job. The appearance of security can be more important than the sophistication of the security itself. These kinds of places would have plenty of guards and cameras, but no real technology.

In the Capitol, though, there was nothing. And Cam knew it wasn't because the US government was being exceedingly clever in their protection systems, keeping their state-of-the-art equipment well hidden. They were clever and professional in their military ops, not in their domestic security.

After a few moments of observation, they all nodded wordlessly to each other and walked back down the steps to join their tour group. Cam gave a glance back over his shoulder at the mold of the Statue of Freedom. Maybe it was his imagination, but she looked tired. Her sword was sheathed, as if she knew more violence would solve nothing. Her shield was by her side, as if she knew defensiveness was not the solution, either. The laurel wreath hanging loosely from her hand at her hip showed that past victories are worthless if the future tears down everything that was won at such great cost. And from Cam's angle, her shoulders seemed to slouch, as if fatigued by the weight of the blanket and the helmet and the burden she bore.

But above all, what struck Cam was the expression Freedom wore. To him, her wide-eyed, unguarded face seemed slack-jawed and incredulous, as if she couldn't believe that after all this time, after all that America and the world had fought for and endured, that we were now fighting amongst ourselves over the inventions of our own egos. We stood on ground soaked with the blood of those who had died for our freedom, and yet we used that freedom to fight each other for money and power. In the land of the free and the home of the brave, we bellowed and threatened and bullied to force our worldviews on each other.

Cam looked up at Freedom's face as he walked away.

I'm right there with you, lady.

After a brief video orientation in one of two huge theater rooms, they met their tour guide, a middle-aged man with thinning hair bleached blond and cut close on the sides, accompanied by shaggy dark-brown sideburns and a thin goatee. He wore a flag-blue tie with white stars that fell straight down from the hollow of his neck, then curved steeply over his prodigious paunch. From the right angle, his tie and torso outlined a lowercase letter *b*.

A red polyester blazer hung down at his sides, since there was little chance it would button, even if he tried. Hung from a lanyard around his neck was a large name tag with a picture of the man's photo-stunned face and the name CHRISTOPHER emblazoned beneath. Between the blue tie, the red blazer, and his rumpled white shirt, CHRISTOPHER looked like an action figure from the USA Everyday Heroes collection. Available in the gift shop to your left. Collect them all.

Behind the name tag was a black transmitter connected to

an earpiece and a thin microphone that curled around his cheek. It was the kind of rig worn by pop stars while they danced and sang on stage. As Cam collected a receiver and headphones from CHRISTOPHER's outstretched hand, Cam had the distinct sense that once, many years and many pounds ago—and maybe still—CHRISTOPHER had harbored dreams of being some kind of a star himself.

And now he was a star tour guide at the US Capitol.

And a damn good one, too, as it turned out. Regardless of what broken dreams may have littered the ground at his feet, as the tour progressed, CHRISTOPHER's passion for US history was evident, and his knowledge of the Capitol building was outstanding. He fielded every question from the tour group with relish, providing colorful and complete answers, often using the questions as a launching point for tangential, but fascinating, historical anecdotes.

He led them up the stairs beside Freedom, Cam giving the poor lady a mental nod as he passed, then up an escalator and through a series of narrow hallways to stand in a round vestibule outside the old Supreme Court chambers. Several pillars ringed the room, age-yellowed and ridged vertically like giant churros. The chambers themselves looked more like a moneylender's counting house than the highest court in the land, but that's probably why they decided to erect an entire building for the Supreme Court a short tunnel's walk away.

They walked through a small rotunda into the Capitol crypt. An array of single and double columns carved from sandstone provided structural support for the Rotunda and the massive Capitol Dome high above them. The roof that connected the columns in the crypt was set with a series of arches, the centuries-old hand-tooled craftsmanship as smooth and creamy white as French vanilla ice cream. Cam shook his head in amazement again at what we humans could achieve if we stopped squabbling and set our minds to a common purpose.

He wandered through the crypt as CHRISTOPER's voice came through his headphones, describing the architecture. Various chandeliers hung from the ceiling, mismatched like the government had picked them up at various liquidation sales. Some looked like Home Depot cast-offs. Others like they'd been purchased five-for-a-dollar at an elderly woman's estate sale.

A hodgepodge of statues ringed the room. CHRISTO-PHER explained that there was no longer room for all of the statues in the National Statuary Hall above them, so Congress had decided to bring some down here. There seemed to be no rhyme or reason to the selections. Samuel Adams, the father of beer, held a place of honor near a doorway. Some guy from Delaware named Caesar Rodney—a founding father, according to the sign underneath the statue—stood next to a bust of Lincoln. Lincoln's disembodied head wore a morose expression, like Rodney had slain Lincoln with a slingshot and Lincoln was feeling depressed about his failure.

More importantly, Cam saw little in the way of security in the crypt. Just one guard, standing with hands clasped before him and legs spread wide in the universal posture of bored men trying not to fall asleep. He didn't even carry a taser, let alone a gun. The security here was a joke.

From there, they went upstairs to the Capitol Rotunda. Here, the view was far more inspiring. They were inside the Capitol dome in a round room that had to be a hundred feet across. The sandstone walls were lined with massive paintings of historical events in John Trumbull's unmistakable Revolu-tion-era style. They were flat paintings inset into curved, gilded frames, so that the sides of the frame extended beyond the edges of the painting, giving each one the dramatic appearance of pushing out of the wall toward the viewer.

Around the room, more of the ubiquitous statues stood, though not as crowded or haphazard as in the crypt below. George Washington, President Eisenhower, a bust of Martin Luther King, Jr., a monument to several of the key suffragettes, including Susan B. Anthony and Elizabeth Cady Stanton. The room was intended to inspire, and it did not fail.

Even more inspiring was the space above them. The sandstone walls rose two hundred feet above Cam's head to an arched and coffered canopy finished in gold. It shone upon them like an indoor sun.

In the center of the canopy was Constantino Brumidi's *Apotheosis of Washington*, the crown jewel of the Capitol, in Cam's opinion. It rested in a place of honor, watching over the proceedings below. Its bright colors and shadows were visible even from the Rotunda floor. The painting consisted of two concentric rings. According to the informational plaque on the wall, the inner ring showed George Washington exalted, flanked by the goddesses of Victory and Liberty and thirteen maidens representing the thirteen original American colonies. The outer ring depicted the concepts of War, Science, Marine, Commerce, Mechanics, and Agriculture, skills that would be useful to a newly established America.

The composition of the painting suited the location perfectly, directing the eye to the pale round space in the center, through which the viewer far below could contemplate God or the sun or the emptiness of existence or their minuscule place in history or whatever fancy their mind might take.

For Cam, once again, the beauty of the architecture, the design, and the artwork led his thoughts to admiration and amazement. Humans were complex, terrible, wonderful creatures, capable in one breath of deep hatred, violence, and anger, and in the next breath of sublime compassion and transcendent beauty. The Capitol building seemed the perfect battleground for the war within our nature. In the midst of all this beauty, would Congress work from a place of selfish greed and corruption, or would they work from a place of selflessness, pushing to further a world that promoted equality, liberty, and justice for all?

And in that same place, Cam had his own choice to make. Celina had a plan, one that she still hadn't fully outlined for Cam or Paulie. She said she wanted to steal something from the Capitol, something easily portable and of great value. But she hadn't said what it was, where it was, or how she wanted to get it.

And Cam hadn't agreed to help her. Not yet, anyway.

From what Cam had seen, stealing from the Capitol would be as easy as stealing from the 7-11 on the corner. But as he stood in the center of the Capitol Rotunda, craning his neck to look straight up at Brumidi's masterpiece and contemplating the choice between good and evil that was offered to every human being in every moment of their lives, he wondered why he would even want to.

10

THE CAPITOL BUILDING looked like a giant fucking butt plug.

As Celina stood in the Rotunda, watching Cam gawk up at the fresco on the ceiling, she had to admit it was a beautiful butt plug. But it was still just a butt plug.

A beautiful, inspiring butt plug.

Which was fitting, since most of the elected officials inside the building were complete fucking assholes. Kind of like the original architects had anticipated the future and designed a building that fit the proctological theme.

On the positive side, the security was just as ass as the congresspeople and the design.

There was nothing there. She'd known security at the Capitol was a joke, but that was before the dipshit in the face paint and the fur hat brought a sharpened flagpole and two thousand of his friends into the building on January 6, 2021. Celina had heard that security had been beefed up since then. This was the first time she'd visited in person to see what had been done.

In a word, nothing. Not in the tourist areas, anyway.

A few more guards, mostly outside the building. A few more of the barricades that the mob had literally used to push down police officers. In other words, in its infinite wisdom and fervent desire to protect the Capitol and its skulking denizens, the government decided to provide more weapons to future insurrectionists.

Inside the building, there were some cameras here and there. A smattering of guards, mostly unarmed. But many of the areas that were roped off and closed to tourists were guarded only by docents, aging volunteers in red blazers, armed only with the authority of their indignation and the strength of their enfeebled arms.

Celina watched Cam's face as he stood in the center of the Rotunda, admiring the *Apotheosis of Washington* in the ceiling high above. It was a beautiful work, but one that stood for all the wrong things. Elevating a US President to the status of a god, for one thing. The power of that office was corrupting enough. Did we really want any of its holders to entertain the notion of themselves as God? And in the painting, Washington was surrounded by symbols of knowledge and industry: science, maritime studies, mechanics, and agriculture.

But also by symbols of war and greed.

Everywhere Celina looked in the room, she saw war and greed. The frieze of American history carved halfway up the dome depicted the glory of colonization and appropriation, of war and death and greed. The only scene that didn't glorify one of these horrible traits was the one showing the Wright brothers at Kitty Hawk, and even that conjured thoughts of modern airlines packing adult customers into seats sized for middle school students, then price-gouging them for the privilege.

At ground level, there were some well-intentioned paintings around the walls, such as the signing of the Declaration of Independence and one of General Washington willingly resigning his commission and giving up the power he held as commander-in-chief of the army—though he took it all back, with interest, when he became president. But the others showed even more war, even more colonization.

There was even a painting showing the baptism of Pocahontas. The poor woman was captured by invaders, held hostage, forced to change her religion and even her name, then forced into a political marriage to a slave-owning tobacco farmer to save her own people, who were later slaughtered anyway for the wealth of their land and the inconvenience of their existence. Then, she was carted all the way to England by her husband so she could be paraded around in front of rich, white people—who called themselves nobles, without a trace of irony—to try to drum up investment money for the colony back home.

This was what America chose to enshrine in its Capitol building? Sexism, enslavement, colonization, greed, and violence? They threw a bust of Martin Luther King, Jr. in there in the eighties to assuage their white guilt. Celina wondered whose job it was to clean up the marble chunks Dr. King's bust no doubt barfed up every day after having to look at all the bullshit around him.

And oh, by the way, the bust was black. Nothing wrong with that. But in that room, with all those references to colonialism and enslavement, where every single other statue is milky white? A little too on the nose for Celina's tastes.

The only statue of a woman in the whole massive room had the heads of three women on it. They couldn't even be bothered to single out one woman. Or, heaven forbid, erect three different statues to three different women. No, they're just women. We can lump them all together. Kill three women with one patriarchal stone. That should get the feminazi's off our backs.

Celina watched Cam turn in a circle, gawking in wonder at what he saw around him. She spun in her own circle, then swallowed her anger and choked down her bile. Her gaze drifted back up to the golden ceiling, to that Great Colander of Democracy. The way the afternoon light came through the cupola windows in that moment, the ceiling seemed to invert and come toward her, the apotheosis at the center bulging down like the pupil of some great alien eyeball, watching humanity and wondering, no doubt, what the fuck all the fuss was about.

Celina loved her country. She did. She was proud to be an American. She was just disappointed in the way its leaders—political and economic—were fucking it all up.

The tour moved on to the National Statuary Hall. With the way the statues were jumbled throughout the room, piled on top of each other and shoved into corners and doorways, it looked more like the storage room at Statue Warehouse—going out of business sale! Everything must go!—than an esteemed room at the U.S. Capitol. The statues were the usual rag-tag mix of racists, sexists, assholes, weirdos, and rich losers. There was Junipero Serra, who forced Christianity down the throats of millions of unsuspecting Mexicans and Native Americans. Over there was Barry Goldwater, famous for getting his ass kicked in a presidential election.

There was the usual lip service, too. Nebraska sent the statue of Chief Standing Bear, who just looked pissed, holding out his hand. A statue of Helen Keller as a young girl. The woman lived into her late eighties and spent her life advocating for the abilities of the disabled. To honor that life, they chose to depict her as a little girl clinging to a water pump as if she was too scared to find her way as a blind woman in the big, scary Capitol.

The best statue of all was the one of Amelia Earhart. Not a bad statue. Amelia standing tall in her aviator's outfit, hair cut short, a sassy smile on her face. But the good ol' state of Kansas could leave it alone. They had to engrave "Amelia Earhart, Famous Aviatrix" on the base.

Aviatrix? Celina could imagine the Kansas politician with the billiard ball body and the stinking stogie clamped in his jaws. *What should we put on the base?*, his simpering underling would ask. Anticipating with cum-staining glee getting tied up and whipped later that evening by his dom, Mistress Brunhilda, the rancid pol pulled his stogue from his mouth, the end black and wet and chewed to shreds, gave a yellow-toothed grin, and said, *Let's call the uppity bitch an aviatrix.*

But Celina wasn't there to mock the inane choices of American politicians. She could do that from anywhere. She was there for recon. She glanced around the room, checking for the guards. There was a guard at the entrance from the Rotunda, facing away from the Statuary Hall. Celina could see no other guards. Just two tour guides chatting with each other in the far corner, paying little attention to the tour members cluttering the room.

Celina worked her way toward the far end of the hall, closest to the chamber of the House of Representatives. There was a long, narrow corridor there that led to a warning sign, a red velvet rope on portable gold posts that served as a barrier, and a set of double-doors guarded by two attendants in blue blazers. Through those doors were the House chamber and the offices and meeting rooms that surrounded it.

Congress was in recess at that moment, for some undoubtedly ridiculous reason, so the population at work should be lighter than usual, but there were always staffers and maintenance staff and the few elected officials who actually tried to get real work done. The attendants were there to keep out unauthorized people—that would be the nosy tourists—and to hold the doors when congresspeople and their staff decided to parade through the aisle formed by two parallel chains of velvet ropes stretching through the center of the Statuary Hall.

Seeing her movement, Cam and Paulie drifted toward Celina.

The number of guards was low in the tourist areas of the Capitol, but the guards who were there were trained and dedicated. They weren't armed, likely just to set the tourists at ease, but Celina was sure they had access to weaponry, if needed. Like the tour guides and attendants, they were proud to work in the U.S. Capitol and took their jobs very seriously.

Celina also knew that there were armed police officers who escorted the senators and representatives from place to place within the Capitol. That force was likely what had been beefed up more than anything. The force might be lighter today on this side of the Capitol than normal, since the House wasn't in session, but there would still be some officers roaming around.

The attendants who guarded the doors were not tour guides or volunteers. They looked harmless enough, but they would have been trained and told not to open the doors for anyone who wasn't authorized. If she threatened them, Celina was sure they would let her through, but then they'd alert the police. Celina didn't want to attract any attention, if she could avoid it. If the credentials she'd forged couldn't get them through without being noticed, Celina would have to come back another day.

She checked once more for anyone watching, either a guard, a tour guide, or a nosy tourist who seemed like they would take See Something, Say Something as a personal motto. Seeing no one, she and Cam hung their credentials around their necks and slipped down the hallway at the quick, business-like pace of two harried, type-A congressional staffers.

Paulie stayed behind to deflect any attention they might have garnered, and to keep watch for any trouble that might head their way.

As they strode down the hallway, Celina saw the attendants scan them from head to toe. Cam looked rumpled and professional in an off-the-rack casual suit without the tie. She had worn a cream-colored silk blouse over dark grey pants with pumps and an elegant camel-brown open-front coat. Maybe a bit dressy for an off-season Capitol tourist, but convincing enough for a staffer.

She and Cam held up their credentials as they approached. The attendants had the doors halfway open before they were even close enough to scan the laminated cards. They smiled and nodded as Cam and Celina waltzed through.

"Okay," said Cam, once the doors had shut behind them. "We're here. Now what?"

They stood in a long marble-tiled hallway outside the House chambers. Celina saw a few staffers milling about, heads down in sheafs of paper. No one gave them a second glance.

Celina smiled and pointed down the hallway to her left.

"The speaker's office is this way," she said.

11

Celina led them down the hallway and around the corner, striding quickly and keeping her head up like she knew where she was going and she needed to get there quickly. Just like most of the other staffers that prowled around the Capitol.

She kept her eyes roving for any suspicious glances or any armed police officers, but found nothing. As she'd hoped, the population was much lower with the House not in session. The office buildings that surrounded the Capitol, where the Congresspeople did the majority of the work that didn't involve floor votes or debates or the like, were probably more crowded, but the House side of the Capitol was relatively quiet that day, thankfully.

They strode to the end of the hall to the southeast corner of the building. A small closet stood ahead of them. Behind and to the right was the House chamber. Immediately to Celina's right was the speaker's lobby, a long hallway that ran along the back of the House chamber. On the left side of the hallway were a series of rooms that used to serve as the offices of the Speaker of the House, back in the late 1800s. Now, they were retiring rooms for the members.

To Celina's right were two plain wooden doors. A placard

above one read *Speaker of the House, Madeline Kinkaid*. Celina took a deep breath and looked around her. No one was in the hall they'd just traversed. No one seemed to be in the long hallway of the speaker's lobby, either.

She knocked softly on the first door, leaning her ear against the wood for a response. She heard nothing.

She moved to her left, away from the view of the speaker's lobby, to stand before the second door. Both doors led to the same place, the ceremonial office of the Speaker of the House. It was a two roomed chamber where the Speaker of the House could host photo ops or retire during long sessions on the floor. The speaker had several offices in the Capitol complex, including a small office connected to the House floor, this ceremonial office across the hall, and a sprawling set of more functional offices adjacent to the Rotunda, as well as an office in one of the congressional office buildings across the street.

All of the 435 US representatives and 100 senators had office space in one of the buildings surrounding the Capitol. The leaders of the parties in the House and Senate, including the current House speaker, were given additional office space inside the Capitol building. The surrounding buildings were close, just a short ride on the Capitol subway, followed by a quick jaunt through the Capitol tunnel system. But power had its privilege, and a room to call their own inside the Capitol was one of them.

Celina knocked on the second door to the ceremonial offices. Hearing nothing, and seeing no one around them, she looked at Cam and nodded toward the door lock. Cam's eyes widened briefly. He glanced around, then pulled a slim, hard-shell case the size of a pack of gum from his jacket pocket and bent down to pick the lock.

Celina knew Cam was good. She'd worked with him on the Picasso job and seen him act cool under pressure. He said he'd been picking locks since he was in diapers, and she'd chosen to trust him on that point.

That was very weird for Celina. She'd only ever trusted one person before: her father. It wasn't in her nature to trust.

But she loved Cam. It surprised her to even think that without recoiling in horror or laughing out loud. But it was true. She had loved him within weeks of meeting him. That was also very weird. Celina never fell for anyone, let alone falling that hard that fast.

And sometimes love made people do stupid things. She hoped trusting Cam's lock-picking skills wasn't one of them. They were standing in the U.S. Capitol, committing a felony in the middle of the afternoon. She really didn't want to walk out of there in handcuffs.

As Cam worked, Celina turned her back to him, shielding him from view as much as possible while keeping a wary eye on the two hallways that could cause trouble if someone came around either corner. In her mind, she was working furiously through a series of contingency plans if they got caught.

As it turned out, she needn't have bothered. Ten seconds after he bent down, Cam stood and opened the office door. They both slipped inside, and Celina shut and locked the door behind them.

They had broken into the ceremonial offices of the speaker of the U.S. House of Representatives, the person third in line for the Presidency of the United States.

Celina took a beat to take in the space. A thick indigo carpet lined the floor. On the wall opposite the door was a large window, gauze curtains filtering a soft white light that filled the space. Comfortable couches and chairs with striped upholstery were arranged around the room. The feel of the room was elegant, but in an old-fashioned sort of way. Sort of a wealthy grandmother kind of vibe.

On the right, a large mirror with a gold frame covered one wall above an ornate fireplace. A small doorway led to the adjacent office, where someone on the speaker's staff could sit. Celina could see the edge of a small desk through the doorway.

To her left was another desk. There was nothing small about this one. It was at least eight feet wide and made of rich oak wood with carved feet and ornate ornamentation along the sides. The surface was empty, gleaming in the light from the window, the only adornment a small bouquet of flowers in one corner of the desk. They were fresh. Celina could smell their fragrance from the doorway.

Behind the desk stood an equally ornate wooden chair padded in a colonial style with a floral-embroidered cushion that was in keeping with the design scheme.

The only things that broke the pattern were a phalanx of American flags with ornate gold fringe that stood guard against the wall behind the desk and a battery of cameras, lights, and softboxes on tall mounts in front and on either side of it, facing the desk.

"This is where they come to get photos when the speaker signs important bills or hosts visiting dignitaries," Celina said to Cam.

Her voice was hushed. She didn't know why. It was unlikely anyone would hear them if they walked by outside. But the room seemed to command hushed tones, even from Celina.

Fuck that.

She cleared her throat, then spoke loudly, almost too loud to be prudent.

"Fucking photo ops," she said. "They keep this whole space for photo ops. At taxpayer expense."

Cam gave her a strange look, but just nodded.

Beneath the window was a sumptuous cherry-wood

bureau. Celina felt a thrill shiver her spine. In the shock of being in the room, she'd almost forgotten why she'd come.

She stepped across the room to the bureau. Three velvet boxes of various sizes and colors sat atop it, each one propped open to reveal ceremonial medals and awards set in velvet linings. Beside each box was a note, two of them formal, one handwritten, set on small easels. They were letters from dignitaries of various countries, awarding various ceremonial honors to the speaker for acts of service or aid to their countries.

Celina's eyes roved quickly over the awards, her mouth pursing in disdain. As usual, the speaker had accepted awards in her own name, taking credit for the work of hundreds of other people. No surprises there.

There was nothing else on the bureau. Celina frowned and turned in a circle, surveying the rest of the room. There were photos and framed documents on the walls. The mantle above the fireplace held a few small baubles, but she didn't see any other objects of note in the room. She turned back to the bureau and opened the doors below, checking the shelves within. They were all empty.

"It isn't here," she whispered. The thrill that earlier had shivered her spine became a flood of irritation.

"What's not here?" asked Cam.

Celina balled her fists. "It's not fucking here," she hissed through clenched teeth.

"What are you looking for?"

"A statue," Celina muttered. She set her hands above one another, about a foot apart. "A small statue."

She must have moved it. Celina had seen the statue in a photo taken in the room, but that photo had been taken years ago. Before the insurrection.

She must have moved it to another location after the insurrection, to keep it safe.

"What kind of statue?" asked Cam.

She fucking moved it. That bitch. Celina huffed out a breath and set her jaw.

"A valuable one," she muttered as she stalked back toward the door, trying in vain to control her emotions, with little success.

Her head felt thick and her temples throbbed. In the thickening haze of her anger, she didn't think twice about striding through the speaker's lobby, into the House chamber, and straight into the speaker's floor office. She saw no one, and no one tried to stop her.

The statue wasn't in that office, either.

That made Celina even angrier.

She stalked up the center aisle, past the representatives' seats and out the back door of the chamber, then straight down the hallway, through the double doors, and back into Statuary Hall. The attendants at the door jumped when she burst through the doors, but they held them open and went back to their jobs.

Celina stalked down the aisle of velvet ropes that ran through the center of Statuary Hall. Paulie was there, loitering by one of the statues. She looked up in surprise as Celina and Cam came through, but Celina didn't break stride. She gave Paulie a subtle shake of the head and continued on.

She passed their tour guide, who startled when he looked at them. Celina stared him down until he averted his eyes. He had recognized them, thought they'd been part of his tour a few minutes ago, but now they were striding through the Capitol with lanyards around their necks like they worked there. She knew he would question what he thought he saw, then assume he'd been mistaken. But it would probably nag at him for days. If anything happened to arouse suspicion and the tour guide was questioned, the information he'd provide would be valuable. Might even lead the authorities to Celina and Cam and Paulie.

But nothing would happen. Celina was angry, but she wasn't stupid.

Not very stupid, at least. Just stupid and angry enough to turn left after Statuary Hall and burst through the doorway in the small hallway that connected Statuary Hall to the Rotunda. Above the door was a sign just like the one above the ceremonial offices. *Speaker of the House, Madeline Kinkaid.*

The door led to the actual working offices of the speaker. This time, Celina knew she'd be noticed. It was unlikely the speaker herself would be in the office today, but Celina had no doubt that her staff would be there.

And she was right. There were at least a dozen staffers roaming through the ten or so rooms that comprised the speaker's Capitol office. A few of them glanced at Celina and Cam. Some even frowned slightly, but they averted their eyes quickly. In Washington, staffers quickly learned not to challenge the people in power unless you had power behind you. They followed the fucking laws of the savannah. Kill or be killed. Don't rock the boat, and if you challenge authority, you'd better be able to take them down in a fight.

Celina wielded the authority of her anger and the power of her fearlessness, and she was banking on the fact that none of the staffers working there would be senior enough to stop and question her.

She strode into each room in turn. They fell into two types, each one either a too-small room stuffed with paper-strewn desks and filing cabinets or a meeting room with quilted leather couches and elegant paintings on the walls. Celina scanned each room quickly. She didn't take the time to scour through cabinets and drawers searching for the statue. She already knew in her gut that it wasn't there. She knew she was wasting her time, and risking their discovery for no reason.

But she couldn't stop. She had to be sure. And the movement helped her. It both assuaged her anger and, when she didn't find the statue in each successive room, fueled it.

She worked her way down the hallway through the rooms until she arrived at the biggest room with the neatest, largest desk. It had to be the speaker's personal office.

The sight of the office finally stopped Celina. All the anger and irritation drained from her. The statue wasn't there. She could see that right away. There wasn't much in the way of personal decoration in the room, aside from a framed photograph on the desk. She moved behind the desk, touched lightly the corners of the neat piles of paper stacked on it. The photo was of the speaker with her late husband, Senator Robert Kinkaid, a fellow Democrat from the speaker's home state of Virginia.

Celina picked up the photo and looked down at it. The couple was on some kind of mountaintop in baseball caps and windproof shells, like they'd just hiked the mountain and reached the summit. They looked happy.

Senator Kinkaid had died in a plane crash twelve years ago, six years after he and the speaker were married.

Good. Celina hoped the bitch still cried herself to sleep every night.

"Excuse me."

A sharp voice came from the doorway. Celina set the photograph back down and looked up to see a round-bellied man with glasses in a rumpled tan suit and a blue tie. Around a balding pate, he had a ring of rumpled hair desperately in need of a trim.

The junior staffers outside had called their parents.

"Who are you," said the man, "and what do you think you're doing?"

He did not sound friendly.

And Celina did not care. She knew the speaker had

another office across the street, just like all the other congress-people. She'd had that office for all twenty-three years she'd been a member of Congress. If the statue were anywhere on site, it would be there. Celina would check that next.

"Sorry," she said, coming around the desk. "I took a wrong turn."

She pushed past the man and out the doorway, Cam following close behind her.

"Took a wro— Hey," called the man as he followed them down the hall. "What's your name? Are you with Senator Deacon's staff?"

Celina ignored the man as she and Cam strode down the hall.

"You can't come in here like this."

Celina kept walking toward the door.

The man stopped in the hallway and called after them. "Tell your boss the speaker will hear about this," he said, "and she will not be happy."

Celina burst out the door and back into Statuary Hall again, looking for Paulie. It was time for them to leave.

The speaker wouldn't be happy? Celina hoped that was true.

She smiled grimly to herself. If her plan succeeded, the speaker would be a fuck of a lot less happy.

12

Paulie had always liked visiting Washington. Sure, it had a troubled history. Slavery, arrogance, corruption. That was America's cross to bear. And those were still problems today, in various forms.

And the politics. It had always been contentious, but when Paulie was younger, politicians would argue all day, then go out for a beer and talk about their kids. Now, it was pure bile 24-7, and nothing was getting done.

But amidst all that negativity, Washington D.C. was a symbol of the promise of America, and a demonstration of what could be achieved in spite of all the negatives.

Paulie had never spent as much time in the Capitol as she did that day. The Rotunda was amazing, a massive space with an echoing ambiance and cool air that had the musty, dry smell of historic buildings everywhere. As if the bones of the builders were still there somewhere.

Paulie liked that thought. People didn't take as much pride in their work anymore. It was hard to do. Society had drained everything of value. Most of the stuff for sale was made as cheaply as possible to maximize some corporation's profit margin. When something was well made, the price was sky high, out of reach of the average person.

But no one talked about quality, anyway. The only things that mattered anymore, if you believed all the advertising and propaganda, were what your possessions said about your wealth or your stature. And those kinds of things were all designed to lose their value as soon as the next sales season came around. You buy a fancy computer or phone and it's obsolete a year later. You buy a fancy car and the new model comes out and makes your year-old ride seem out of fashion. You spend an obscene amount of money on a handbag or a pair of shoes or a watch and something comes down the line that makes you want something newer and even more expensive.

It's all just a big hamster wheel that keeps everyone running and puffing, chasing a carrot that they can never catch. The process is designed to keep the normal people unhappy, constantly striving, while the rich people watch, laugh, and get richer and richer with every turn of the wheel.

But it wasn't always like that. There was a time when people used what they made, and the value was in the quality and the longevity. Paulie could feel that kind of pride of workmanship in the walls of the Capitol.

Not so much in the statues, especially the modern ones. Those were all just vanity projects. Some politician trying to curry favor or court a big donation by honoring some fat cat from the old days. Or someone trying to win over a portion of the electorate by commissioning a statue of a Native American or a woman or a black person. Those statues felt smarmy and disingenuous.

But not the building itself. Not the old paintings, and not the architecture. Even the modern additions like the Visitors Center, which was only twenty years old, showed a thoughtfulness and a quality that gave Paulie hope. The people who had worked on that project hadn't opted for the cheapest, fastest solution, the one that would minimize costs. They got a lot of shit for that, Paulie remembered, but they had held firm. They'd built for history, a project that they hoped would awe visitors two hundred years from now, in exactly the same way that the Capitol Rotunda still awed visitors today.

The Visitors Center was no Rotunda, of course, but it had its dramatic highlights, like the two huge skylights that let you look up and see the Capitol dome from underground. Overall, it was just a place for people to come into the Capitol without adding a structure that would ruin the original design. But Paulie still appreciated the effort.

Just as she appreciated the Statuary Hall, not for the statues, but for the architecture. The checkerboard marble tiles, the variegated marble columns, the beautiful curtains draping down the walls. She loved the sight lines, the way the space pulled your eye straight down the hallways as you entered the door, but pulled it around the room and up to the heavens if you stopped to look around.

According to the tour guide, the space used to be the chamber of the House of Representatives in the earlier days of the country, and it still bore the majesty befitting not the practice, but the dream of such a deliberative body. The old balcony that still had seats for visitors. The fireplaces in the corners for warmth amid all that stone on cold days in the Washington winters. The plaques on the floor where the desks of Abraham Lincoln and John Quincy Adams once stood. Presidents had been inaugurated there. Luminaries had lain in state there. And Paulie could feel that history all around her.

But above all, she loved the ceiling. The double-sunk coffers and the lantern in the center that let in all that gorgeous afternoon light. It wasn't as grand as the Rotunda dome, nor as inspiring, but it still lifted Paulie's mind to thoughts beyond herself. And wasn't that the point of politics? The original point? Politics wasn't supposed to serve the politician. Politicians in America were elected to serve the people, both in the present and, even more importantly, in the future.

Everyone seemed to have lost that foresight. Not just politicians. Everyone. After fifteen years in prison, Paulie had come out into a changed world. Cell phones and the internet and streaming television and social media. Nothing wrong with any of those things, but they seemed to be splitting everyone apart, shrinking people's worlds even as they opened people's access to it.

It felt good to be in a space that lifted Paulie's vision higher. If she closed her eyes and pulled in a deep breath, she could smell the history and taste the idealism. Life was about more than power or money or followers or influence. And the Capitol—the bones, not the flesh—reminded her of that fact.

Paulie heard the echoes of someone walking fast through the hall, their shoes clacking on the tiles. She opened her eyes and turned to see Celina and Cam banging down the center aisle. Celina gave Paulie a fierce look and a tiny shake of her head.

That girl was a firecracker, and something had lit her fuse.

Cam shrugged from behind her. He was clearly just following Celina's lead.

Celina stared daggers through the eyes of their poor tour guide, Chris, as she passed. The color drained from his face once she'd gone by. Celina might as well have held a gun to his head or threatened to murder his family. The poor man looked like he might piss his pants.

Paulie saw Celina and Cam walk through the hall and turn through the archway with the name of the Speaker of the House on a wooden placard fixed to the sandstone above. They breezed in as smooth and as quick as you please, like they owned the place and the speaker owed them back rent.

Chris frowned for a second. He must have recognized Cam and Celina. The tour group wasn't that big. But he couldn't square the circle of two of his tourists storming around the Capitol like they belonged there, with ID badges swinging from their necks.

He must have found some way to make it sit neat in his brain, because he seemed to collect himself for a second, then gathered the tour group together again. Paulie could see him counting heads once, then again, and frowning to himself. His eyes found Paulie's, and they narrowed a little. Paulie gave him a soft look and sent him comforting vibes. It seemed to settle the poor man a bit.

He herded them all up and led them back through the Rotunda. Paulie peeled off the back of the line and watched the group traipse back through the Rotunda and down the stairs to the Visitors Center. The tour was over.

But Paulie had never been there for the tour.

And she certainly didn't mind hanging out in the Rotunda for a bit while she waited for Celina and Cam to return. She found a harmless space to stand in, let her eyes walk all the way up to the beautiful artwork on the ceiling, and just soaked it all in. The colors, the scents, the sounds of the murmuring and the echoing, like the whispers of the ancients.

She didn't get to enjoy it for long. A few minutes later, Cam and Celina came back out of the same archway they'd gone in. She could feel the emotion flooding out of Celina. Anger and frustration, and some kind of deeper hurt.

Paulie still didn't know what the hell they were doing there. Celina had been keeping her plans close to her vest. That was her right. She was leading this one and Paulie was happy to go along for the ride. It wasn't the way she or her husband had run their crews, and probably wasn't how Cam ran his, but this was Celina's crew. Celina could run it however she liked. If Paulie didn't like it, she was free to step out.

But she wanted to be there. Paulie would support Celina however she needed support.

And right now, Celina looked like she needed to cool off for a while. A glance at Cam told her he was thinking the same thing.

"Let's head back," said Paulie once Celina and Cam had gathered around her.

Celina huffed once, then shook her head.

"You two go back," she said. "I need to check one more place."

"I'll go with you," said Cam immediately.

"We'll both go," said Paulie.

"No." Celina's voice was quick and her eyes were sharp. Then she looked at both of them and softened. "Thank you," she said, "but it'll be easier if there's just one of us."

Cam stared hard at Celina for a long moment. Paulie waited to see what he would say. It was obvious that he didn't want to let Celina go alone. He wanted to support her, too, and he was clearly worried about her mindset. But Celina was a smart, independent woman. Cam couldn't control her. And he shouldn't try, even if his intentions were good.

He knew that. Paulie had taught him that. She held her breath to see if his respect for Celina was strong enough to overcome his concern for her.

He released a long breath. "Okay," he nodded. "We'll meet you back at the house."

That's my boy.

"But if you haven't come back or checked in after an hour," he looked at his phone, "I'm coming after you."

Celina smiled grimly. "You don't know where I'm going."

"You've checked every office the speaker has in this building," Cam said. "I know where you're going."

Celina stared hard at him for a long moment, then nodded once and stalked away, heading toward a stairwell.

Paulie watched Cam follow her with his eyes, looking after her long after she'd disappeared from view.

She reached out and held his arm. His eyes tracked back to hers, clouded with worry.

Paulie squeezed his arm once. "Let's go home," she said softly.

With another long glance toward where Celina had been, Cam nodded, and they walked away together.

Love was a complicated thing, and Celina was a complicated woman. Paulie knew what she hoped would happen with Cam and Celina, but love took its own path, and sometimes that path led into the jungle.

She just hoped she could help Cam and Celina cut through the vines.

13

Cam paced back and forth in the kitchen, his mother sitting on a barstool watching him, her head in her hand propped on the counter. His mind raced with worry. His ears strained for the sound of sirens or gunshots. He checked his phone every minute for notifications of an incident at the Capitol complex. He checked social media for the same thing.

He realized he was just working himself into a frenzy. He had no idea what was going on, and no way to know. Wearing a groove into the floor and imagining all the worst outcomes was going to do no one any favors.

If he was actually on the job with Celina, he'd be fine. He'd be focused on the objective, keeping his body and mind relaxed and extending his senses for input. He forced himself to do that now. He sat down on the couch in front of the fire, closed his eyes, and focused on his breath. Just like his parents had taught him since he was a kid.

His heart rate slowed, the pulsing in his temple receded. He became more aware of the volume of the space around him, of the cool temperature of the air, of the faint smells of omelette it still carried from breakfast. He could feel his moth-

88

er's presence, though whether he was actually sensing her energy or just remembering she was there, he didn't know.

Unfortunately, extending his senses like that made it very obvious just how uncomfortable the damn couch actually was. The cushion, which looked fluffy and soft, was hard as a rock. It bulged against his back and made him arch awkwardly. Within minutes, his lower back was aching.

Cam opened his eyes and stood with an irritated huff. All the anxious thoughts picked up again right where they'd left off.

He checked his watch. They'd left Celina thirty minutes ago.

Thirty minutes until check-in.

Cam considered waiting outside the Longworth House Office Building. He knew that's where Celina had gone. That's where the speaker's only other office was, the original office she'd been given when she was first elected. As the youngest member of Congress since the early 1800s, and a female, to boot, it had been in all the papers. To the press, Madeline Kinkaid was a wunderkind.

Cam had only been ten-years-old at the time, but she'd been in the news when her husband had died a decade or so ago. When she became Speaker in the current Congress, they'd done a bunch of retrospective pieces. Kinkaid was only the second female Speaker of the House in U.S. history, following in Nancy Pelosi's very large footsteps. And she was young, only forty-five or so when she took the gavel two years earlier. The wunderkind was being wunderful yet again.

So Cam knew all about the cluttered, utilitarian office space across the street from the Capitol building. They'd played it up in all the retrospectives. A rags-to-riches kind of thing, even though a cluttered two-room office in downtown DC was hardly what Horatio Alger would have called rags.

And he knew that's where Celina had gone. Through the Capitol, down the stairs to the basement, through a footpath tunnel under Independence Ave into Cannon House Office Building, then another short pedestrian tunnel into Longworth.

Which was probably crawling with staffers and congresspeople.

And armed cops.

Cam started pacing back and forth across the kitchen again.

"What should we have for dinner?"

He halted mid-pace and looked at his mother. She raised her eyebrows.

"It's getting toward dinnertime," she said. "Sneaking around is hard work. Celina will probably be hungry when she gets here."

Cam took a deep breath and let it out in a heavy sigh.

"Yeah," he said, turning his mind to the question. It seized on the idea like a thirsty man seizes a glass of water. He pulled open the fridge. As he focused on dinner plans, his mind spinning through the possible dishes he could make with the ingredients he saw before him, he felt his chest loosen, his shoulders relax. The anxiety was still there. He could feel it lurking just below the surface of his mind. But at least he had something to do. Something to focus on until Celina returned.

If she returned.

Cam checked his watch. Twenty-nine minutes to check-in.

He sighed again and set to work.

Piles of chopped herbs and vegetables surrounded him. Carrots and onion, minced garlic and thyme. Chicken thighs were already marinating in a bowl with red wine, chicken stock, and brandy. He was working on the bacon, cutting it into half-inch pieces, when his phone buzzed on the counter.

Cam realized he had lost track of time. He checked his watch. One minute before check-in time.

He wiped his hands on a towel and tapped his phone. A text from Celina.

On my way.

Cam let out a sigh that carried the weight of a thousand worries. Tension drained from his body like water draining from a spilled bucket.

Paulie reached across the counter and spun the phone around so she could read it. She nodded once, then looked up at Cam.

"Wouldn't it be nice if she could walk in the door and smell a delicious dinner cooking?" she said.

A smile twisted Cam's mouth. He shook his head.

"Wouldn't it be nice if my own mother would pitch in to help instead of just sitting there watching?"

Paulie shrugged. "You seemed like you needed something to do."

Cam's smile faded, and he nodded slowly.

"I did," he said, then looked up at Paulie. "Thanks."

Paulie slid off her stool, came around the large center island, and held Cam's face in her hands. Cam could feel the love pouring from her eyes into him, filling the space the draining tension had left behind. He felt warm and safe and soft, like Paulie was wrapping him in a warm blanket, then hugging him close.

God, he'd missed his mother.

"That's what mothers are for," she said, then patted his cheek and turned to the counter. "Okay, what are we making here?"

By the time Celina came through the front door, the bacon was crisp, the chicken was seared, and the mirepoix was sauteing. The house had filled with the rich scent of dinner in progress.

"Smells incredible," said Celina as she sat heavily on a barstool. She reached across the counter to steal a few pieces of bacon from the plate where it rested. Paulie smacked her hand lightly with the back of a wooden spoon. Celina grinned and popped the stolen pieces into her mouth.

Celina surveyed the counter and the stove for a moment. "Coq au vin?"

Cam was at the stove, his back toward the center island. Since he'd heard the keys in the front door lock, he'd been fighting the urge to drop everything and run to Celina, pull her into his arms and check her everywhere for bruises, stare into her eyes for any hint of what might have happened.

But he knew she'd just be pissed off if he did that. And he knew he had to learn to keep his shit together. If he and Celina were going to stay together—and he sincerely hoped they would—this situation was going to happen again. Celina was not the type of woman to stay by Cam's side every hour of every day, and he wouldn't want her to be. He had to learn to give her space and control his fears. No one wanted to be with a partner who freaked out whenever they left the house.

Of course, breaking into a Congressperson's office in a busy government building on a weekday afternoon isn't quite the same as just leaving the house, but the principle still applied. He desperately wanted to ask her how it went, grill her for details, admonish her for taking foolish risks. But he knew he needed to be patient. She would tell them when the time was right for her.

"Yep," Cam said over his shoulder. He'd just added the garlic to the pan, and it required stirring to keep it from burning.

"Did you add brandy to the marinade?"

She slid the marinade bowl across the counter, sniffed it, and nodded in approval. Cam pushed the mirepoix to one side of the pan and added tomato paste to the other side, then put a small scoop of mirepoix on the end of a wooden spoon and turned, hand held under the spoon, to give Celina a taste.

She took the spoon in her mouth, her lips closing over it as Cam drew the spoon slowly back. She flicked her emerald-green eyes up, watching him as she bit the spoon in her teeth, held it against the force of Cam's withdrawal, then slowly loosened her grip and let the spoon slip slowly, slowly through her full, soft lips.

The movement might have been innocuous, innocent, if it weren't for the look in her gorgeous eyes. That look was definitely not innocent. In the blink of an eye, Cam's pants became very tight in the crotch.

Damn, that woman.

Celina focused on tasting the food instead of teasing Cam, then nodded. She got up and came around the counter as Cam gave a taste to his mother, who murmured her approval. As Cam mixed the tomato paste in with the mirepoix, Celina stood beside him, then reached back for the marinade and slowly poured it into the pan while Cam stirred.

They stood like that, side by side, listening to the hiss and sizzle of the hot pan settle to a throaty simmer as the liquid poured in and bubbled as it heated. Cam added the chicken, nestling it under the liquid, then sprinkled the thyme over the top and covered the pan to cook.

As they stood and watched the glass cover steam up, Celina slid her hand around Cam's waist and pulled him tight against her. Even through the rich scent of the food, Cam could smell Celina's hair, the light smell of lavender that he would recognize anywhere.

Celina released him, turned, and surveyed the counter.

"You've got the bacon, the pearl onions... Beurre manie?"

Cam pointed to a stick of butter softening on the counter.

"Okay," Celina said. "Mushrooms?"

Cam shook his head. "Haven't gotten there yet."

"I'll start chopping."

Paulie smiled and held out her knife to Celina.

An hour later, the three of them leaned back in their chairs at the table, their bellies full with good food and wine, and their hearts full with good companionship.

"Who's up for a movie?" asked Celina. With a wicked grin, she said, "Mission Impossible?"

Cam laughed, but then his face grew serious.

"I think it's time you told us what's going on, Celina," he said.

Celina nodded and stared at her glass as she swirled the remains of her wine.

"Did you find what you were looking for at Longworth?"

Celina glanced up at Cam and raised her eyebrows. Cam raised his right back.

He knew he should be patient, but he'd been patient. For hours. This wasn't the question of an overly concerned lover. This was the question of a crew member who needed information. Who deserved to know what was going on.

Celina grinned and nodded, then stared back down at her swirling wine. Cam had said he knew where she was going, and he now knew he'd been right.

"No," Celina said. "It wasn't there, either."

"Okay," said Cam, with a glance at his mother. She was watching Celina closely, her face filled with compassion and concern for Celina. Paulie really was a remarkable person.

"You said we're looking for a statue," Cam continued.

Celina nodded toward her wine glass.

"A valuable statue."

Celina nodded again.

Cam laughed and shook his head.

"How about you give us just a little more information?"

Celina raised her eyebrows once more, but still didn't look up from her wine. "What do you want to know?"

"Everything," said Cam, his frustration coming into his voice.

"Everything?" Celine smiled at her glass. "That's an awful lot."

Now she was fucking with them. Okay. Cam could play along. But he wasn't going to bed tonight without getting the answers he needed.

"We've got all night," he said. "But how about you start by telling us your plan."

"My plan?"

"You didn't find the statue. We looked all through the Capitol—the fucking U.S. Capitol—and then you checked the office building."

"Right."

"You're after a statue that Speaker Kinkaid owns."

"Correct."

"But you didn't find it."

"Nope."

Celina still wasn't looking up from her wine glass. Cam looked at his mother, exasperated. She held out both hands palms-down and patted the air, telling him to settle down.

"Okay," said Cam, drawing out the word and doing his best to calm his irritation. He didn't appreciate all the mystery from Celina. It wasn't just because they were intimate. Withholding information was no way to run a crew. In order for the plan to run smoothly, for every crew member to be able to adapt quickly and safely when the plan inevitably went to shit, everyone needed to know everything.

And Celina wasn't telling them everything.

"You didn't find the statue," he said. "Does that mean the plan is off?"

"No." Celina finally stopped swirling her wine, but she still didn't look up. "It means we have to figure out where it is."

Cam sighed. Finally, they were getting somewhere.

"Right. How are we going to do that?"

Finally, Celina looked up at him and at Paulie.

"I have a plan," she said.

"You do?" asked Cam.

A slow smile spread over Celina's face.

"I do," she nodded, her smile turning into a grin. "But we might need to call in a few friends."

14

THEY STOOD on a brick-paved sidewalk in Alexandria, Virginia, about a twenty-minute drive from the Capitol. The air was crisp, the sky clear. A red maple twined above them, filtering the bright sunlight through its vivid orange leaves into dapple and shadow on the red brick.

Cam, Celina, and Paulie, steaming cups of coffee in their hands, huddled around a brochure of Old Town Alexandria as if they were a group of tourists trying to map their route to the next destination.

Instead, they were observing the house across the street from them.

The house was gorgeous, a historic three-story townhouse on a massive double lot. Unlike most houses on that street, which were built shoulder-to-shoulder, this one had no immediate neighbors on either side. Built in the mid-1800s by a wealthy merchant, the home had been protected and well-preserved since. It was even listed on the National Register of Historic Places.

It was also the private home of the current Speaker of the House, Madeline Kinkaid.

The main structure was tall and rectangular. Most of the

97

construction was brick, but the front facade was built from stone blocks, probably sandstone, and painted a tasteful beige. To the right side of the house was a gated entryway watched over by a towering maple and a large guard house. On the left side, surrounded like the rest of the property by an eight-foot brick wall covered in ivy, a lush, well-maintained garden extended the length of the house, with several seating areas, fire pits and heaters, and an outdoor kitchen. In the back, protected by another gate, a short driveway led to a garage.

Like Celina's home, this one exuded elegance and wealth and history, maintaining the feel of its 19th century design with stone steps and wrought-iron railings leading to a heavy oak front door. The doorway and the windows were tall and arched, painted a white that was so brilliant and clean, it must have been repainted twice a year. A scalloped ornamental cornice ran along the roofline, lending the building both a sophisticated air and a hulking presence above the sidewalk.

While the exterior honored the original architecture, from the research Celina had done, Cam knew the inside of the home had been renovated several times to keep in step with modern convenience, aesthetics, and technology. That included security technology. The exterior of the home was covered by numerous cameras around the property and on the house itself, cleverly hidden so as not to distract from the home's historical appearance. It stood to reason that there would be cameras inside the home, as well. But Celina, as talented a hacker as she was, still hadn't been able to get inside the system.

They hunched over the brochure, the smell of the coffee filling Cam's nose and making his stomach growl. He hadn't been hungry for breakfast, but he was hungry now. He took a long swig from his cup. The hot liquid burned down his throat, warming him against the chill mid-morning air.

"High-end security throughout," Celina was saying. "State

of the art, with cameras everywhere, sensors on all the doors and windows, floor sensors at night, even face reco and thermal patterning so she can get up for a glass of water or a piss at night without setting off the alarms."

"Sounds serious," said Paulie.

"How long until you can hack it?" asked Cam.

Celina pressed her lips together. "It's not easy. It's run by a dedicated network admin, and she's good, but she's not that good. Kinkaid must have had expert help when she set it up. Passwords change every three hours, always a random string of fifty characters, with sophisticated obfuscation and intrusion detection. The house is locked down tighter than most banks I've seen."

"Why so much security?" said Cam. "It's not like she's the President."

"She's the third most powerful person in the U.S. government," said Celina. "And some would argue she's second, more powerful than the Vice-President. The speaker can decide what laws get passed, can decide which ones even come up for a vote."

"And she's a woman," muttered Paulie.

"And she's a woman," Celina nodded. "A relatively young one. Pelosi was in her sixties when she became Speaker. Old enough for people to think about her like a grandmother. Kinkaid is forty-seven. She's a threat. You think there aren't crazy fuckers out there who wouldn't love to break into a female Speaker's house at night and show her who really has the power in this country? Put her in her place, show her where women belong? That kind of shit?"

Cam sighed and nodded. "Ok, so we can't break in and we can't hack it. That's gonna be a problem if we're trying to steal a statue from inside the house." He thought through options. "Does she ever take the statue somewhere else, put it on loan or on display somewhere? You said it used to be in the Capitol. Do we even know for sure if it's in the house?"

"That's what we need to figure out."

It was not the answer Cam was hoping for.

From the far end of the sidewalk, a man in a long black overcoat, grey scarf and jeans, and black boots strolled toward them, hands in his pockets. Celina looked up. When she saw him, her face lit up.

"Glad you could make it," she said, stepping away from Cam and Paulie and smiling broadly.

"And miss a chance to see you again?" The man smiled back and kissed Celina on both cheeks before wrapping her in a big hug. "Hello, again, gorgeous."

He had a faint British accent and wore his luxurious dark hair short on the sides and long on top, pushed into a stylish coif. A two-day stubble covered his chiseled jawline. His chest and shoulders were broad and clearly well-muscled, angling down to a slim waist under his well-tailored jacket. He looked like a goddamn movie star.

Cam suddenly felt awkward and ugly. His overcoat felt like a ragged sack, his shoes like second-hand rejects, his hair like it had been cut by a wayward hedge trimmer. Watching Celina hug the man was like watching a red-carpet gala on television.

Cam felt a stab, sharp in his stomach, and clenched his jaw. From the side of his vision, he saw his mother glance toward him and tilt her head, a faint smile on her lips. He ignored her.

"Cam and Paulie Hauk," said Celina, bringing the man toward them with one arm around his shoulder in a way that was far too comfortable for Cam's taste, "this is Simon Walsh, the best recon and infil guy you'll ever meet."

"A pleasure to meet you," Simon said, taking Paulie's hand in his and bowing to kiss it. His voice was like soft silk on skin.

"Oh, I like this one, Celina," she said, pressing her other hand over her heart and winking at Simon.

He laughed, a rich, low laugh that seemed to rumble through Cam's body. "The feeling is absolutely mutual, my dear."

Why was it that everything said in a British accent sounded suave and sophisticated? The man was hitting on his mother, his fifty-six-year-old mother, right in front of him.

"Cam," Simon said, turning toward Cam and extending his hand. His eyes were the vivid blue of the ocean in Cancun. "It's a pleasure to finally meet you in person. Celina has told me a lot about you."

"Has she?" Cam said, shaking Simon's hand and glancing at Celina. "Do you two talk often?"

Simon's eyebrows went up briefly in surprise, then his face shifted into a broad grin, his eyes shining. He pulled Cam toward him and leaned in. "Not as often as I'd like, mate, believe me," he said conspiratorially.

"Simon..." said Celina, shaking her head.

Simon straightened and winked at Cam before releasing his grip. Cam glanced back and forth between Celina and Simon. Celina punched Simon playfully in that broad chest of his before Simon pulled her back into a warm, familiar, one-armed hug.

Cam's guts roiled. Celina had never mentioned anyone named Simon, but clearly the man was important to her. A friend. A good friend, even, from the looks of it. Maybe even more than a good friend.

He felt an acid twinge in his stomach. The coffee he'd drunk earlier crept up the back of his throat.

"Is that it, then?" asked Simon, turning to face the house across the street.

Celina turned with him and nodded.

Simon regarded the home for a moment. "Come in through the roof?"

Celina shook her head. "Ray guarded."

"We can use a drone."

"You can drill that precisely with a drone?"

Simon smirked at Celina.

"You insult me, darling. Of course I can."

"My apologies, your lordship."

Simon frowned at her, then turned back to the house. "Keep your lordships to yourself, madam," he said under his breath, so faintly Cam could barely hear it.

Celina chuckled softly.

What the hell, was this guy some kind of English nobleman or something?

"Wouldn't a drill be too loud?" said Cam. "Especially at night. Someone would wake up."

Simon and Celina both looked at Cam for a long beat. Cam felt his cheeks grow hot under their gazes.

"It's just a term," said Celina. "Slang."

"Not an actual drill, mate," Simon explained. The friendliness in his voice made Cam hate him even more. "It's an electromagnetic beam that can penetrate standard building materials—commercial and residential—to create an image of the interior."

"Like sonar," said Paulie.

"Exactly like sonar, love," said Simon, then regarded Paulie with an appraising eye that made Cam want to punch him right in his perfectly sculpted nose. "Beauty and brains. Celina, why didn't you warn me about this wicked siren on your team?"

"Some things you have to discover all on your own," said Celina.

Paulie grinned at Simon.

Even his own mother was seduced by the man's infernal

charms. The acid in the back of Cam's throat crept a little higher.

Simon craned his head back to look at the sky.

"Tonight, then?" he said. "Weather looks good." He leaned toward Paulie. "Bad weather can throw off the sonar signature."

Cam noticed that, when he leaned, Simon had made sure his arm and shoulder pressed against Paulie. He didn't have to do that, the fucker.

Paulie nodded sagely.

"Tonight," said Celina, nodding.

"Excellent." Simon clapped his hands and rubbed them together. "Who's hungry for a bite to eat? No sense working on an empty stomach, eh?"

He put one arm around Celina's waist and the other around Paulie's, then led them both down the sidewalk.

Cam, trailing behind, had suddenly lost his appetite.

15

THEY HAD A LONG LUNCH, then a wander around Old Town Alexandria, followed by an even longer dinner filled with charming stories from Simon and far too many bottles of wine before a night job that was just hours away. Cam largely sulked in his chair at the meals or hung behind the group when walking down the sidewalk.

And the others largely let him. After a few odd looks from Celina and a few attempts by Paulie to pull him out of his funk, they let him sulk and went back to enjoying Simon's company.

And he was good company, Cam had to admit. He was handsome, he was British. And, from the way he ordered expensive wine and picked up all the checks without a blink, he was rich. But he was also charming and entertaining. He showed interest in Celina and Paulie, and even did his best to engage Cam. By the end of the evening, against his will, Cam found himself laughing along with the others at Simon's stories.

He was an English lord, as it turned out. The second son of a minor duke in England.

"Second son of a non-royal noble," said Simon, correcting

Celina. "Worth practically nothing at all." He lifted his glass and gave a roguish leer. "But occasionally helpful with women." He winked at Paulie, who lifted one eyebrow in response.

"When have you ever needed help with women?" Celina muttered as she took a sip from her wine glass.

Simon turned toward her. His eyes lost focus for a moment, his smile turning wistful as he seemed to slip into his memories. Then he returned to the present moment and shrugged. "From time to time," he said quietly before taking a long drink.

By the end of the evening, Cam had managed to shake off his mood. Celina and Simon were obviously close, but Cam didn't know if there was a romantic history between them. If there was, Celina would tell him in her own time, if she wanted to.

Cam knew he wasn't the first man Celina had slept with. Maybe not even the first man she'd fallen in love with. He had no right to be upset if she came across a former lover or boyfriend.

And he shouldn't be surprised if they were handsome. Celina was drop-dead gorgeous. Of course she would attract men with movie star looks. That just made sense.

Honestly, the only thing that didn't make sense was why Celina was with Cam. He didn't have movie star good looks. He wasn't the second son of an English duke, minor or otherwise. Celina could do so much better.

And maybe that was the real problem.

Cam knew he was overreacting. He knew he was acting petty, petulant, and jealous. And he knew it wasn't a good look, for Celina or for himself. It was toxic. And there was nowhere to go with it but down. What did he think he would do, demand that Celina never see an old flame? Demand that she only associate with men who were less handsome and less accomplished than Cam? It was ridiculous. It was time to pull his head out of his own ass and act like a grown man.

That didn't mean he trusted Simon. For all he knew, Simon had taken the job so he could woo Celina back.

And Cam might not be good enough for her, but that didn't mean he'd give up without a fight.

But he didn't have to be a pouty, jealous asshole, either. That would not help his cause.

"Simon," he said after the latest round of laughter had subsided, "how did you gain your... expertise?" He waited a beat. "At recon and infil, I mean," he added with a grin.

Celina turned toward Cam with a sly smile and a wicked shine in her eyes. Paulie smiled at him, too, exuding calm and love, as always.

Simon's eyebrows rose at hearing Cam finally speak. He chuckled at the joke, then frowned in thought as he considered his response.

"That, my friend"—he tilted his head toward Cam to emphasize the word—"is an excellent question. And it has a very complicated answer involving two Australian women, a Russian-made RPG, and a wallaby drunk on fermented kiwis." He raised his hand to the waiter, who rushed toward the table. "We're going to need another bottle of wine."

By the bottom of the next bottle, Cam was laughing along with everyone else, laughing so hard the muscles in his side actually hurt.

The laughter drifted into a congenial silence. It hung heavy in the air for a long moment, and Cam could feel something shift in the mood. A quick glance around the table told him everyone else had felt it, too.

The sun had gone down hours ago and the windows were dark. Their bellies were full, their appetites sated. It was as if a switch had been thrown in the universe. The wine-fueled joviality of the last few hours slid to the background.

They'd met. They'd bonded. And now it was time to focus.

Simon insisted on paying the hefty bill. They all stood, went into the night, and went to work.

Celina had done some research. The house across the street from their target was owned by a wealthy older couple in their seventies. Despite the relatively mild winters in Washington, the couple chose to winter in their palazzo in Pozallo on the southern coast of Sicily, where the low temperatures at night rarely dropped below fifty degrees.

Though the couple had hired a security service and had a modern security system installed, it was no match for Celina. Cam and the others were inside within minutes.

They set up in the second-floor study, which had two large windows facing the street. They left the house lights off. Celina had provided everyone with a pair of AR glasses that let them see in the dark as if the lights were blazing. They spoke in whispers, the sound technology in the glasses amplifying the softest sub-vocalization, just as they had done for Cam on the Picasso job.

Celina looked through the glasses at the windows of the speaker's home across the street, starting on the top floor, looking for any sign of movement and any sign of the statue. No sense in mounting a huge recon operation if you can see what you need just by looking.

"The top floor windows are covered," she said.

The glasses would provide a visual of any people moving around inside, but they didn't show inanimate objects like the statue. Without an unobstructed view, they couldn't see inside.

She shifted her gaze down to the second floor. She peered closely for a moment, then removed her glasses and looked again.

Frowning, she took a pair of small binoculars from the small equipment bag she'd brought. Beside the high-tech glasses, the binoculars looked as anachronistic as a sextant on a modern megayacht. Celina looked through the binoculars, then dropped them to her waist.

Celina shook her head. "It can't be," she muttered.

"What is it?" Cam asked.

She put the AR glasses on again and checked the other windows, moving methodically from window to window before stepping back, arms folded across her chest.

"What's wrong?" Cam asked again.

"I don't know yet," said Celina. "Simon, what's the longest lens you have on that drone?"

"100x digital zoom," he said. "Equivalent to a ten thousand millimeter lens. I can see a fly on a table one hundred yards away like it's crawling up my palm."

From his steady gaze and straight face, Cam knew he wasn't exaggerating.

"How is it in low light?" asked Celina.

Simon scoffed. "Once again, you insult me, darling. I taught you how to write interpolation algorithms, remember? My camera can see as well the dark as these fancy glasses you've given us."

"Good," said Celina. "Get your drone in the air, just above our building." She pointed across the street. "I want your cameras to look through their windows."

Simon frowned, appeared about to say something to Celina. Instead, he just nodded and turned toward the door.

Cam started toward the window to get a look for himself and see what had concerned Celina so much. Simon clapped him on the shoulder as he passed.

"Give me a hand, mate, alright?" He slung a bag over one shoulder and picked up a large metal briefcase he'd carried in from his car. He pointed to a smaller case beside it. "Grab that one, would you?"

He led Cam down the stairs and out into the backyard. The AR glasses provided a perfect view of the yard, but the sky was clear and the moon was half-full. It provided just enough light for anyone to see, if their eyes were well-adjusted to the dark. Thankfully, a high stone wall and a ring of mature maple trees blocked any view the neighbors might have had.

Simon set his shoulder bag on a chair and put the metal case down on a stone dining table set on a wide deck in the backyard and gestured for Cam to set the smaller case beside it.

The midnight air had become frigid. The owners of the home had timed their move to Italy well. Cam buttoned his overcoat and flipped up his collar against the cold.

"Here," said Simon, unwinding his scarf from his neck. He held it out to Cam. "Take this." When Cam didn't reach out for it, Simon added, "It'll just get in my way."

Cam hesitated for a moment, then took the scarf with a nod of thanks and wrapped it around his neck. It was still warm from Simon's body heat, and Cam's shivering muscles immediately relaxed.

Cam peered over Simon's shoulder as he opened the larger case and saw a massive drone set in a foam holder, carved to the exact shape of the object. Several accessories were set in their own custom holders on both sides of the drone.

Simon lifted the drone carefully out of the case and set it on the table. One by one, he took out the accessories and set them on the table beside the drone, then shut the now-empty case and set it down on the deck.

He picked up one of the accessories and bent over the drone to attach it.

"Have you and Celina been together long?" he asked without looking up. His voice was a low whisper, but Cam could hear him loud and clear.

Cam stuffed his hands in his pockets and looked down at

his feet, shuffling them on the decking with a soft shushing sound.

"Since March," he said.

Simon over his shoulder at Cam, impressed.

"That might be the longest relationship she's ever had."

He turned back to his work.

"This is the camera processor," he said as he twisted four knobs to screw a large flat box into the frame of the drone. "It handles all the computations to convert the raw camera signal to enhanced images before sending it down to the receiver."

"Why is it so big?"

Simon glanced over his shoulder at Cam.

"It's a lot of computations."

He turned back to the table and picked up a squat cylindrical object. He held it up for Cam.

"The lens."

Cam nodded as Simon screwed the lens into place.

"We never dated," said Simon casually. "In case you're wondering." He looked back at Cam again.

All the replies going through Cam's head sounded like high-school bravado. *I wasn't wondering. Didn't think of it. Never crossed my mind.* So he just didn't say anything.

And he considered that silence to be progress. Funny how much you can see when your head isn't in your ass.

"Optical scrambler," said Simon, holding up a small box the size of a pack of gum.

"What does that do?"

"Emits a field that deflects any rays that come at the drone. Infrared, electromagnetic, that kind of thing. So it can't be detected with those methods."

"Doesn't that interfere with your own scans? Those are electromagnetic, too, right?"

"Yes, that's right," said Simon as he snapped the box into a holder on the side of the drone. "And, yes, it would normally interfere."

When he didn't say anything else, Cam said, "Why doesn't it interfere, then?"

Simon finished attaching the box, straightened up, and looked at Cam. In the moonlight, his face was half in shadow, half lit in silver. The dramatic shading made his features stand out even more. The smooth nose, the angular jaw. He looked even more handsome in the half-dark. The fucker.

"Because I'm good at what I do," he said.

He picked up the last part and bent down once more to affix it.

A question nagged at the back of Cam's mind. Against his will, it crawled down and sat on his tongue, pushing to get out.

"Did you want to?" Cam blurted.

Cam knew the question made little sense, but Simon didn't turn, didn't stop what he was doing.

And didn't answer.

"Date her," Cam added. "Did you want to date her?"

Simon finished attaching the last part, set the drone carefully in the center of the table, stood and turned to face Cam. His back was to the moonlight, casting his face completely in shadow.

"You love her, don't you?" he asked.

Cam could feel Simon inspecting his face, waiting for an answer. Cam straightened his back and stood tall. This was one answer he could give with total confidence.

"I do," he said.

Simon studied him for a moment, then nodded and turned back to the table.

"I know I look young," he said, "but I'm closer to your mother's age than to yours."

"Wha—" stammered Cam. The man couldn't be older than his early forties. Cam's mom was fifty-six. "How old are you?"

Simon opened the smaller case. Inside, also encased in custom-molded protective foam, was a large box with a stubby antenna and two joysticks. Simon lifted it out carefully and held it in both hands. He turned back toward Cam.

"I'll be fifty-five in December," he said.

He flipped a switch on the box and pushed both joysticks up. Instantly, the drone shot into the air with astonishing speed... and almost total silence. If Cam hadn't seen it, he wouldn't have believed it. He looked up, watching the drone recede to a tiny speck, then grow larger again as Simon brought it down to hover ten feet above them.

"Take off your glasses," said Simon. "Keep watching the drone and take off your glasses."

Cam kept his eyes on the drone. When he removed his glasses, he could see nothing but empty sky above him. He put the glasses back on, the drone was there, the sound of its rotors a quiet shushing in his enhanced hearing. He took the glasses off, the drone disappeared and he couldn't hear a thing at all.

Granted, it was nighttime and the sky was dark, but Cam had a feeling he'd have trouble seeing the drone even if it was the middle of the day.

"That's what the last box was for," said Simon casually. "It's essentially a very good projector, but I like to call it a cloaking device."

Cam put his glasses back on as Simon sent the drone soaring straight up, high into the dark sky above them.

Simon hadn't lied. He really was good at what he did.

16

Simon's voice came through the small speaker on the earpiece of Celina's glasses.

"She's up."

Celina and Paulie stood in the dark second-floor study of the Honorable Thomas Wilkins, former Chief Justice of the U.S. Court of Appeals for the Fourth Circuit. The smell of cigar smoke and leather permeated the entire room, the walls lined with law books, perfectly arranged and uniform in appearance. An ornate oak desk with a green blotter and a leather swivel chair filled one half of the room, a leather couch, a high-backed leather armchair, and a side table stood in the other, with a thick, dark Persian-style rug on the floor. The room was as dull and unimaginative as the man himself.

Justice Wilkins had been retired for almost a decade now, and he and his wife had fallen into a very predictable and very helpful travel routine. You know what they say. One man's summer home is another woman's base of operations.

In her glasses, in the lower corner of the viewscreen, Celina opened a small window that displayed the video feed from Simon's drone. Right now it was mostly dark, with a faint view of the lights of Alexandria far below and Washington, D.C. in the distance. Simon was flying high.

"Give me a visual on the windows," Celina said.

"Roger that," came Simon's reply.

All four of them were able to watch the video feed on their individual glasses. The city lights enlarged with ferocious speed, the outlines of buildings becoming visible as the drone dropped. Simon was an expert at piloting that thing, but he was a bit of a daredevil. That was fine with Celina. It was his toy. He could break it if he wanted to, just as long as he didn't fuck up the job before he did it.

The buildings and lights grew larger and larger. Washington was no longer visible, then Old Town Alexandria slid away as the buildings of their street filled the screen. The drone came to a smooth stop at a vantage point just above the roof of their building, looking down on the speaker's house.

The lens of the drone aligned with the windows of the house, then zoomed in tighter and tighter until the leftmost window on the top floor was all Celina could see.

Only she couldn't see anything.

When she looked across the street with her naked eye, she could see a faint yellow light burning behind a white curtain. She couldn't see through the curtain, but she could see the glow of the light.

When she looked through her glasses, however, or at the camera view from the drone, she could see only a wash of pale beige, like the whole window was covered in a shroud.

"Something's wrong." Simon sounded confused. Celina could hear him pull his laptop out of his bag and start clacking away on the keys.

She'd need to get him a new keyboard, one that wasn't so fucking loud. And she knew whatever he was tweaking was pointless.

"Give me a view of the second-floor window," she said.

"Hold on," Simon replied. "I've almost got it."

"No, you don't." Celina was pretty sure she knew what was happening, and she knew Simon wasn't going to fix it with a few keystrokes on his laptop. "Second-floor window, Simon."

"One second."

"Now."

Celina took a deep breath. Simon was a friend, and he wasn't doing anything wrong. She shouldn't talk to friends like that.

"Please," she added.

A long pause, then a quiet voice.

"Right."

As the camera shifted down from the top-floor window, Celina could see the facade of the house as clear as day. Crystal clear, in fact. Simon's camera feed was super high-resolution, and his night-vision algorithms were every bit as good as he claimed.

But when the view got down to the second-floor window, it all went beige again.

Fuck.

"Okay, Simon. That's enough."

Goddamn motherfucking fucking fuck.

"Wha—" Simon began.

"Drill it," said Celina.

A brief pause, then Simon replied, "Yep, you got it."

The view on the drone peeled back again. If the window in the viewscreen on Celina's glasses were any larger, she would have felt her stomach drop with the speed that Simon sent his drone back up into the sky. She could feel his frustration in the way he piloted the drone.

"Scanning now," he said.

Before the drone got close to any building, Simon would scan the area for any proximity sensors that the drone might trigger.

Like most lessons, he'd learned that one the hard way. It had taken quite a bit of the influence a minor English lord could muster to appease the Belgian Marquis du Conte Marbré when an alert caused him to look out the bedroom window of his castle in Charleroi one evening and find a drone spying on him and his latest mistress.

In fact, Simon hadn't been trying to catch the Marquis at all. He'd been planning to watch his lover, the Marquise, perform various acts of self-gratification for the camera. She enjoyed voyeurism, as it turned out.

But her plans had changed, and she hadn't thought to inform Simon.

As it turned out, she also enjoyed pissing off the Marquis.

So, now Simon knew better. Given the location of the speaker's home on a street in a city, the sensor perimeter would have to be fairly tight to the property line. Otherwise, it would go off whenever someone walked down the sidewalk or threw a crushed beer can over the wall into the garden.

Simon confirmed that guess.

"Perimeter sensors at five feet on the sides and... fifty feet above."

Fifty feet was high, high enough to prevent most people from any surveillance scans. But Simon wasn't most people. His drill tech was much more powerful than most. At fifty feet, he could stay outside the sensor range and still get what they needed.

"Okay," said Celina. "You know the drill."

Simon chuckled at the pun. Celina smiled grimly.

She expanded the drone's camera feed to fill half of her viewscreen in her glasses. She watched the drone settle into a stable position high above the roof of the speaker's house.

"What happens now?" asked Paulie, standing at the window looking out.

"He'll work in a grid, starting at one corner of the house

and moving slowly over its footprint. The drill will send an electromagnetic beam—"

"The sonar," said Paulie.

"The sonar, right," Celina nodded, smiling faintly. A lot had changed with technology in the fifteen years Paulie had been in prison, but nothing had changed with her mind. She was still as sharp as the tip of a knife.

"The sonar beam will penetrate all the way through the house from the top and slowly build a three-dimensional image of what's inside."

"It can go through all the floors at once?"

Celina nodded. "Simon can control the depth of the beam. That's why it's easiest to come down from the top, get everything in one shot." She flipped open a laptop, turning it away from the windows with the screen brightness dimmed all the way down so the glow wouldn't be visible from the street. "You can watch the scan build here. It works kind of like a 3-D printer, but with a three-dimensional image instead of a physical object."

Paulie came to stand behind the laptop. "I've never seen a 3-D printer."

"It builds layer by layer," said Celina. "Kind of cool to watch, actually."

"The printer or the drill?"

Celina smiled. "Both."

She clicked to fill the laptop screen with the output of the drill. Right now it was pitch black, but shadowy green lines would soon start to work their way across the screen, building up a three-dimensional model of the speaker's house, like a dollhouse that had been cracked open.

There wouldn't be any colors, and the drill would filter out anything that moved too much for an accurate scan, like people or pets that were walking around. But it would show the layout and the location of inanimate objects with remark-able clarity.

And for the sneaky ones who liked to build false walls and secret doorways, the drill would show all of those, too.

People bitch and moan about the loss of privacy, and some tech companies claim to be the champion of the little guy, that privacy is a basic human right. But that's just a marketing spiel. There is no privacy any more. Not in a tech-centric world. Technology knows all our secrets.

They stood watching the black screen for a minute or two, waiting.

"How long does it take?" asked Paulie.

"For a house this size, the full scan will probably take half an hour, if there are no interruptions."

"That's a long time." Paulie went back to the window and peered out. "Won't someone see the drone?"

"Simon's tech is pretty amazing. If you were standing right next to the drone, you wouldn't be able to see it at all. He's got cloaking technology so good he could fly it right up and use the blades to chop your nose off and you wouldn't even know he was coming."

"That's a lovely image." Paulie came back to watch the laptop. "What about the noise? And the wind?"

Knife-sharp.

"Even Simon can't get rid of those," Celina said. "But he's got the noise down to a whisper. And he can minimize the wind by controlling the speed of the rotors. Can't get rid of it completely or the drone would fall to the ground, but he can minimize it. And right now, he's a hundred feet off the ground. Noise and wind aren't really an issue."

"Better watch out for birds."

Celina laughed. "Actually, I think he's putting off some kind of EM field to keep them away."

"Won't keep away the human birds," said Paulie, then

glanced at Celina and winked. "Isn't that what they call them in England? Simon's handsome."

"You interested?" Celina nudged Paulie with her shoulder.

Paulie laughed, the sound like warm sunshine on a frigid day. "Girl, I've been in prison for fifteen years. A fine cut of beef like that comes along? Of course I'm interested. I'm old, not dead."

Celina tried to mute her laughter, then gave up and laughed long and loud at that. Far too long and far too loud for being on a job in someone else's house, but she felt like she hadn't laughed in weeks. Simon always got her laughing, and he'd done it again at dinner. But those were just funny stories. This was a laugh that felt like it came from her soul.

"I'll put in a good word," she said once she got control of herself again. She wiped tears from her cheeks.

The laptop screen flickered.

"Okay, looks like something's coming up," said Celina.

They both leaned down toward the laptop. A long green line appeared on the left side of the screen. It flickered once, then again, then went dark.

"Damn it." Through her earpiece, Celina could hear the frustration in Simon's voice. "Celina, we have a problem."

In the viewscreen of her glasses, Celina could see the drone ascend at speed from the roof of the speaker's house, then move across the street and drop like a stone toward Simon and Cam in the backyard.

"What are you doing?" she said. "What's the problem?"

The drone came to an abrupt hovering stop, then landed gently on the table in front of Simon and Cam. The camera was pointed at Cam and Simon. Through the feed, Celina could see Cam's face, creased in confusion and concern.

Simon's face came into frame and filled the view as he bent down to address the drone's camera.

"This lady, the speaker?" he said. "She knows what she's doing. Or her security person does, at least."

Simon stood, leaving Celina staring at his waist. She saw his hand reach toward the camera, and then the feed went dark. She dismissed the window in her viewscreen.

"Why?" she asked, though a suspicion was already forming in the back of her mind.

She hoped it wasn't true. With a historic home like the speaker's, it would take deliberate knowledge and extensive planning, not to mention funds, to retrofit.

"It's shielded," said Simon.

"Shielded how?"

Simon sighed in frustration. "You know how, Celina."

Celina stepped back from the laptop and swore under her breath.

"My thoughts exactly," said Simon.

The only way to shield a structure from a drill like Simon's was to surround the frame of the structure with an extremely dense metal. The densest metals tended to be either too heavy for practical application in a structural project, requiring a great deal of reinforcement, or they were toxic, highly reactive, or straight-up radioactive, like uranium or plutonium.

But, while most of these metals could shield commercial drills, none could shield Simon's drill. Except one.

Osmium was the densest metal on earth. It could, with difficulty, be beaten out into extremely thin sheets that would reduce weight while maintaining their shielding capabilities. But osmium was also volatile, toxic, and extremely rare. That meant it was also unbelievably expensive. Especially pure osmium. One ounce of pure osmium was worth a kilogram of gold.

Not a lot of people knew about EM drills, and those that did usually weren't worried about protecting themselves from them. They considered their proximity alarms to be security enough.

But Celina knew of exactly two people who were concerned enough about EM drills to guard their homes against them: Dr. Christopher Nestrom, the late genius tech wizard who had invented the prototype glasses Cam wore, and Celina's father, Perry Maxwell.

And now one more. The Speaker of the House, Madeline Kinkaid.

All three of them had taken the time and spent the money to shield their homes from EM drills.

All three of them had lined the exterior walls of their entire homes with sheets of pure osmium.

17

THE CAR WAS silent as they drove back to Celina's house. The city was deathly quiet. The headlights pierced the dark to reveal empty streets, empty sidewalks. It was nearly four AM, and Washington was passing through the veil between late night and early morning, the in-between when all breath quieted, all hearts stopped, and all dark souls sought cover.

Cam was at the wheel, with Simon and Paulie following behind in Simon's truck. Celina stared out the window from the passenger seat.

She'd learned long ago to keep her emotions to herself, especially when she was angry or frustrated. When she was younger, she would have acted out. She might have smashed a lamp or a side table with a baseball bat or thrown dishes or a vase to the floor or, her personal favorite, punched holes in the drywall with her fists or her bare feet.

Her father had corrected that behavior. He'd let her vent, then he would make her repair the damage herself. The process was therapeutic, but it was also a pain in the ass. For years, Celina's bedroom walls looked like a favela shanty with all the shitty patch jobs everywhere.

Over the years, her drywall skills had improved, and so

had her anger management skills. Now, she could stay calm and quiet on the outside, even as her guts burned with frustration.

She opened the door from the garage calmly and left it open for the others. Celina walked straight to the kitchen and opened a bottle of Sauvignon Blanc from the cooler, then took down four wine glasses and drained the bottle into them. She brought her glass into the sitting area by the fireplace and sat calmly on the couch.

Once by one, the others came in and did the same. Cam sat on the couch beside her. Simon and Paulie each sat in one of the armchairs on either side. Celina started the gas fireplace with a remote control, more to have something to look at than for the heat. The house was cool, but Celina was still hot with anger.

They sat in silence for a while. The cool wine, the mesmerizing flames, and the silence helped Celina settle herself down. She heard Simon quietly pulling in deep breaths through his nose and letting them out his mouth. It was his way of calming himself, by meditating, focusing on his breaths. Everyone had their own way.

By the time she'd drunk half her wine, Celina's anger had cooled enough to talk. She shifted on the couch, then sat forward on the edge of the cushion. Noticing her movement, the others perked up, too.

"No drill," Celina said simply.

"No drill." Simon nodded his head.

Silence. The finality settled in Celina's stomach like a hard, cold sphere of glass. They needed to find other options.

"Cable guy?" Simon suggested.

Celina shook her head. "They have a book."

At most homes, even high-end ones—especially high-end ones—you could pretend to be a maintenance worker, like a cable guy, to gain entry to the home. At the speaker's house, they kept a schedule book at the guard house. No unscheduled worker was ever allowed onto the property.

"Paparazzi?" said Paulie.

Again, Celina shook her head. "The windows are obfuscated." At the confusion on Paulie's face, she said, "They scramble any digital cameras. It's why Simon's drone camera couldn't see through the windows."

Paulie still looked confused, but Celina didn't want to get into the details at that moment. Thankfully, she noticed Celina's mood and nodded in acceptance.

"Peeping Tom?" suggested Simon.

Simon waited a beat, then grinned.

Celina gave him a half-smile. "In that neighborhood? Not a chance. Some neighborhood watch blue-hair would see you peeping through the windows and call the cops in a heartbeat."

"Who said I'd be the one doing the peeping?" said Simon, feigning offense.

"Sorry," Cam said. "Why no drill? What the hell happened out there?"

Celina nodded to Simon, who frowned in thought before speaking.

"The drill uses an electromagnetic beam to scan the structure and contents of the building," he said. "Radio frequencies with very long wavelengths. Anything fixed in place for the duration of the scan will be detected. That usually means inanimate objects, but if a pet or a person is sleeping and not moving, the scan will pick them up, too."

"Okay," said Cam. "Then what went wrong?"

"EM drills can penetrate the most common building materials. Wood, plaster, stucco, and so on."

Cam nodded.

"My drill can penetrate even more. Stone, most metals.

Materials that are too dense for commercial EM drills are no problem for mine."

"EM drills are used commercially?"

"Sure," said Simon. "Plumbers use them to detect pipes. Carpenters look inside finished walls. Electricians, surveyors, those kinds of people use them all the time. A lot of drills use radio frequencies, but they tend to be scattered and weak. Good for a foot or two, but no more. The better ones, like mine, use more focused radio frequencies."

"So, your drill is more powerful than theirs?"

"Much, much more powerful." Simon pressed his lips into a weak smile. "My drill can penetrate more dense materials to a greater depth and from a greater distance than any commercial drill could even dream of."

"You're good at what you do," Cam said with a smile.

Simon smiled back, but then his smile faded again.

"There are some metals even my drill can't penetrate. Those metals are very dense, and they tend to be very rare or very dangerous. But, there are a couple of dense metals that aren't rare or dangerous. Iridium, rhenium, and platinum are common and cheap. They're used in engine parts, electronics, even medicine."

"Is that what was in the house?"

Simon shook his head. "Those metals all have pros and cons. As building materials, though, they tend to be impractical. But there's one metal that's readily available, highly malleable, and non-toxic, and it shields drills better than the others."

"What's that?" asked Cam.

"Gold," Simon replied.

Cam looked confused. He glanced from Simon to Celina and back to Simon.

"Gold," he said. "Like, gold gold? Like wedding ring gold?"

Celina felt a weird heat in her stomach when Cam said that. She ignored it.

"Yes," said Simon. "Gold gold."

"Gold isn't a building material," said Paulie.

"Not a common one."

"I don't understand," Cam said. "How was gold used as a building material? That house was made of brick and sandstone."

"The Speaker of the House," said Celina softly, "has lined the roof of her home with gold."

Cam's mouth gaped open.

"Like bricks of gold or something?"

Simon shook his head. "Bricks are far too heavy, and unnecessarily thick. All you need to shield a drill would be a thin sheet of gold. An eighth of an inch is enough. But it has to be very pure. Even twenty-four carat is dicey if the purity isn't absolutely precise."

"So you're saying the speaker has eighth-inch sheets of twenty-four carat gold under her roof?"

Simon nodded.

"That can't be cheap," said Paulie.

"Prohibitively expensive," said Simon. "That's why I haven't bothered trying to get my drill to penetrate it."

"Can you tune your drill to get through?" asked Celina.

Simon shook his head. "It will take longer than you want to wait," he said. "But believe me, I'll be working on it starting tomorrow."

"Why would the speaker do that to her house?" Cam asked. "Why would she even know to do that?"

Simon looked to Celina.

She breathed deep.

"I know of two other people who did that. One was my father. The other," she looked pointedly at Cam, "was Christopher Nestrom."

"Dr. Nestrom?" Cam thought for a moment. When he looked up, his eyes were wide. "His lab? Is that why the cell and wi-fi signals couldn't get through?"

Celina nodded. "Nestrom and my father were close. It's possible that Nestrom was close with the speaker, somehow, as well."

Celina kept her eyes on Cam, but she could feel Simon's gaze shift to her, then away again.

"Okay." Cam pulled in a slow breath and released it. He rubbed his hands over his thighs and fell back against the couch, absorbing this new information.

"What about the walls?" he asked. "Can't we drill sideways, through the walls?"

Simon shook his head slowly. "Also shielded."

"Underneath? Is the floor shielded, too?"

Simon stared at Cam for a beat, then looked at Celina and shrugged.

It was an idea.

Celina stood and paced back and forth behind the couch.

It was a brilliant idea, and Celina was pissed she hadn't already thought of it.

"The metro stop is a long way from the house," she said. "Ten blocks, at least. And I think it comes in from the northeast. But I'll pull up the city maps, see if there are any access tunnels that run nearby."

"Doesn't have to be big," said Simon. "*We* don't need to get in there. Just the drill. And without the drone, the drill itself is small. A sewer pipe could be big enough."

For the first time since they'd left the speaker's house, Celina had hope.

She looked at Cam and smiled. Hot, cute, and brilliant.

And not an asshole. The bar for a good man was shockingly low, but, still, so few managed to clear it. But Cam flew over it like a jet at cruising altitude.

She leaned over the back of the couch, clinked her wine glass against his. They both drank, and then Celina gave him a long, slow, delicious kiss. His lips were cold and tasted of Sauvignon Blanc.

It was a definite turn-on.

And his eyes had that smoky look in them that made Celina want to tear his clothes off.

Then the smoke dissipated. Cam looked uncomfortable and squirmed in his seat on the couch.

"Can we sit somewhere else?" he said. "These couches are torture."

Celina took him by the hand and led him to somewhere much more comfortable.

Some quick research the next morning showed that there were no metro tunnels near the speaker's house. However, a sewer pipe ran under the alley behind it, accessible through a manhole on the two-lane street that bordered the property to the east.

Unfortunately, the pipe behind the house was the start of a branch line, so it was small, only eight inches in diameter. It fed into a pipe under the two-lane street that was only slightly larger, twelve inches wide.

If the speaker had lived in a different part of town, further down the sewer grid, the pipes might have been five or six feet in diameter, plenty large enough for Simon and the team to recon without risk of detection. As it was, they had to burn time picking up traffic cones and City of Alexandria uniforms to create the appearance that they were doing sewer mainte-nance, then squat in a huddle over the manhole in the middle of backed-up late-afternoon traffic while Simon fed his drill through the pipes.

It wasn't hard to find cones or uniforms, but any disrup-tion of traffic would eventually alert the authorities, who would quickly discover that there was no sewer maintenance scheduled on that street on that day. It was still less obtrusive than a night job, but the cops would eventually come to investigate. Celina and team needed to be long gone before they did. The clock was ticking.

They parked their fake maintenance van on the curb and set up three cones around the manhole. Cam directed traffic while Celina removed the manhole cover and set it to one side. Simon pulled on a pair of nitrile gloves and squatted over the hole with his drill and a coil of fiber optic cable.

It was a straight shot from the manhole through the eight-inch pipe to the sewer line coming from the speaker's house. Simon had rigged his drill to the cable with a wire guide that let him maneuver with decent precision. There was a camera on the end of the cable. The live camera feed was sending to everyone's AR glasses.

Celina and Cam stood watch while Simon worked. Paulie had stayed behind at Celina's house, but, like everyone else, she was watching the camera feed on her glasses and staying in touch with the others during the operation.

The cable snaked, inch by agonizing inch, through the sewer pipe. A thin line of brown liquid ran down the bottom center of the rusted metal pipe. Black sludge lined the sides, along with some kind of gelatinous white mass that Celina tried not to think too hard about. Occasionally, someone would flush their toilet or run a faucet and a flood of water would rush down, flooding the camera and obscuring their view until the flood passed by.

Exposed in the middle of the street, clock ticking, it felt to Celina like they had been there for an hour. But Simon was quick and efficient. He overshot the opening to the house pipe when an ill-timed flush splattered the camera lens with a fleck of shit. By the time it had washed off, the opening was behind them.

But before they started, Simon had measured the distance

along the street from the manhole to the house, and he was keeping track of how much cable he'd fed out. He quickly realized his mistake and backtracked, quickly finding the opening and making the turn into the house pipe without trouble.

The pipe to the house ran slightly uphill, limiting visibility slightly and making Simon's progress even slower. But eventually, checking his measurements, Simon knew they were only a few feet from the house. Celina checked her watch as Cam stepped out to untangle a snarl in the traffic. What felt like an hour had only been twenty minutes.

"Almost there," said Simon. "Switching on the drill now."

Celina had the camera feed in one window of the viewscreen of her glasses. She opened another window, connected to her laptop back in the maintenance van. It showed a dark screen, like it had the night before.

She stepped out into the street to help Cam direct traffic, more to occupy herself than because he needed the help. She hated waiting, and it would look pretty odd if she started to pace back and forth in the middle of traffic.

Simon inched the drill forward. In her view of the laptop screen, Celina could see shadowy green outline of grass and the edge of a tree trunk, some sprinkler lines and a sprinkler head, then a small deck box loaded with gloves, hats, hedge clippers, and what looked like a small wagon.

"Coming under the foundation... now," said Simon.

The view of the laptop screen went black.

If Simon swore, Celina couldn't hear it. She was too busy swearing herself. She banged on the hood of a car stopped in front of her. Through the windshield, the driver, a soccer mom who had been texting on her phone, looked like she'd just shit a brick. Celina didn't give a fuck. She waved the woman forward angrily. The woman quickly dropped her phone and drove away.

"Pulling back," muttered Simon.

It had taken twenty minutes to get through the pipes to the house. Simon did the reverse in three, his gloves getting slimier and slimier as he slid the cable back through them. Ten minutes later, they were packed up, in the van, and halfway back to the city.

"Motherfuck," shouted Celina, banging her hands against the steering wheel as she drove. She'd learned not to break shit when she was mad, but swearing didn't hurt anything. And it sure as fuck helped. "Fuck, fuck, motherfucking fuck."

By the time they'd dropped off the van, ditched the uniforms, and gotten home, Celina had calmed herself down.

Paulie opened the door for them when they arrived.

"They shielded the fucking floor," said Celina as she stomped past. "Those rich fucks lined their fucking floor with pure gold."

"Aren't you even richer than the speaker?" asked Paulie.

Celina spun back to Paulie, ready to spit fire.

Paulie just raised her eyebrows. "And isn't your floor lined with gold, too?"

Celina had been ready to lash into Paulie, but when she saw her, when she saw that kind, beautiful face and felt the love pouring out of her, she lost the urge to say something cutting. Instead, as Cam and Simon came in and shut the door, Paulie's words sunk in.

"Yes," she grumbled, "and yes." She sighed and flopped down on the couch. "I'm a rich fuck, too." She pressed the heels of her hands against her eyes. "I fucking hate rich fucks," she shouted.

The couch cushion pushed against her back, pressing it into an uncomfortable arch. She slid backward, trying to find a more comfortable position. It was worse. She rolled onto one hip and crossed one leg over the other. The cushion gouged into her side. She stood and kicked the couch with her boot, shifting it back a few inches along the wood floor with a loud screech.

"These fucking couches suck ass," she said.

Cam came over, stood directly in front of Celina, put a hand on each shoulder, and ducked to find her gaze, pulling it up with his as he straightened.

"Yes," he said, "they do. They really fucking do."

He pulled her into his arms.

Celina stiffened, resisting. She didn't want to be hugged. She wanted to break something or shout at someone or take a knife from the kitchen and shred every stupid fucking ass-sucking couch in the whole fucking house.

But as Cam held on, his embrace loose, but firm, his heat seeped into Celina's body. She felt her anger cool as Cam's heat washed through her. Celina's stiff body relaxed, then melted against Cam.

His embrace tightened around her. She closed her eyes and felt the firmness of his chest against hers. She pulled in the smell of him, like sandalwood and sun-warmed earth. She filled her lungs with that scent that had so quickly become so familiar to her. She slid her hands around his waist, under his shirt, and pulled him hard against her. She felt him stiffen against her upper thigh.

Yeah. That was one way to get over her frustration. Why hadn't she thought of that before?

"What now?"

The voice sounded far away.

Celina looked up into Cam's eyes. He was looking back at her, his eyes filled with the same heat she knew he would see in hers.

"Celina?"

It wasn't Cam's voice. His lips hadn't moved. Those soft lips, and that very talented tongue behind them.

"You two can fuck in a minute, okay?"

Simon.

Celina turned her head. Paulie and Simon were standing there, watching. Paulie looked amused. Simon looked annoyed.

"Right now," Simon said, "I'd like to know the plan."

Celina grabbed Cam's ass cheek and gave it a hard squeeze. He jerked involuntarily forward, grinding against her.

Oh, yeah. He was ready.

She turned toward Simon.

"You want to know the plan? Here's the plan. First," she pointed back and forth between her and Cam, "we are gonna fuck, so fuck off."

Simon rolled his eyes.

"Okay, good for you. Then what?"

"Then," Celina sighed, "we go with the nuclear option."

Simon frowned.

"The nuclear option? What's that?"

Celina turned back toward Cam, slid one hand over his ass again, the other up behind his neck. She pulled those soft lips down toward hers.

"I'll tell you later," she muttered.

18

IT DID Paulie good to see the passion Cam and Celina shared with each other. The way the look in their eyes shifted from a normal, everyday awareness to an intense need for each other, it took Paulie's breath away. She and Sam had been like that when they were younger. Even when they were older, before he died. It was chemical. Emotional, but those emotions led to some kind of chemical reaction that made them forget the entire world and just dive into each other.

When it happened with Cam and Celina, Paulie could feel it. The air became electric. She could smell their sexuality in the air, the pheromones. She loved to see it. She loved knowing that Cam had that. He'd wanted it so badly for so long, and Paulie had been stuck in prison with no way to help him except by giving advice once a week during their visits, like she was some kind of Dear Abby column in the newspaper.

But he'd found it, all on his own. And now that Paulie was out and surrounded by it every day, it reminded her of what she and Sam had had.

And how long it had been since Paulie had felt that for herself.

Her memories of Sam were full-color, high-definition. They were as vivid today as they had been when she'd first experienced them. That was a trick she'd learned in prison. Meditation was one thing, but learning to access your memories, to crawl back into them like crawling under the bedcovers on a cold night, that had kept her soul alive.

She'd spent hours, in the beginning, teasing fragments of memory together. She thought of it like walking down a long beach where some glass object had been shattered. As she walked, her heels sinking in the wet sand, she picked up the pieces of broken glass, worn smooth by the sea over time. Bit by sea-smooth bit, she puzzled them together until, one day, the memory clicked whole and came to life in her mind.

She'd gotten better at it over time, faster. And then she'd spent those hours not rebuilding the memories, but reliving them. Like watching a home movie in full immersion.

And now she was seeing it in real life. The passion she and Sam had shared was replaying before her eyes through Cam and Celina. It filled Paulie with peace and joy and love and warmth. As a mother, she was thrilled.

As a widow, she still grieved, deep in her heart. She knew a part of her always would.

And as a woman, she was lonely. Touch-starved.

She felt as alive and vivid as she had when she was thirty years younger. Getting out of prison after fifteen long years had that effect. But criminals tended to have a short life expectancy. Sam was gone. Many of her oldest friends were dead or in prison themselves. Cam and Celina were wonderful, but they had each other.

And they made the most of every moment together. Paulie could hear them sometimes. Late in the evening, in the middle of the night, early in the morning. Hell, anytime really. In prison, Paulie had gotten used to the sound of other people's orgasms, of people finding that one little bit of happiness, with another or by themselves. Hearing Cam and Celina finding that bliss together made Paulie smile.

It was also really annoying.

Celina was a passionate woman. That much was obvious. That's one of the many things Paulie loved about her, and she could see that Cam loved it, too.

Celina wasn't just passionate about sex or her love for Cam. She was passionate about everything. Paulie could see it in her drive, her determination, her loyalty.

And yes, in her temper, too. Paulie was pretty sure anger had been a problem for Celina when she was younger. She didn't know where it came from, but someone, probably her father, had taught her how to control it. And Celina did control it, to a degree. But that anger still threatened to get the best of her sometimes.

When it did, Paulie was glad she was here to help. Unchecked anger was almost always destructive. Anger could be helpful, if channeled in constructive ways. But unchecked anger was never a good thing.

There was something driving Celina, something dark. Something that stoked her anger more than Paulie had ever seen. In the few months that Paulie had known her, Celina had always had an edge. But this D.C. job had honed that edge to a deadly gleam, and it drew blood whenever anyone got close.

So far, Celina had managed to control it, barely. But how long would that control last? Would something tip her over the edge, make her lose control? Would that anger become unchecked and destructive?

Paulie hoped not. But either way, she was there to help. She loved Celina, and she loved how Celina loved Cam. She would do anything, anything, to help them make it as a couple.

"Well, that's always fun," said Simon.

"What is?" asked Paulie.

Simon gestured toward the stairs, where Celina and Cam had just gone to their bedroom.

"Watching other people's foreplay."

Paulie laughed.

"Don't you remember when you were that age, Simon?"

Simon smiled. He had a beautiful smile. It suited his beautiful face.

"I do," he nodded, his eyes clouded with memory for a moment. "I suppose I'm just jealous, really."

"I can't imagine you have trouble finding women to sleep with," Paulie said.

"It's about more than that, though, isn't it?"

He gestured for Paulie to follow him into the kitchen, where he pulled a corkscrew from a drawer and a bottle of red from the wine rack. He slit the foil over the cork and peeled it off the neck of the bottle.

"At my age," he said, "it's not about sex. It's about companionship."

He pulled the cork with a soft pop, set it on the counter, and thought for a beat.

"Companionship *and* sex." He grinned in a way that made him look roguish and irresistibly charming. "But mostly companionship."

He filled both glasses and set the bottle down.

"You're still too young to know," he said to Paulie as he held one glass out to her, "but you'll understand one day."

Paulie laughed as she took the glass. "Don't bullshit a con artist, Simon."

They clinked their glasses together.

"The only way to fool a con artist is to tell them the truth," he said.

He grinned that irresistible grin again, held up his glass to her, and took a long pull, his eyes fixed on hers over the rim of the glass.

Paulie regarded him for a long moment while he drank. He looked young, but she knew he was older. Probably only a few years younger than her. He still had a full head of hair, thick and dark and thoroughly gorgeous. And his body was as trim and muscular as a man in his thirties. But there was a weary wisdom in his eyes and a learned restraint in his manner that could only come from living life. And behind all of that was a humor and a hopefulness that could only come from living well.

As Simon took his glass from his lips, Paulie brought her glass up to hers. She watched Simon watch her sip her wine. His eyes twinkled and the corners of his mouth twisted up.

"Well," he said, "seems like we've got some time to ourselves. What should we do?"

Paulie tilted her head. Several options ran through her mind, some of them R-rated. A few of them very R-rated.

She smiled to herself. One of the other benefits of age? Patience. Savoring the small moments, the delicious little feelings, and letting them unfold in their own time.

"How much do you know about cooking?" she asked.

Simon's eyebrows went up and a smile—a genuine smile of surprise and delight—spread over his face.

"My darling woman," he said, "please allow me to show you exactly what I know. Would you care to collaborate?"

Paulie was more than happy to oblige.

19

WHEN HE MADE love to Celina, Cam lost all track of time. He lost all sense of place. He lost all sense of anything except Celina. Nothing else mattered. His world became one woman, infinite.

Often, it wasn't until hours later that he would become conscious of any fatigue or hunger or any physical needs at all beyond the need to satisfy and be satisfied by Celina.

And so he had no clue how long they'd been upstairs in the bedroom when the smell of food cooking wafted into the room, faint, but intense. His senses were already heightened, filled beyond the point of ecstasy with the feel of Celina, the smell of Celina, the sound of Celina. They'd gone together quickly, then taken their time to build again to the point of release. As always, they found their rhythm together, each one feeling and responding to the other, attuned to the other as if she slid into his mind and he into hers.

And now, as one, they sat up, sweating and slick with each other's pleasure.

"That smells really good," said Cam.

"I'm fucking starving," said Celina.

Two minutes later they were in the kitchen, barefoot and disheveled and stinking of sex, Cam still pulling on his t-shirt.

"Look, Simon," said Paulie, setting the table for four. "The kids decided to join us."

"And what an honor it is, indeed," said Simon over his shoulder.

He crouched in front of the open oven, mitts on his hands, an apron tied around his waist, a kitchen towel set neatly over one shoulder. When he stood, he held a baking dish in his hands. Paulie set a hot pad in the center of the table and Simon rested the dish neatly on top. They both smiled, seeming very pleased with themselves.

"Perfect timing," said Paulie.

"Oh my fuck it smells amazing," said Celina, sitting down and pulling her napkin over her lap.

She leaned over the dish and took a long sniff. The mashed potatoes and cheese on top were a beautiful golden-brown color, darker at the edges and on the tips of potato whipped like meringue. Through the glass sides of the baking dish, Cam could see several layers of dark minced meat, bright green peas, and roasted carrots.

"Shepherd's pie?" asked Celina.

"Cottage pie, technically," said Simon. "We didn't have lamb, so we used beef."

"A family recipe," said Paulie, looking at Simon with a bright smile. "I didn't know English lords had family recipes."

"A minor, non-royal lord," said Simon, grinning back at her. "We have to fend for ourselves, you know."

"Well I don't care if it's a family recipe or you flew your fucking cook in from bloody England," said Celina, holding her plate and fork over the baking dish, ready to serve herself. "It smells incredible and I'm hungry."

They ate and drank and talked and laughed for hours. The cottage pie was as delicious as it smelled, as were the pan rolls they'd made to go with it. For dessert, Celina dug several pints of ice cream from the freezer in different flavors, along with chocolate syrup, nuts, and Maraschino cherries. She made sundaes to order for everyone.

Finally satiated, they cleaned up and adjourned to one of the theater rooms upstairs, where the couches had enough throw pillows to simulate a comfortable seating area. They let Paulie and Simon pick the movie. After a heated debate with a lot of laughter, they settled on Die Hard. Cam and Celina snuggled in with each other on the couch.

Afterward, they went back down to the kitchen. Cam made coffee for everyone. They sat around the kitchen table and sipped in silence.

"Okay, Celina." It was Simon who broke the silence. "Enough mystery. What is the nuclear option?"

"And what are we trying to steal, anyway?" said Cam.

Celina laughed, without humor.

"I'll start with the second one," she said.

"And don't say it's a statue," said Paulie, holding up one finger. "We already know that."

"It is a statue," said Celina, then smiled as Paulie shot her a dark look. "But it's more than just that."

She stared down into her coffee for a long moment, thinking, then sighed heavily. She looked at Cam.

"Did I ever tell you about my great-great-grandfather?"

Celina hadn't talked about her family much at all. Cam knew a bit about her father, that he had worked in tech, started a company and sold it for a hell of a lot of money, then started another one and sold that for even more. He knew that he and Celina had been very close, and that her mother had never been in the picture, though he didn't know why. Other than that, she hadn't really told him anything.

He shook his head. Celina looked at Simon, who shook his head, too.

"His name," she began, "was Tommaso Albertini. Italian. Jewish. An artist." She shrugged. "Good, but not great."

She leaned forward, forearms on the table, and looked down at her coffee cup as she turned it slowly between her hands.

"He grew up in Livorno, not far from Florence, and he knew at a young age he wanted to be an artist. Pestered his parents about it. They wanted him to be a cobbler, like his father and his grandfather, but Tommaso wouldn't listen."

"Now I see where it comes from," said Simon. "It's a family trait."

Celina smiled faintly.

"They sent him to Paris to apprentice with the son of some friends from town, a painter who'd just moved there himself."

She paused and looked them each in the eye.

"Amedeo Modigliani."

Cam sat back in his chair. The others looked as surprised as he felt. Cam had no clue that Celina's family had ties to the famous painter and sculptor.

Celina looked pleased by their response.

"Tommaso moved to France when he was sixteen. Slept in the corner of Modigliani's studio in Montmartre for three years. He did all the usual apprentice shit. Cleaned brushes, stretched canvases. That kind of stuff.

"Modigliani was hanging around with Picasso, Brâncuşi, Severini, Juan Gris," said Cam. "Tommaso must have met them, too."

Celina nodded. Cam couldn't believe it. He'd just stolen a Picasso, and that was incredible enough. Someone in Celina's family line had actually met the man, and Modigliani, and who knows how many other greats. It would have been more than a hundred years ago, but it still awed Cam to think that Celina had that connection with history.

"He tried to be a painter," Celina continued. "Got pretty

good. I've got a few of his paintings back at the house in San Francisco. But when you're hanging around with Picasso..."

"That'd make anyone feel inadequate," said Paulie.

"When Tommaso was nineteen or so, Modigliani left Paris and went home to Livorno for a while. He was strung out, sick, could barely work. Tommaso stayed in Paris and moved to a little flat in Montparnasse. He got interested in sculpture, especially African sculpture, and started exploring.

"Modigliani came back after a few months and crashed with Tommaso for a few weeks until he found his own place. Tommaso turned Modigliani on to African sculpture, too, and Modigliani threw himself into it for a few years before he gave up sculpting and went back to painting."

"Some of those sculptures are worth a lot of money," said Simon. "One of them just sold at Sotheby's for almost ninety million."

"Tête," nodded Celina. "A two-foot limestone sculpture of the head of an African woman in a tribal mask."

"Don't tell me that's the statue," said Simon, leaning forward, his eyes large. He was practically salivating onto the table. "The buyer and the seller were both anonymous. Did you hack into Sotheby's and get the names? Did the speaker buy it?" He frowned. "She's not that rich, is she?"

Celina smiled. "It's not Tête," she said quietly.

Simon slumped back, clearly disappointed.

"Tommaso was selling portraits on the street and by commission. That's how he lived, and he did pretty well. Like I said, he was good. No Picasso," she smiled, "but good.

"Like Modigliani—and every other male painter in Paris— he painted nudes. And, naturally, he didn't just paint them."

She raised an eyebrow at Paulie, who laughed out loud.

"He fell in love with one of his models, Vivienne, and before long my great-grandfather, Arnaldo, was born. Tommaso was twenty-one. He opened his own portrait studio in Paris and he and Vivienne raised a healthy, happy family together."

Celina stared down into her coffee again.

"Good story," said Simon. "How does this relate to what we're all doing here?"

Cam had been wondering the same thing, but he knew Celina would come to it in her own time. He was content to listen and watch and let the story unfold.

"Modigliani was in his sculpture phase when Arnaldo was born. He and Tommaso were still close friends. Former apprentice, same hometown, both Italian Jews in Paris, that kind of thing. They were tight.

"Tête had already been sold, but as a wedding present-slash-baby shower gift-slash-thank you gift, Modigliani gave Tommaso and Vivienne one of the studies."

She didn't look up from her coffee, just swirled it, the coffee mug making a quiet, rhythmic scraping sound against the tabletop.

"The last study, actually," she said. "Looks exactly like the real thing, but about half the size."

Her eyes swung to Cam. He felt the same subtle thrill deep in his core that he always felt when those gorgeous green eyes settled on him. This time, he felt another thrill along with it.

"One-foot tall," Celina continued, "instead of two."

Simon whistled softly.

"It's been in my family ever since, passed down from generation to generation, all the way down to my father."

"Then how did Madeline Kinkaid end up with it?" asked Simon.

Celina stopped swirling her coffee mug. The silence was like the quiet before a bomb explodes.

"She fucking stole it," Celina said.

She pushed back her chair with a screech and stood, towering over them all. Her stance was fierce. When she spoke, her voice was changed. Where before she'd been relating a charming, exciting family story, now the more familiar Celina was back. Driven. Purposeful. Determined.

Angry.

"And we're going to steal it the fuck back," she said.

Cam's mind reeled. Tête was a well-known piece, one of only twenty-seven sculptures Modigliani had ever made. That ninety million dollar auction had only happened nine or ten years ago. Four years before that, Tête had changed hands for eighty million, which meant the value had gone up ten million dollars in four years. It was probably worth at least a hundred million today.

But that was for the sculpture that everyone knew, a sculpture that had been in circulation, more or less, for over a hundred years.

Now, Celina was saying there was another sculpture. A new sculpture, so to speak.

Putting a value on anything was a subjective thing. A house was worth whatever someone was willing to pay for it. But art valuation was even more subjective. And the kind of people who paid nine-figure sums for a piece of art tended to be competitive. Like the tech douchebag with the Picasso, they tended to buy the art more to impress their friends and assuage their insecurities than for their appreciation of the art itself. Not all art collectors were like that, of course, but a surprisingly high percentage was.

Now here was a heretofore unknown sculpture, attached to a major piece from a major artist. If it looked like Tête, it was beautiful. If it was the last study, it was historic. Every original work of art is one-of-a-kind, but a piece becomes familiar when it has been in circulation for a while. This study would be brand new. It would feel incredibly rare.

And, thus, would be incredibly valuable.

A hundred fifty million? Two hundred million? No one could say until it was sold.

Cam watched Celina pace back and forth as he and Simon and Paulie thought through the implications of what she'd told them.

When she'd brought up the Picasso job, she'd paced just like that. Determined. Calculating.

Only then, she'd been excited, too. She'd wanted to stick it to the tech douchebag, but she'd also initially wanted to sell the piece. She was excited for the haul. She didn't need the money, but the higher the take, the higher the stakes. And that got her juices flowing.

This time, she seemed just as determined, just as calculating. But Cam had finally put his finger on the thing that had been bothering him since they first stepped on the plane in New York, headed for DC.

Celina didn't seem excited.

Not in the same way.

This time, instead of the rush of the stakes and the glee in giving an asshole the hit he deserved, she just seemed angry.

"You don't want to sell it," Cam said quietly.

Simon and Paulie looked up.

Celina stopped pacing, her back toward Cam.

"You want to reclaim it," Cam continued. "Bring it back into the family."

Cam saw Celina's back rise slowly, then fall as she gave a heavy sigh. She turned back to them.

"Yes," she said quietly. "And I understand if any of you don't want to participate." She shook her head in frustration. "It was unfair of me to let you go this far without telling you everything."

Cam glanced at Simon and Paulie, trying to read their expressions. He didn't see any anger there at all. They seemed to feel exactly like he did.

Cam stood and took Celina by the shoulders, just like he'd done earlier that day. Just like then, he ducked his head, found her eyes, and pulled her head upright with his gaze.

"This statue is a part of your history," he said. "Your family's history."

Celina's stared back at him, those emerald eyes wide and shimmering.

"This woman stole it from you," he said. "And we're here to help you get it back. Period."

Celina turned to look at Simon and Paulie, still seated at the table. They both nodded at her.

"Are you sure?" Celina said. "It's a lot to ask. You don't have to do this." She stared hard at Cam to make sure he understood that she meant it. "Any one of you can back out at any time with no hard feelings. At all."

"I'm not going anywhere," said Cam.

Paulie stood and touched Celina's cheeks. "This is the most fun I've had in fifteen years, sweetie. I'm not going anywhere, either."

Celina laughed.

Everyone looked at Simon.

"You and I go way back, Celina," he said, his voice deep and serious. "Your father was my dear friend."

He stood from his chair, slowly, with solemn gravity.

"What kind of an asshole do you think I am?" he cracked. "How can I say no? Especially with these two fools jumping in headfirst."

They all laughed.

Once the laughter had died down, Simon said, "Okay, so that's the statue. That's what we're stealing. Now what's this nuclear option thing?"

"Oh," said Celina, taking a deep breath. "That."

She motioned for them to sit down, but remained standing herself. She leaned on the back of her chair with both hands.

"The drill didn't work. None of the other ideas are feasible. But we have to get inside somehow. We have to know if the statue is even in there."

Cam suddenly had a very bad feeling. Celina was incredible, more capable than anyone he'd ever met. But sometimes she had a tendency to be reckless. He had a feeling this would be one of those times.

"So we try the nuclear option." Celina shrugged. "I'm going in myself."

"Alone?" Cam asked.

Celina nodded.

"How?" said Simon.

Celina grinned.

"I'm going to knock on the front door."

20

"THIS IS A TERRIBLE IDEA."

It was late in the afternoon, the sun shallow and slanting through the glass doors in the bedroom. Since dinner the previous night, Cam had been trying desperately to talk Celina out of her plan.

She had acknowledged all of his points. Yes, it was risky. Yes, they could arrest her for harassment. Yes, they could detain her for accosting a public official. Yes, they could run her identity and potentially attach her to any number of schemes she'd run over the years, including the scam she'd run just a few blocks away earlier that year, when she'd faked her transcripts to graduate top of her class in the criminology program at McFadden University.

And yes, even if she did get in the house somehow, she still might not be able to determine for sure if the statue was in there. It might be hidden, might be in a locked room, might not be there at all.

Celina didn't care.

"I'll be alright, Cam," she said for the hundredth time as she went through her closet, trying to pick out an appropriate outfit. "I'm just knocking on a door. I'm not doing anything illegal. We'll see where it goes from there."

Cam grumbled in frustration. He had a bad feeling about this one. But trying to convince Celina when her mind was set was like trying to stop a boulder from falling down a mountain when it had already tipped over the edge.

She turned to him, slipped both arms around his neck and stared at him in that very distracting way of hers. Her hands were warm and her scent washed over him, lilac and fresh air. He was instantly intoxicated, as always.

"Besides," she said, her gaze sliding back and forth between Cam's eyes and his lips. Very distracting. "I'll have all of you nearby, watching and listening. If something goes bad, you'll find a way to get me out."

She brought her head closer, her breath warm on his lips.

"I trust you," she said.

And then she kissed him, and all the usual effects her kisses had on his body kicked in.

This time, though, instead of pressing forward like Cam desperately wanted her to do, she pulled back, a wicked smile teasing the corners of her mouth.

She knew exactly what she did to him.

She always knew exactly what she was doing.

Why should he think this time was any different?

"Okay," Cam said. "I trust you, too."

She kissed him again, soft and slow. "Good," she said, then turned back to her closet. "Now tell me, what the hell do you wear when you're trying to get invited into the private home of the Speaker of the House?"

"Um," said Cam. "Something nice?"

The something nice turned out to be black tights that hugged every one of Celina's dazzling curves, and a stunning black tunic adorned with a pattern of gold, pearl, and azure circles reminiscent of the Aztecs, with a low collar and a deep but tasteful opening in the front that left Cam licking his lips and dreaming about taking the tunic off later that evening.

Cam sat on the side of the bed while Celina finished dressing. When she came out, her hair was up and she'd put on tall black heels. A necklace and earrings in the same azure and gold as the tunic completed the outfit.

Cam's mouth went dry as he took in the finished look.

"You are..." he stammered.

"What?" Celina said with a slow smile. She came to the bed, straddled Cam's thighs, and sat on his lap, one tall heel on either side of him.

Cam was instantly rock hard. He was helpless when it came to this woman. With a glance, she could send his mind and his body into a tailspin in the very best way possible. With a whisper, he would give her his soul.

He already had.

Celina ran her hands through Cam's hair, down the side of his face, her hand soft against his cheek.

"What am I?" she said.

"Indescribable," Cam whispered.

And then she kissed him, soft at first, then harder and deeper. Her fingers in his hair closed into a tight grip, pulling his head back, arching his neck so she could kiss him more fully. Cam lost himself in the feel of her, the smell of her, the thought of her.

Hopeless. He was hopeless. There was no hope for him any longer. He belonged to Celina now.

She broke their kiss at last, her breath ragged, her eyes hooded, her skin flush. Cam knew he looked the same. His heart was racing and all he could think about was undoing the outfit Celina had spent the last hour putting together.

Celina looked down at him. Cam could see the battle in her eyes. He knew she wanted more. He knew she wanted him, and the thought, as always, sent an incredulous thrill racing through his blood.

But the look in her eyes cooled, receded. Cam felt a sharp stab of disappointment. The look was replaced by something else. A simmering, something waiting, restrained, ready to explode.

Celina slid off his lap, took his hand, and pulled him upright. She led him out of the bedroom and down the stairs to the kitchen, where Simon and Paulie were speaking quietly and laughing about something.

Seeing them come in, Simon looked up and the laughter immediately fell from his face. He was all business now.

"Alright," he said. "Let's go over the plan."

Celina nodded.

"Everyone has their glasses?" Simon said.

They all nodded.

Good. I'll have the drone up nearby. It has some features I can use for distraction if the shit hits the fan."

Cam had no idea what those "features" might be, but he was sure they would be effective, whatever they were. Simon hadn't been boasting when he said he was good.

"Paulie and I will set up in the house across the street to the south," Simon continued, "like before. Cam will be on the northwest corner. He'll be the first responder."

Cam nodded.

"Celina, you'll start on the northeast corner. That way, Cam will have a clear view of anyone approaching you from behind. When Paulie and I are set up and ready," Simon said, "we'll give you the signal. You can then approach the speaker's door and knock."

"From there," Paulie said softly, "it'll be up to you."

That same bad feeling came back to Cam. Something wasn't right about all this.

"This is a terrible plan," he said.

"Of course it's a terrible plan," said Simon. "It's a terrible idea. Celina, for the last time, can we please figure something else out?"

Celina's face was serene, almost Zen-like. But in her eyes was a fierceness, a sharp focus that Cam knew all too well. There would be no talking Celina out of this one.

"Let's go through the failure scenarios," Cam said, his tongue thick in his dry mouth.

Simon sighed. "Right. If there's a problem at the front door, Celina will disengage. Cam will come in for distraction and innocent opposition."

"The bumbling bystander," said Cam.

Simon nodded. "That should buy Celina time to disappear."

"And if she makes it inside?" said Paulie. "Then what?"

"The signal from Celina's glasses should penetrate the gold lining," Simon said. He swallowed hard. "Hopefully."

"If it doesn't?" asked Cam.

"If it doesn't, we wait for a visual from Celina."

"I'll flash a light or flip a window shade," Celina said.

"You'll have the drone circling to watch all the windows?" Cam asked Simon.

"Yes," he said, "but I don't think we would see a window shade fluttering. Whatever is obfuscating the windows would foul the camera view. She'd have to get to a front window for that. And we don't know if the obfuscation would apply to the light or not." He looked at Celina. "Front window would be best. We'll have someone watching at all times. Eyes, not cameras."

Celina nodded.

Cam didn't like it. So many things could prevent Celina from getting to a front window once she was inside the house. Once she stepped inside, the odds of her getting to a front window were extremely low.

"I'll move closer," Cam said. "When she gets inside, I'll come to the gate and watch the windows on the east side. I can see through the bars."

"Good," nodded Simon. "That gives Celina another option for signaling."

"If you stand too close to the gate," said Celina, "a guard might try to get you to move. You'll attract attention."

"I'll stand across the street. I'll be able to see from there."

Celina thought for a moment, then nodded.

"What if all goes well and the signal from the glasses does come through?" asked Paulie.

"Then I scan the house and you all help me look for the statue," said Celina. "We'll get a detailed floor plan as well as a precise location for the statue."

"And once you have that, you get the hell out," said Cam. "Don't waste any more time in there than you have to."

Celina patted Cam softly on one cheek and smiled at him.

"I won't," she said. "I promise."

"How much time do you think you'll need?" asked Simon.

"An hour," Celina replied. "Tops."

"How are you going to convince the Speaker of the House to let you into her house at night for a whole hour?" asked Paulie.

Celina grinned at her. "I'll think of something."

"One hour," said Cam. "If worse comes to worst, we'll break the door down and get you out of there."

"Cam..." said Celina.

"Easy there, mate," said Simon. "It's not an enemy bunker in Fallujah. We can't go in with flashbangs and tear gas."

"Why not?" said Cam. He heard his voice rising. A part of his brain knew he was being unreasonable, but he couldn't stop himself. "Are you just going to let them have her? Take her away to prison?" He shook his head. "Fuck no. Uh-uh. If shit goes sideways, I'll go through a fucking window if I have to."

Celina turned to him. Cam tried to avoid her eyes. He knew what would happen if she caught him with those eyes.

Celina put a hand on each cheek and forced him to look at her.

"Cam," she said.

The softness of her voice, the depth in her eyes, the beauty, the compassion he saw there. It shattered his already fractured heart.

"I can't lose you," Cam said, a hoarse whisper.

"It'll be alright, Cam."

"I won't let them take you to prison."

His eyes flicked involuntarily toward Paulie. Celina pulled them back to hers.

"I'll be alright."

Cam looked down and shook his head. Celina tightened her grip on his cheeks and bent his head back up. She kissed him, a kiss unlike any they'd shared before. This one wasn't sexual. It wasn't hot or hungry. It wasn't a soft kiss of satiety or contentment.

This was a kiss of love. Compassion. Trust. This was a kiss that lit up Cam's body like he'd never felt before.

His muscles relaxed. He was afraid, but that wasn't going to change the course of events. He had to push that fear to the side and focus on the job. Celina was the smartest, most capable person he had ever met. He had to trust her.

Celina's eyes were searching his. When she saw acceptance come into Cam's eyes, when she felt his body relax, she kissed him again. A quick, gentle kiss.

"Okay," she said, turning to the others, "let's get to work."

21

IT WAS ONLY eight o'clock in the evening, but the street was already deserted. It was Monday, a school night and a work night. And a storm was blowing in. Dry, fallen leaves skittered across the road. Thick grey clouds obscured the stars. The moon was just a faint glowing dot in the sky. Even the street-lights seemed muted in the breathless air.

And the temperature had dropped precipitously. Cam stood in the backyard with Simon while he set up the drone. Celina was in the study with Paulie, setting up the laptop. Celina had brought an overcoat, an elegant black jacket that suited her elegant outfit perfectly. Cam, like an idiot, had only brought a scarf and a light blazer. He buttoned his blazer, flipped up the collar, and wrapped the scarf twice around his neck.

"You ok, mate?" said Simon as he assembled the drone. This time, he'd brought a third case, filled with different accessories, each set in a snug foam holder like the others. He fit them to the drone one by one.

"I'll be fine."

"*She'll* be fine," said Simon, giving Cam a pointed look.

156

"This is a weird one, but I've seen Celina on jobs a hell of a lot weirder than this. This is a walk in the park."

Cam snorted. "It would be, if she wasn't knocking on the door of the third most powerful person in the world."

Simon shook his head. "You Americans," he said. "Saviors of the world." The sarcasm dripped onto Cam's shoe.

Simon attached a piece onto the drone chassis, then straightened and looked at Cam. "Do you really think the Speaker of the U.S. House of Representatives is more powerful than the Prime Minister of the UK or the president of the European Union or the president of China? Your speaker can't even pass legislation half the time. She's got power, sure, but two people would have to die before she touched the kind of power that could lead a nation."

Cam stuffed his hands in his pockets and shook his head. He didn't give a shit about power, and he didn't care to squabble with Simon about it.

"There are guards there," Cam muttered. "And a Capitol Police detail. That's all I'm saying. People are watching."

"People are always watching," said Simon, taking another accessory from the case and bending down to attach it underneath the drone. "You think Celina doesn't know that? You think she doesn't know how to handle herself? You should know better than that by now."

Cam had never heard Simon this argumentative before. His tone, his movements, everything smooth and genteel about the man had become sharp-edged and abrasive.

A thought struck Cam.

Simon was nervous, too.

Cam could see it now, in Simon's harsh tone, in his sharp movements, in the way he would try to attach a piece to the drone and have to try two or three times to get the alignment right.

Simon was nervous about this job, too. That explained his edginess.

But it didn't make Cam feel any better.

Cam nodded toward the drone. "What kind of distraction features does this thing have?"

Simon stood, glanced at Cam, and sighed heavily. The change of topic was an offer of truce, and Simon was accepting the terms.

"Flares, sirens and horns, some harmless projectiles. Enough to scramble a security force and make them forget about some random intruder, but not enough to land anyone in prison." Simon took the controller from its case and worked the two joysticks around to loosen them. "It'll seem like some kid pranking in the wrong place."

Cam nodded.

"We're done down here," he said. "Let's go back up."

Simon brought the controller with him as they went up to the study on the second floor to join Celina and Paulie. Two folding director chairs stood by the window. On a portable stand beside one, a laptop was set up to record the feed from Celina's glasses. That would give them a detailed record of the floor plan of the house, including the location of the furniture, security cameras, anything visible or detectable by the technology in the glasses.

A second laptop was set up on a stand beside the other chair. That one would display information coming from the drone, including position and altitude, as well as the camera feed. Simon had put all of this in the viewscreen of his glasses the last time, but no one wanted any distractions that night. Setting up the laptop allowed Simon to keep his viewscreen focused on Celina and what she was seeing and hearing.

"Drone is set and ready," said Simon.

Celina nodded.

"The feed from my glasses is set up and ready to record." She looked at Paulie. "As soon as I'm inside."

Paulie nodded.

Simon went to the second laptop, fiddled with his drone controller, and checked the output on the screen.

"I'll set the drone to maintain a position above the front door," he said over his shoulder. "Once you're inside, I'll switch it to a perimeter sweep, but it's cloudy and windy tonight." He looked around at Celina. "I'll need a moment to calibrate it to conditions once you're outside and in place."

Celina nodded.

Simon looked hard at her. "That means you'll need to wait for my signal before you go up to the door."

"Okay," said Celina, "Jesus."

Simon stared at her for a moment longer. "Fine," he said at last. "Glasses check."

They all put on their augmented-reality glasses and turned them on. Cam saw a familiar blue N hover in front of his eyes. The logo of Nestech, Inc., Christopher Nestrom's company. Celina had modified the device so much that it bore only a passing resemblance to the prototype Cam had stolen from Nestrom years ago, but she'd kept the start screen in place. Kind of an inside joke. Every time he heard Celina's voice saying "Hello, Sam Davis" in one ear and "Hello, Cameron Hauk" in the other, it made him smile.

Every time except that night.

Cam flipped through a series of windows showing the views from everyone else's glasses. He saw Paulie through Simon's eyes and Simon through Paulie's eyes. Then he saw himself through Celina's eyes. In his viewscreen window, Cam saw himself looking directly at Celina.

He looked tense. The bags under his eyes were visible even with the glasses on. The study was pitch dark, but in the enhanced imaging of the glasses, his skin looked pale. He needed to relax, to get his head into the right space. Regardless of his concern for Celina, he was going on a job and he needed to act like it. His worrying would only put Celina in more danger.

He closed the window. He'd open it again once they were all set and in position outside.

"I just need a minute," said Cam.

He left the room and went into the bedroom next door. The only light was the dim light of the cloud-filtered moon and the streetlamps outside, but with his glasses still on, Cam could see easily.

A doorway on one side of the room led to a prep area with a mirror and a makeup table, with two large closets beyond. A doorway on the opposite side led to a bathroom. In between, the hulking shadow of a king bed with a scrolled-wood headboard dominated the surprisingly small room, stacked with pillows and a thick bedcover. A cedar chest sat on another thick Persian carpet that lay under the bed and over the wood floors.

Two small nightstands flanked the bed, the time glaring in red numbers from a clock on each one. The surface of each nightstand held a book, each one perfectly aligned with the corner of the nightstand, reading glasses tightly folded and set just so on top of the books. On one nightstand was a coaster and a small plastic cup, upside-down. The odd emptiness of a home closed for the season.

Cam perched on the edge of the cedar chest. He put his elbows on his knees and his head in his hands and rubbed his face, trying to work out the tension. Then he sat up, straight-backed, squared his legs and closed his eyes. He breathed in deep, then slowly out, over and over, trying to calm himself, to center his mind.

Every job carried risk, even the smallest ones. Every job created fear. Cam didn't try to get rid of the fear. He couldn't.

No one could. He just pushed it to one side and focused instead on the job itself. He visualized the street corner where he would wait for Celina, standing in the shadow of a street-lamp, his phone in his hand as a plausible explanation if someone stopped to ask why he was loitering alone on a street corner at night.

In his mind, he watched Celina enter the house, then exit again an hour later and walk away from him. No one followed her. No alarms were triggered. All went safely.

He didn't bother imagining all the failure scenarios. Every plan failed at some point. He would deal with those failures when they arose. He just needed to stay relaxed enough and focused enough to deal with them quickly and efficiently when they did.

He took more deep in-breaths, more slow out-breaths. He could feel his mind unknotting, could feel the tension in his muscles dissipating. Gradually, his heart rate slowed and steadied.

When he opened his eyes, Celina was there, standing in the doorway. They looked at each other for a long moment, there in the quiet and the dark, their vision augmented by the glasses they both wore.

Celina broke the silence.

"It's time," she said, quietly.

A few minutes later, Cam stood on his corner in his assigned position. The air had grown thick with the approaching storm. Cam could feel an electricity in it, as if the air itself were charged.

"Drone is up," said Simon's voice in his earpiece. "Hold positions. Give me a moment to calibrate."

The wind at street level was picking up, already blowing the ends of Cam's scarf gently to the side. At drone height, it must have been whipping.

Cam held his phone up and scrolled idly through his

Instagram feed. He wasn't paying any attention to what was on the screen, but he needed to appear like he was doing something on his phone. Neighbors were still awake. They might look out their windows, might wonder about the man on the corner. He was well-dressed enough. He looked innocuous enough. But he needed to keep up appearances.

What he really wanted to do was stare down the street where Celina would be coming from. He resisted. He couldn't be seen staring down the street for an hour. That might attract attention. Besides, until Simon gave the signal, Celina would still be around the far corner, out of sight.

"This bloody wind," Simon muttered. "Hold position."

Cam couldn't help himself. He moved out of the shadows and glanced down the street, even though he knew he would see nothing but blowing leaves and bare sidewalk.

Instead he saw Celina, just steps from the speaker's front steps.

"Celina," said Cam, involuntarily moving toward her. "Celina, hold position."

"Celina, goddamn it," Simon said, "the drone isn't ready yet."

In the corner of his viewscreen, Cam opened a window showing the camera feed from Celina's glasses. He could see the door of the speaker's house, saw it grow larger as Celina climbed the front steps.

"Return to position, Celina," said Simon sharply.

As he strode down the sidewalk toward her, Cam saw Celina reach one hand up to her ear. Her camera feed went black.

"Celina, I've lost your feed," said Simon, frustration and a hint of panic in his voice. "Celina? Celina, come in. Do you read me?"

She turned it off. On purpose.

Cam picked up his pace. He could see the speaker's house,

could see the front door, Celina's form in front of it. It was only halfway down the block, but it seemed like a mile.

Cam watched as Celina reached the top step, straightened her back, and knocked three times sharply on the door. The sound was faint in the wind. Cam picked up his pace. He wanted to sprint to the door, but he didn't want to break cover.

The door opened. Celina blocked Cam's view. He could only see a woman's black hair and part of her shoulder.

He lengthened his stride.

"Come in, Celina," said Simon.

Celina and the woman stared at each other for a long moment.

Cam drew closer, now just a few strides away. The silence in the night contrasted with the pounding in his ears.

"It's you," said the woman simply.

Her voice died quickly in the charged night air, but Cam was close enough to hear it.

He could see the woman now, standing in the doorway. It was the speaker, Madeline Kinkaid. She wore a soft black jumpsuit with a long beige sweater coat. Her outfit was casual, but she wore elegant flats with a black and gold pattern.

The speaker was beautiful. Cam had seen her picture in the news a hundred times. But in person, it was more striking. And even here, at home at night, caught unawares, her beauty was unmistakable.

And oddly familiar, though in that moment Cam couldn't think why.

The speaker tilted her head to one side, regarding Celina with curiosity on her face. Behind her, in the yellow glow of the lights in her home, Cam could see a security guard in a black suit.

"I wondered when you'd come," the speaker continued.

Cam was almost there. He saw the guard clock him, reach up to his earpiece.

He heard Celina's voice, icy and stiff.

"Hello, mother," she said.

Cam nearly tripped, nearly sprawled out flat, right there on the sidewalk.

Somehow, he kept his balance, managed to force himself to stride on, past the doorway. From the corner of his eye, he saw the guard take his hand down from his ear.

Cam's mind buzzed and spun like it was filled with a thousand bees.

Celina's camera feed came back on. Through her camera, Cam watched her step inside the house. The speaker closed the door behind her.

He slowed his stride. He came to the curb on the opposite corner. The corner where Celina should still have been waiting. Images from Celina's camera were still moving. He could hear Celina and the speaker talking. But none of it registered.

"Cam."

It was Paulie's voice. His mother's voice. Soft, caring, soothing.

"Cam," she said in his earpiece, "come back. Come up here."

Why had she called the speaker *mother*?

Cam's mind slowed, as if each thought had to fight through a sea of molasses to get to his consciousness. The wind picked up. A handful of dry leaves chattered across the road.

Cam barely noticed.

Dully, automatically, he did what his mother said.

22

Celina was not expecting her mother to recognize her.

She recognized her mother, of course. Her mother was the speaker of the U.S. House of Representatives. Her face was in the news nearly every day. Celina saw her all the time.

And she'd known from the beginning that Madeline Brooks—Madeline Kinkaid, once she married the senator from Virginia—was her mother. Celina's father hadn't told her any tales. He'd never lied to her. When a four-year-old Celina asked why other kids had mothers and she didn't, her father had told her the truth, right from the start.

They'd spent a lot of time talking about it over the years. Celina's father was clearly still in love with her mother, right up until the day he died. He never condemned her for her choice, always explaining to Celina the reasons for Madeline's decision with the utmost empathy for what Madeline had been going through.

Celina's feelings about the matter were different.

Very fucking different.

But she hadn't thought her mother knew anything about her. Or cared to know.

Instead, after a brief flicker in her eyes—not surprise,

really, but something. Recognition? Resignation? Rueful amusement?—Madeline had just opened the door and let Celina inside.

The door opened to a long, narrow entryway with high ceilings ringed in ornate white painted crown molding. Walls painted butternut yellow led to a floor tiled in grey marble, with a thick, tightly woven grey runner over the top. A bench with a butternut cushion squatted against the wall beneath a wide mirror in an ornate mahogany frame. Stairs painted white rose at the far end, with a mahogany rail and baluster. A security guard hulked beside ten-foot mahogany double doors that formed the only doorway leading out of the vestibule.

For such an elegant home, Celina had expected a more extravagant entryway. But maybe people in 1860 didn't try to impress each other with their homes the way they did now.

"May I take your coat?" Madeline asked. Celina shrugged it off. Madeline hung it on a wrought-iron coat rack in the corner and nodded for Celina to follow her inside.

Celina glanced at the security guard as she passed. Why were they all tall and bald? Didn't any short men with good hair know how to act self-important and pretend to be able to protect people?

The guard regarded Celina with the same cool suspicion she felt for him.

"Your taste in men has really gone downhill," she said.

The speaker said nothing. Celina followed her through the double doors into a wide, airy room with fifteen-foot ceilings. On the wall to Celina's right, another mirror stood floor-to-ceiling, flanked by windows almost as tall. Two doorways opened at the far end of the room and in the center of the wall to Celina's left.

A set of French doors beside the mirror led to an outdoor sitting area. Soft exterior lights cast a warm glow over a park bench of iron and wood, surrounded by pots of pansies and mums blooming in purples, pinks, and yellows. Fall flowers giving a last memory of summer before winter fell. The area was surrounded by a tall brick wall, giving a sense of total privacy.

In contrast to the brightly colored flowers, the decor inside the room was white. White walls, white couches, white coffee table, thick white carpet from wall to wall. That was the mother Celina knew. Everything in black and white.

"Have a seat," Madeline said. "I'll prepare some tea."

She didn't ask Celina if she wanted tea, just assumed as much and left the room. The security guard stood in the corner like a cardboard cutout from an action movie. One of the evil minions that would get his anonymous ass kicked by the hero en route to the real villain.

But Celina didn't sit. She walked around the room instead. The walls were covered with artwork and photographs. Several paintings, mostly baroque or romantic. A few abstract sculptures. One wall held a series of twenty square photos in identical square mattes and frames, arranged in a four by five grid that covered the wall from floor to ceiling. Celina expected them to be photographs of the speaker meeting with foreign dignitaries, ex-presidents, and celebrities.

Instead, as she drew closer she saw that they were black-and-white photos of women. One photo a woman sitting in a frilly evening gown, one arm thrown over the back of her chair, the other arm holding a shotgun by the barrel, stock on the floor, staring daggers at the camera. Another of a gorgeous plus-sized woman in an elegant crop top, braless, ample breasts resting on her belly, with hands on hips, daring the viewer to deny her beauty.

Another photo showed a tattooed woman standing in thigh-high water wearing high-waisted bikini briefs. Her t-shirt was pulled over her head, shrouding her face but exposing the bottom of her full breasts. The pose was sensual.

Might have even been sexual were it not for the woman's arm stuck straight in the air, giving the middle finger to the camera.

Every image was artistically gorgeous. Every image was of a woman. Every image subverted or challenged or mocked the stereotypical societal conception of the woman as decoration or as baby factory or as domestic servant. Every image showed women as strong, confident, thoughtful, determined, or rebellious. It was a wall of women.

Celina was impressed. Madeline had good taste in art.

She peered closer at the photos, adjusting her glasses to make sure the incoming sound was off, but the outgoing sounds and images were transmitting, then continued around the room, admiring more of the artwork. The Tête study was not in the room, though Celina hadn't expected it to be. It would likely be in a private study, or perhaps in Madeline's bedroom.

She checked the corners of the ceiling for cameras. There were none.

Celina glanced at the security guard, who regarded her coolly, but attentively. She wandered toward the door the speaker had gone out, hoping to slip away to explore the rest of the house. But as she got closer, Madeline returned carrying a wooden tray laden with two mugs, a ceramic teapot, a sugar bowl, a milk carafe, and a plate of shortbread cookies.

"Do you like art?" she asked as she set the tray on the coffee table. The couches were arranged parallel to each other and to the wall of windows, with the coffee table between them. Madeline set a cloth napkin on the table before Celina, another on her side, then sat on one couch and gestured for Celina to sit on the other.

Celina glanced at the couch warily. She hoped it was more comfortable than the ones at the DC house.

"Of course you like art," Madeline continued. "You're Perry's daughter."

"I'm your daughter, too," Celina said. "Isn't that usually how that works?"

Madeline hummed neutrally in response. She sat forward on the edge of the couch and poured tea into her mug, releasing billows of steam into the air.

Celina gingerly took a seat on the edge of the opposite couch and was surprised when it yielded to her weight. She sat further back and found the couch to be soft and comfortable. The complete opposite of the stone ledges that passed for furniture in the other house.

"Do you take cream and sugar in your tea?" Madeline asked.

"I can fix my own tea," said Celina, crossing her legs and throwing one arm over the back of the couch.

She regarded the speaker carefully, watching her face for any clues to what she was thinking. The woman was a practiced, experienced politician at the top of her game. She would be doing whatever she could to play Celina. She'd already hidden her surprise at seeing her long-lost daughter. Now she was playing the gracious hostess. Celina didn't know what Madeline's game might be, but she knew exactly where Madeline could be hurt.

Like every other politician, her fatal flaw was her need to cling to power.

Like every other politician, her hidden secrets were her weakness.

Madeline nodded deferentially, added one cube of sugar and a splash of milk to the mug she had poured, and took it as her own. She sat back on her couch and sipped slowly from the steaming mug. She closed her eyes and savored it, murmuring in pleasure.

"I love a good cup of tea in the evening," she said, letting her eyes open slowly, drowsily. "Nothing with caffeine. And none of that chamomile or mint. This one," she tapped the side of the mug with one well-manicured nail, "is an orange tea with lemon and ginger and some valerian root."

Celina didn't respond. The speaker continued.

"I discovered it while I was in Luxembourg, if you can believe it. During a liaison with the European Commission. I finally had an hour to myself and found this tea in a little tea shop on the banks of the Alzette, run by an Armenian woman named Azadouhi. She was fascinating and her tea was incredible. I bought as much as she would sell me. When that ran out, I tried to contact her again, but couldn't find her. So I found this as a substitute. It's not quite the same, but it's still delicious, don't you think?"

Celina hadn't moved from the couch. She'd just been staring at the speaker while she delivered her monologue.

"Are you surprised to see me?" Celina asked.

Madeline smiled faintly and took another sip of her tea. Steam clouded her face for a moment, then dissipated as it rose toward the ceiling.

"I figured you would contact me, eventually," she said, "though I didn't know when that might be."

"Why would you think that?"

Madeline shrugged. "A child wants to know her mother. It's human nature."

She stared at Celina, her eyes wide and cool, her face relaxed. Her hair was straight and black and cut square to her shoulders. Business-like, while still maintaining a hint of femininity. Her cheekbones were razor sharp, her body lithe and strong. Celina had to admit, she still looked hot for a woman pushing fifty.

And Celina was sure Madeline used that sexuality to her advantage. Celina would. Celina did. All the time.

Madeline didn't seem the least bit afraid to look people in

the eye. Celina could imagine her spearing arrogant congressmen and senators with those hazel eyes, dazzling them with her beauty, throwing them off balance as their male urges took over their feeble mental faculties, then spearing them in the heart with her drive and her logic.

But Celina wasn't an insecure man-boy in a shitty suit and a shittier elected position. In Celina, Madeline would find a tougher opponent than she was used to.

Celina stared back at her, her own eyes just as cool, just as unwavering.

"My mother abandoned me and pretended I didn't exist," she said. "For my whole life. Why would you think I would want to talk to her?"

Madeline kept her face completely neutral. She took another sip of her tea, sipping the steaming drink slowly and easily, as if Celina had asked who she thought might win the Super Bowl or the next presidential election.

Her whole demeanor was maddeningly calm and friendly. There was no hint of regret or remorse, no tinge of shame or guilt. Instead of sounding like a woman who had wrecked Celina's life, she sounded like a beloved aunt trying to help Celina work through the pain.

It made Celina even angrier. She hadn't planned on being angry. Provocative, yes. She'd wanted to put Madeline on her back foot, press on the guilt angle, then maybe start a minor spat and storm off, saying she needed a moment alone, saying she needed the bathroom or something. The guard would start to follow her, a guilt-ridden Madeline would wave him off, and Celina would be free to roam the house, map the floor plan, and find the statue.

Instead, it was Celina who was getting riled up and Madeline who seemed in complete control. Celina could handle being given up. Adoptions happened all the time, and Celina had been lucky enough to be taken in by her own father. Madeline hadn't wrecked her life at all. Not even a little.

But what kind of a mother abandons her kid, then pretends in public that she'd never had a kid at all?

It was even part of her political platform, for fuck's sake. She'd gotten pregnant with that senator, had complications that led to the loss of the baby and a complete hysterectomy. She milked that sob story and leaned into the female angle she was already working. She became the childless champion of women's rights, the tragic mother never-to-be who now fought tirelessly for the rights of other mothers, for the rights of all women everywhere.

It was a good story. Celina had to give her that. And it became even more powerful when her husband died. Celina wouldn't have been surprised if Madeline herself had cut a hose or loosened a bolt in the engine of her husband's twin-prop plane, just so she could get the sympathy vote. She'd ridden that little tragedy all the way to the minority leader-ship, then to the speakership. The woman was ruthless. Heart-less. She would do anything to increase her power.

A part of Celina admired that in her.

A bigger part despised it.

Celina's blood began to boil and she felt steam coming from her ears like it was still coming from Madeline's mug of tea. She pulled in a long breath. Cam did that all the time, and it seemed to work for him. She pulled in the breath, then let it out slowly, quietly through her nose, so Madeline wouldn't know she was calming herself, wouldn't know she needed to calm herself.

It worked. Her clenched fists loosened a bit, the tight ball in her chest unwound just a little.

She leaned forward, pouring herself a full cup of tea. She took it without milk or sugar, leaned back on the couch and sipped it, staring through the steam at Madeline. At her mother.

The temperature was perfect, just shy of burning. The tea scalded her tongue just the way Celina liked it. And her mother was right. It was delicious. The orange and lemon provided a citrus tang, countering the bitter earthiness of the valerian root, while the ginger left a pleasant echo of spice on her tongue.

Valerian was supposed to aid sleep and ease anxiety. Probably why Madeline liked to drink it at night. Possibly why she chose to serve it to Celina.

She'd need a hell of a lot more than valerian to dull Celina's anger, but Celina appreciated the subtle deviousness.

Madeline looked down at her tea mug in her lap and nodded slowly.

"I suppose," she said, "there's only one question someone in your position would want to ask their mother."

Celina held back her scoff, but barely. This woman who had never known Celina, not even for a second, was about to tell her what she was thinking and feeling? This ought to be good.

"Yeah?" said Celina. "What question is that?"

Madeline sipped slowly from her mug, staring calmly at Celina over the edge. She set the mug back down in her lap and swallowed her tea, never dropping Celina's gaze.

"I suppose," she said with that same maddening, friendly calm, "you want to know if I regret my decision."

She tilted her head, regarding Celina like the subject of a fucking psychology experiment.

"You want to know," Madeline continued, "if I ever loved you at all."

23

CELINA WAS GOING TO PUKE. Her body went ice-cold even as sweat broke out on the back of her neck. She felt weak, broken, like all of her nerves had suddenly detached from her muscles and were dangling loose, leaving her helpless and floppy on the couch. Her eyes grew hot and her throat felt thick, like she'd swallowed a ball of socks.

And she knew Madeline could see it all. Madeline was watching for it, hoping for just this response.

Celina stared back at her, couldn't look away. She felt observed. She wanted to be alone.

She brought her tea to her mouth, trying to hide herself behind the mug.

Her hand was shaking. She missed her mouth. The lip of the mug caught on her chin and spilled hot tea down the front of her blouse. The scalding liquid didn't burn her skin, but her skin burned anyway.

Celina jumped and spilled more tea, on her stomach, on her thighs.

She set the mug down on the table and stood, swiping at her front, trying to brush away the burning.

Madeline stood with her.

"My goodness," she said, "are you alright, dear?"

Madeline set down her own mug and picked up her napkin, walking around the coffee table to try to pat Celina's blouse.

Standing up brought Celina's body back online, her nerves reconnecting to their muscles. She choked down the thickness in her throat and savored the heat of the spilled tea soaking through her blouse.

Madeline had caught her off-guard. Bravo. Good for fucking her. She'd scored a hit.

It was the last one she would ever get.

"I'm fine," said Celina. She grabbed the napkin from Madeline's hand and wiped at her blouse herself, then threw the napkin down on the table. "I need to use the bathroom," she said. She pushed past the speaker, toward the two doorways leading out of the room. "Which way is it?"

She knew the way. She'd studied the floor plans.

When she turned back toward the speaker, she saw the security guard in the corner step forward, saw the subtle hand sign from the speaker that send him back into the corner.

Like a good guard doggie. Sit. Stay.

Madeline pointed toward the doorway directly behind Celina. "Down the hall, second door on the left," she said.

Celina didn't start shaking until she was out of the room, out of sight, halfway down the hall. Then her body shook all over. She couldn't walk. She leaned one shoulder against the wall and waited for the shaking to pass.

It didn't. Not fast enough.

She calmed enough to ignore it and pushed herself forward.

Dark oak floors lined the long hallway, with crisp white walls and molding. Several tall doors opened on either side, with a large archway at the end.

Celina knew the layout by heart. The two doors on the

right led to a dining room, then a kitchen. Through the kitchen, a large pantry opened beyond that.

On the left were two more doors. The first led to a closet, the second to the bathroom. She passed them both by.

She passed the wide staircase that came next and continued to the end of the hallway. It opened through a wood-cased archway into a formal sitting room with a fireplace set in the far wall between two large windows that overlooked the garden. Scalloped wood shelves were set into the walls, filled with monolithic rows of books, as if someone had collected every set of encyclopedias known to man and used them to line these shelves. Armchairs and side tables were arrayed around the room in pairs and trios. It was the kind of place the menfolk would retire to after dinner to drink brandy and smoke cigars.

Celina scanned the room quickly, but she knew already that the statue wouldn't be there. There was artwork hanging on the walls, but nothing of any real note. The statue Celina was looking for had personal meaning to the speaker, and this was a formal room, not a personal one.

The personal rooms would be upstairs.

She left the sitting room and climbed the stairs as quickly and quietly as she could.

The second floor had three large bedrooms of roughly equal size, each with a private bath. Celina darted into each one, scanning the room quickly, knowing that she could review the footage in detail later. She was looking for the statue. Everything else was recon.

The second-floor bedrooms were beautiful, tasteful. Celina was surprised to see that they were far more colorful than the room she'd had tea in downstairs, and far more colorful than the house in Washington. The walls were painted in bold umbers and blues, with matching bedcovers, throws, and pillows. There were paintings and photographs everywhere in a variety of styles and subjects. It had a homier feel than Celina had expected, and the decor evinced an artistic taste that mirrored Celina's own.

Her stomach roiled and burned at the thought.

She moved on to the third floor. This was where she expected the statue to be.

Celina had studied the history of the house, looking up the original floor plans and all the building permits that had been obtained since. She knew the third floor had originally been identical to the second floor, with three large bedrooms that had been fitted with private bathrooms over the years. The merchant who built the house must have had a large family, or frequent visitors.

When the speaker had bought the house, she'd renovated it extensively. That must have been when she'd installed the gold shielding, which was *not* mentioned in any of the building permits. The permits showed that the speaker had torn down most of the third-floor walls and created a large master bedroom suite with a private bath and dressing area on one side and a large private study on the other.

She and her husband had shared the space when he was alive, but now the massive study belonged entirely to Madeline. If the profiles and interviews were to be believed, that was where she spent the majority of her personal time, staying up late reading or working on some bill or other, then flopping into bed for a few hours of rest.

Celina slipped up the stairs into a long hallway like the ones on the other floors, this time with only two doors on one side. The door to Celina's right would lead to the bedroom, the other to the study. Celina went to the right, first.

She scanned the bedroom. No statue. She scanned the bathroom and the dressing area. She didn't expect the statue to be in either, but she wanted to be as complete as possible.

Finding nothing, she moved back into the bedroom. The

private study was accessible from the hallway, but a short passage opened into it from the bedroom, as well, with doors on either end and storage rooms in the space between.

A tingling rose in Celina's stomach as she stepped through the first door into the wide, dark passage. She'd figured the statue must be in the study, and now she'd ruled out any other reasonable location, both within the house and outside of it. The statue wasn't in any of the speaker's external offices, and it was too valuable and too sentimental—or so Celina assumed —for the speaker to keep it anywhere else. It had to be here.

Celina stepped lightly and quickly down the passageway. She slipped through the door to the study, shutting it silently behind her. The tingling in her stomach had reached her head. Her whole body felt like it was quivering. Unlike before, this quivering wasn't from anger. It was excitement, triumph. She turned to scan the room.

A pair of desks stood together in front of Celina, their sides facing her. The speaker was standing at the desk on the right, calmly shuffling papers, occasionally lifting one to peer at it more closely.

"I suppose I should have been more clear in my directions," the speaker said without looking over at Celina. "I meant the second door on the left on the first floor." She finally looked up, reading glasses perched on the end of her nose, a calm smile on her lips. "Not the third floor."

Celina's blood immediately boiled again. She clenched her fists so hard she thought her knuckles would burst through her skin.

But she couldn't let Madeline see her emotion. She'd shown far too much earlier. Madeline had scored a hit. Never again.

Celina ground her teeth and pulled in a deep breath through her nose.

"I couldn't help it," she said, her voice as airy and light as a debutante at a cotillion. "Your house is so beautiful, I got distracted after using the restroom and had to explore." She approached the speaker and held out one hand. "I hope you'll forgive me."

Madeline's eyebrows lifted. "Of course I don't mind, dear," she said. Her pleasantness was a slap in Celina's face. "You are always welcome here."

Madeline turned back to the paper she was studying. Celina stared at her profile, lit in gold from below by a lamp on the desk. Madeline was using her pleasant attitude like an épée, jabbing at Celina, trying to provoke her. So far, she'd been succeeding.

But what was with the maternal hospitality? *You are always welcome here?* Celina had never been welcome there before. The sentiment made Celina uncomfortable and confused.

Madeline was messing with her head. That fucking bitch. Celina had expected her to be good. You don't become Speaker of the House without knowing how to manipulate people. But she was fucking supervillain good.

But every supervillain had the same fatal flaw: overconfidence. Now that she was on to Madeline, Celina could play dumb and use that confidence against her.

She strolled around, examining the room. A fireplace and hearth stood against the far wall, a low fire crackling. Two wing-backed leather chairs with ottomans stood in front of the fireplace, a round side table between them. One chair looked recently used, with a blanket tossed haphazardly across the seat and a book angled toward it on the side table. That must be the speaker's chair. The other would have belonged to her late husband.

Idly, Celina scanned the book title as she walked by. A history of politics in the Levant. The speaker was working on her Nobel Peace Prize in her spare time.

The roof of the study was pitched, with three skylights set

into it, allowing all four walls to be lined with bookshelves from floor to ceiling. Unlike the shelves in the sitting area on the first floor, which had been lined with leather-spined volumes designed more for appearance than for use, these shelves were overflowing with books of all colors and sized and bindings. Hardcover, paperback, and mass market. Fiction and non-fiction, reference books and coffee-table books. They were stacked two deep on some shelves, laying on top of each other on others.

Celina was surprised not to find any cameras mounted along the ceiling. Like the rest of the house, the study was completely unsurveilled. The speaker must have assumed the external security system was robust enough that they didn't need internal cameras. That was a mistake.

Opposite the fireplace, closest to the passageway to the bedroom, the pair of desks stood back-to-back. The speaker and the senator would have worked together, facing each other. Both desks were messy, but one was now clearly used only as a staging area, with books and stacks of paper arranged neatly on its surface.

The other desk, where the speaker stood, looked like it was used often. A laptop and monitor sat on one side. Papers were strewn around, along with an empty mug, several coasters, a cylinder filled with pens.

And a statue.

The speaker's body had hidden it from Celina's view earlier, but now she could see it, as plain as day. A simple, small statue of pale brown limestone. Only one foot tall, it was little more than an elaborate paperweight. From a block carved square at the base, a graceful neck rose to a woman's long face. Small lips pursed above a sharp chin. An impossibly long, slender nose rose to the woman's narrow eyes, closed. Her hair swept straight back behind her head in a stiff, blocky bun.

The statue was plain, simple, straightforward.

And breathtaking.

Celina stepped to the side for a clearer scan of the statue and the area around it. It was just sitting on the desk amidst the coasters and papers. She didn't see any kind of security. She hadn't really expected any. The security on the house would be enough to discourage any intruders.

Celina glanced up at the skylights, surprised that they were even there. Too much risk. Maybe they were guarded with sensors. Maybe the glass was bulletproof and shatterproof. There had to be some kind of protection on them. They must have been obfuscated like the other windows, or else Simon's drill would have been able to get through. They would figure out the details later, but the skylights provided another option for entry.

"I'm afraid I'll have to bring our evening to a close, Celina," said the speaker, putting down her paper and setting her reading glasses on top of it. "Congress is back in session tomorrow and I'd like to get some sleep." She gave a twisted smile. "The people's work never stops."

Celina nodded and moved immediately toward the door to the hallway. She had what she needed.

The speaker followed her down both flights of stairs to the front door, where the security guard was waiting. Celina hadn't seen any other guards inside the house, but she knew they were there. They would be roaming the grounds, for sure. The old floor plans showed a small basement, probably used only for laundry and food storage, but there would be a surveillance room in the guard house outside. There could be one in the attic, too, or above the garage. Maybe even a bunk for security guards to stay the night.

The guard moved to one side as Celina put on her jacket. The speaker held the front door open for her.

"Thank you for coming," said Madeline. She paused for a moment. "It was lovely to see you."

Her voice was so sincere, Celina almost believed her.

The woman was truly a master of manipulation. No wonder she'd gotten as far as she had.

Celina nodded and moved past her.

"Celina," said Madeline, stopping Celina on the porch. "When did you start wearing glasses?"

Odd question. It caught Celina aback for a moment. Thankfully, her back was to the speaker. She gathered herself and turned back toward the front door.

Madeline stood in the doorway, arms crossed over her chest, wrapping her beige sweater tight against the cold night air. She looked like any soccer mom anywhere in America.

"I didn't know you wore them," Madeline said.

Celina tilted her head at the speaker, doing her best imitation. She wore the calmest, friendliest expression she could muster.

"There's a lot you don't know about me, Madeline."

Celina walked down the front steps and away down the sidewalk.

She didn't look back.

24

MADELINE WATCHED Celina until she was out of sight, then shut the front door quietly.

That had certainly been interesting.

"Do you want me to set a detail to follow her?"

The young security guard's face was alight, eager. He had one hand on his earpiece, ready to set things in motion.

Madeline shook her head. "Thank you, Edward. That won't be necessary."

Her security detail was thorough and professional, and well-trained to identify and assess potential threats. But they had a tendency to be a little overzealous when it came to ambiguous interpersonal relations.

Unfortunately for them, dealing with ambiguous interpersonal relations was Madeline's job description.

"I'll be turning in for the night now."

"Good night, ma'am."

"Good night, Edward."

Madeline climbed the stairs to her study. She didn't really need the security guards at the house. She certainly didn't want them there. But ever since the attack on Speaker Pelosi's San Francisco house years ago, not to mention the January 6 madness in 2021, the Capitol police had taken to erring on the side of caution.

But Madeline's house was no ordinary home. Perry had personally overseen the security appointments when she'd bought the home years ago and started renovations. He'd paid an unconscionable amount of money for sheets of gold—pure gold!—to be installed in the walls and ceilings. Even under the floor. Something about intrusion shielding. It helped to have a tech genius designing your home security system.

And he'd done something to the windows, too. Scramble glass, he'd called it. Again, something about thwarting intruders. Probably something he would bring to market one day.

Something he would have brought to market.

Madeline flopped down in her desk chair and sighed.

She had lost two good men now, two men who were near and dear to her heart. First, her husband in the plane crash. He shouldn't have been flying in that tiny plane anyway, let alone over a mountain range in a thunderstorm. But he'd always liked to fly, had always liked adrenaline a little too much. It was part of what Madeline loved about him, so different from her own bookish ways.

Then Perry's death almost two years ago. Only fifty-four and in perfect health, yet he'd died of a heart attack in his home. Life was strange and cruel.

Her first thought when she heard the news had been of Celina. Madeline had thought about flying to California to be with her, but she kept to the arrangement. It would have been disorienting for Celina, anyway, if her mother appeared from nowhere. She didn't even try to reach out.

She and Perry had agreed long ago that this arrangement would be best—with Perry raising Celina and Madeline focusing on her work—and Madeline still believed it to be true. So she had waited and grieved in private and hoped, one day, her daughter would seek her out.

And now she had.

She picked up the statue and cradled it in her lap, the stone cool against her palm, as always. She ran her hand over it, the hard edges of the base, the smooth lines of the face, the bumpy texture of the hair. She'd caressed that statue so many times over the years she was afraid the oils on her skin might degrade the limestone somehow.

Perry had given it to her, before she left for good. She'd given him the baby, he said, so he would give her this. A way to remember them.

Celina was going to steal it.

Of course she would. She hadn't come for a social visit or to finally reconnect with the long-lost mother she saw on television every day. Or, more likely, on Instagram or TikTok.

Maybe she'd hoped to shock Madeline by her sudden appearance, but Madeline had known Celina was in town. She'd gotten an alert on her phone when the doors had opened at the Capitol Hill house, had checked the cameras— the hidden cameras that Perry had installed, not the basic cameras—and seen it was Celina. She'd been shocked then.

But from that moment, she'd waited. Half-expecting. Hoping that Celina might knock on her door. She had no idea what the interaction would be like, but she was looking forward to it.

And it had certainly been interesting.

Those glasses Celina had been wearing were definitely not from Lens Crafters. Probably some kind of augmented reality thing. It looked like Perry's work, but maybe Celina had inherited some of Perry's genius.

She had a genius of her own, to be sure. Madeline had followed Celina's life and career closely, even beyond Perry's regular updates. Her staff knew to watch closely for any news from the tech sector, especially San Francisco. They thought Madeline was just keeping up with the times, and that was part of it. But Madeline's chief-of-staff knew the truth. She knew to look for any mention of Celina's name and make sure those articles made it into the news digest Madeline's team prepared for her at the end of each day. Celina had made waves in Silicon Valley with her brash attitude and her technical brilliance, and Madeline had admired her from a distance.

Madeline didn't care if Celina stole the statue. It belonged to Celina, anyway. Part of her family's heritage. Madeline had never wanted to take it in the first place, but Perry had insisted. Madeline never really knew why.

Maybe this was why. Perry was otherworldly brilliant. Maybe somehow, in that incredible mind of his, he'd foreseen this situation and had known the statue would draw Celina to Madeline. Maybe he had hoped it would reunite mother and daughter one day.

Well, it had. Sort of.

Celina would be back. But Madeline had a feeling she wasn't going to want to sit for tea the next time.

25

No MOTHER LIKES to see their child in pain.

But no mother can completely prevent it, either.

Physical pain is easier. Skinned knees, scraped elbows, broken bones. These are painful, but a mother can fix them. A kiss, a band-aid, a visit to the doctor. With some ice cream and medication, the pain goes away.

But when your child's pain is emotional, a mother feels helpless. Doctors rarely help, and medication can make things much worse.

When your child is suffering from emotional pain, a mother can't fix it. All she can do is hurt along with their child.

Across from the speaker's house, Paulie opened the front door for Cam. The wind gusted as he stumbled inside, as if it were blowing Cam along with the dried leaves and the storm clouds. She put her arm around Cam's shoulders and led him up the stairs to the study, where Simon sat in front of the window, the laptops at his side.

Paulie set Cam down in the large leather swivel chair behind the desk, the chair of whoever owned the house they were borrowing for their job. Cam responded easily to her pushes and pulls, moving like a life-size claymation figurine, his face slack, his eyes distant and troubled. He didn't speak. He just slumped in the chair and stared across the dark room at nothing.

Paulie could do no more to help him in that moment. She could only feel his pain with him.

She sat back down at the window with Simon and did her job, checking her laptop to ensure that it was properly recording the feed from Celina's glasses.

She didn't know what Cam had seen that set him off. The feed had been interrupted just when Celina approached the front door and didn't come on again until a minute or two later, as she was stepping inside the speaker's house. Some kind of glitch.

Though in several months of using the glasses, Paulie had never seen them glitch before.

Cam was in no state to explain, at the moment, so Paulie focused on what she could do. The feed was coming through loud and clear. Celina was in a sitting room, admiring the art on the walls.

"Perimeter pattern is locked," said Simon.

On the screen of his laptop, Paulie could see the view from the drone, an enhanced night-vision view of the speaker's house from the air, along with several overlays showing various data.

Simon turned toward Paulie and looked past her at Cam. "He okay?"

"Not at the moment," she sighed, focusing on her laptop.

From the side of her vision, she saw Simon glance at her, then press his lips together and nod grimly before turning back to his own work. He fiddled with his laptop for a moment, then picked up a pair of binoculars and focused them through the window.

"Damn windows are covered," he muttered. "Can't see anything."

"The feed is coming through fine," said Paulie.

Simon put down the binoculars and nodded, staring silently out the window at nothing but blowing leaves and darkness.

Paulie slid her laptop to the wide windowsill between them so they could both watch it together. The feed from Celina's camera filled the screen. Modern technology was wonderful, but it was so isolating. Watching the same thing on separate glasses was not the same as watching the same thing on one screen together.

Simon smiled. They both leaned toward the laptop screen, their shoulders touching, and experienced the speaker's house through Celina's eyes and ears.

The inside of the home was as stately and beautiful as the outside. The speaker clearly loved art, and she seemed to have good taste. When the speaker came into the room with a tea tray, Paulie tapped the laptop to increase the volume.

"Of course you like art," the speaker was saying. "You're Perry's daughter."

"I'm your daughter, too," Celina replied. "Isn't that usually how that works?"

Paulie gasped out loud, but Simon didn't flinch. She turned to him, unbelieving.

"You knew?" Paulie said.

Simon's eyes glinted in the dark, catching some stray beam of faint moonlight, enhanced by the glasses Paulie wore. He nodded quietly.

"I was close with Celina's father, Perry. It was never a secret who Celina's mother was, for me or for Celina. Or why she left."

"Why didn't you say something?"

"Not my information to share." He shook his head. "I tried

to get Celina to tell you both. It's a conflict of interest. Letting emotion into a job." He shook his head again, frustrated. "It wasn't fair for us to keep it from you. From both of you."

He glanced over his shoulder at Cam. Paulie looked over, too. Cam had shifted in the chair, and his face wasn't as stunned and blank as it had been. Now, he just looked angry.

"Why did she leave?"

He waited in silence for a long moment, staring at the laptop screen while Celina and the speaker chatted about tea. It all seemed so surreal. Hiding in the shadows across the street, high-tech surveillance equipment everywhere, listening to the Speaker of the House chat with her long-lost daughter about a tea shop somewhere in Europe.

Life was weird.

"You don't have to tell me," said Paulie.

"No, it's okay," Simon said. He gestured toward the window, toward the speaker's house. "It's all fair game now."

He stared out the window as he spoke.

"They didn't mean to get pregnant. Perry wanted to change the world through technology. She wanted to change it through politics. They figured one of them had to give up their dream in order to raise the baby. Madeline was willing to do it."

"Perry wouldn't let her."

Simon shook his head.

"Why didn't they just get married, then? He raised Celina himself, anyway. Couldn't they do that and be married, too?"

"It was the mid-nineties. Times were changing, but they weren't like they are now. A nineteen-year-old girl and a twenty-six-year-old counter-culture neo-hippie from Silicon Valley having an unplanned child out of wedlock? It wasn't going to play well, politically. Not even in the Virginia 8th."

"So she just left?"

Simon nodded.

Paulie thought about Cam as a baby. She couldn't imagine making that choice. She couldn't imagine looking down at that tiny life in her arms and then choosing to put her career over her child.

But she knew nothing about Madeline Kinkaid. She didn't know if Madeline might have agonized over the choice. If she spent nights awake in the dark, her pillowcase damp and cold from her tears. Or if she left and never looked back, focusing instead on the hunt for political power.

Some politicians were idealist, trying to change the world for the better. Fewer and fewer, it seemed. But some, still. Others were hungry for nothing but power and wealth, and didn't care who they stomped into the ground along the way. She didn't know which of those described Celina's mother.

"She left," Simon continued, "and Perry covered her tracks. Doctored the birth records, the paperwork. Made it so no one would ever trace her back to Celina."

Paulie let out a heavy breath.

"Poor Celina," she said.

"And poor Madeline," said Simon. "She and Perry stayed close. I think she was still in love with him, even after she married that senator." He looked at Paulie. "I know Perry was still in love with her, right up to the end."

"Did Celina know?"

Simon shook his head. "She knew what happened, but there was no way for her to know how her mother felt about it. Celina vilified her mother, despite all the explanations and justifications Perry gave for her leaving."

"Doesn't matter why they left," muttered Paulie. "They still left."

"So this is some kind of revenge, then?" Cam's voice was low, but the anger in it punched through the air between them. "She's trying to get back at her mother for leaving?"

Simon and Paulie turned in their seats to face him.

"That's part of it, I'm sure," Simon said. "But not all of it."

"Why couldn't she tell us this herself?" Cam stood from the chair and stalked to the window, his shoulders hunched as he leaned with both hands on the window sill, glaring through the glass. "Doesn't she trust us?"

"I don't know," said Simon. He glanced at Paulie. After a long pause, he said, "You'll have to ask her that yourself."

Cam laughed, a short, rueful chuckle.

Paulie had never seen Cam like this. Angry. Bitter. Her son weathered every storm, every setback with a good nature and a positive outlook. It's what she and Sam had taught him to do. Anything else was counter-productive, even toxic.

But there was nothing good-natured about his attitude now. Paulie could feel the anger radiating from him. It battered her where she sat.

Without another word, Cam turned from the window and walked out of the room.

"Cam," called Simon.

Cam didn't respond.

Simon put a hand to the earpiece of his glasses, started to get up from his chair.

Paulie set a hand on his arm and pulled him back into the seat.

She had never seen Cam like this, but she knew her son.

He was in pain. And they couldn't do anything to fix it.

All they could do was hurt along with him.

26

CAM WANTED to throw the back door open, to bang it back on its hinges and off the side of the house. He wanted to hear it crunch and splinter.

He wanted to break something.

It was a new feeling for him. He wasn't a violent person, by nature, and he wasn't the type to let things get under his skin.

But Celina had gotten under his skin.

And she'd been lying to him all this time.

They'd been casing the speaker's offices and her home. Celina had been talking about her plans for weeks. And she'd been talking about her mother, too, in the context of the D.C. House.

But she'd never bothered to connect those dots for Cam.

That was an important connection to leave out.

It was a betrayal. Cam felt like someone had ripped out his insides and sewn him back up with a gaping hole inside. He'd thought he and Celina were so close—emotionally, not just physically—and yet she obviously felt like she couldn't trust Cam with this kind of intimate information. What else wasn't she telling him? What other secrets was she keeping?

Cam wanted to break something, but he didn't. He opened

the back door quietly, let it click shut softly behind him. Celina and Simon had made sure to disable all the cameras and sensors in the house, so there would be no intrusion alerts for the owners or their security company, but the last thing he wanted was to leave a broken door for them to wonder about and investigate when they came home.

Celina's words on the speaker's porch echoed in his mind.

Hello, mother.

So calm. So casual.

Like she hadn't just nuked Cam's brain.

His brain had gone offline, catatonic. He had moved purely by instinct and momentum. He followed his mother's voice back to the ops house and let her do the rest.

And then he'd heard Celina's voice again, on the camera feed on Paulie's laptop, and his catatonia reversed. It flared into white-hot anger.

He couldn't stay there. Simon and Paulie were working, Celina was in jeopardy, and Cam was mad enough to do real damage.

So he'd come outside into the cold night air. The temperature had dropped at least thirty degrees since sunset, and the wind had picked up. Even with the walls protecting the backyard of the house, it beat against Cam's side, pushing and smacking him. If the rain ever came, it would be a hell of a storm.

Cam liked the wind. He leaned into it, opened his jacket and loosened his scarf and let it cool him down until he was shivering and his nose and ears had gone numb.

He bundled up again and crossed his arms over his chest, staring into the darkness of the yard, his glasses turning the shadows bright as day. A wide swath of yard extended a hundred feet or so until it met the back wall of the property. A gazebo stood on the left, large box planters ran along the wall on the right.

He took off the glasses and slipped them into his jacket pocket. The world went dark.

He wanted the darkness. He wanted to be alone.

Something glinted, a dull shine at the far end of the yard. Maybe a stray moonbeam on a lawn chair or a table. Cam stepped down off the porch and strode across the grass, keeping the glasses in his pocket. He was stepping into darkness now, into uncharted territory. He hadn't been to the back of the yard, hadn't even seen it in the daytime. Aside from the quick scan he'd just done, he had no idea what was back there.

And that's what he liked. Into the dark, the unknown, unaided. He had to put all his senses to use, push all other thoughts from his mind. He was chasing nothing, investigating empty air, but it was something to do that would make his thoughts go away.

He stepped slowly off the deck, letting his body relax completely, opening his mind and his senses to the night. The wind smelled of impending rain. The grass under his shoes was wiry and stiff. The soil beneath it was spongy.

His eyes adjusted to the darkness. He could see the gazebo to his left, a darker shadow within the shadows. A lighter shadow appeared beneath it. An outdoor kitchen. That might have been what had glinted.

But the sight line wasn't right. The outdoor kitchen was on the left side of the yard. From where Cam had been standing on the deck, the glint had been straight ahead.

The planter boxes ran along the wall to Cam's right, filled with an assortment of shadows in varying heights and widths. Some were bushy and waist-high. Others were tree-like and came up to Cam's shoulder. Others looked like they didn't have anything in them at all, but were probably filled with ground-level plants. It was all probably the usual: herbs, prize-winning roses, dwarf lime trees, something like that. Something for a retired judge and his wife to do to stay active and get outdoors without hurting themselves.

The brick wall at the back of the yard emerged from the night. Cam stepped all the way to it, turned and set his back against it, hands in his pockets.

The brick was cold through his jacket. Cam had thought it would feel supportive, thought he could rest comfortably against it, but it felt rough and unwelcoming instead. He turned and ran his hand along the wall, feeling the rough texture under his fingers in the darkness. The brick was smooth, but the mortar extruded from the joints between. The jagged lumps had been poking into Cam's back. It might have looked good in the daytime, but it didn't feel good at night.

He heard a click to his right, turned his head sharply. His night-adjusted eyes couldn't make anything out. He thought about putting his glasses back on, but he wasn't ready yet to hear Celina's voice again, to see the world through her eyes.

It was probably nothing, anyway. A twig snapping under a raccoon's paw. The wind blowing branches against the brick. Cam was agitated. His mind was jumping at the wind.

He sighed and pushed himself off the wall, letting the mortar dig into his palms and give him momentum to head back toward the house.

He sat at the table on the deck and stared into the night. The cold of the metal chair seeping into his legs as he waited. He tried to clear his mind, to think of nothing at all, and failed miserably.

All he could think of was Celina's face in bed in the morning, the sunlight gilding her cheek and flaring the green of her eyes. Her dark, wild morning hair pushed across her head to cascade down the other side of her face. The swell of closeness and love in his chest. The sense of safety he felt when he was alone with her. Safety and trust.

Cam's heart hitched at the thought. It always did.

Hello, mother.

The image burned like an old filmstrip against a hot projection bulb, browning and distorting from the center out. The taste of bile came to Cam's tongue.

He closed his eyes, tried to re-center.

And then the cycle would repeat. Cam couldn't escape it.

He sat in the dark on the porch, for how long he didn't know, replaying that cycle again and again.

He opened his eyes after another cycle and saw Simon's drone hovering silently in front of him, four feet from his face. It hovered in place for a moment, watching him, then shifted to the other side of the table and landed gently.

The job must be over.

Cam heard the door behind him swing open. Electricity crackled through his body.

He let out a heavy sigh, took one last look into the darkness of the yard, then stood from his chair and turned toward the door.

Celina.

She stared at him in silence. She still wore her glasses, but Cam didn't put his back on.

Her face was in shadow. He couldn't see her expression. Didn't want to.

She didn't move. Didn't shift out of the way so Cam could pass. Didn't even turn her head away or tilt it down in shame or regret. She just stared at him, unmoving, unspeaking.

Cam returned the stare. All he could see was a darkness where her face would be.

He wasn't going to give her the satisfaction of him backing down. He wasn't going to be the first to speak. She owed him an explanation. She owed him an apology.

And if she didn't understand that, then maybe... maybe she didn't owe Cam anything at all. Maybe he'd misinterpreted what he thought they had together.

After a moment, Celina took her own glasses off.

She didn't speak, didn't move, just removed her glasses and held them at her side.

They stood like that, like a showdown in the Old West, neither speaking, each daring the other to make the first move.

Simon emerged from the darkness inside the house, behind Celina, a drone case in each hand and under one arm.

He cleared his throat.

"I need to..."

He nodded over Celina's shoulder toward the deck.

"The drone." He cleared his throat again. "I need to... put it away now."

Celina still didn't move, still didn't speak. Simon shifted awkwardly behind her.

Finally, without a word, she turned and disappeared in the shadows, back inside.

With a nervous glance at Cam, Simon came out and set his cases on the table.

"Chilly out here," he said.

Cam stared at the empty doorway where Celina had been.

"You two... okay?" Simon asked.

Cam didn't respond.

Wordlessly, he pulled an empty case over and helped Simon pack up.

27

CAM SLEPT ALONE THAT NIGHT, in a bedroom on the second floor between Simon's room and his mother's room.

Only he didn't sleep. At all. He lay in bed alone, staring at the ceiling and waiting for dawn.

When the light in his room was finally enough for him to see, he got up, dressed, and went down to the kitchen.

Celina was already there, coffee pouring from the Nespresso machine into a cup. She turned when she heard Cam come in. Without a word, she gave the coffee to him and turned back to make another for herself.

"Did you sleep?" she asked without looking up.

He sipped his coffee.

"No."

He watched her back as she nodded, but she didn't say anything else. Somehow that brief exchange was worse than total silence.

Cam went to the refrigerator and pulled out ingredients. Blueberries and raspberries, milk, butter, eggs. He set them on the counter, bent down and pulled out flour and sugar, baking powder and salt.

Celina turned with her coffee, took one sip while eyeing

the ingredients on the counter, then set the cup down, went to the cupboards behind Cam, and pulled down a large mixing bowl, a sifter, and a wooden spoon.

Cam sifted the dry ingredients, added the wet, and stirred them together with the spoon while Celina pulled out a wide griddle pan and spray oil and heated them on the stove behind him.

When Simon and Paulie came down a short time later, Celina had set the table and the kitchen was filled with the rich scent of blueberry and raspberry pancakes, stacked ten high on a plate on the counter. Cam and Celina were working on more, the griddle hissing as Cam poured more batter onto it.

They still hadn't said another word to each other.

Beside the plate, Celina had set out bottles of maple and boysenberry syrup, a stick of butter, whipped cream in a can, and a bowl of chopped walnuts.

"This is some spread," whistled Paulie.

"Lovely to wake up to the smell of fresh hotcakes," said Simon with a broad smile.

"Pancakes," said Paulie.

"I thought you Americans called them hotcakes."

"Pancakes," said Paulie.

"Flapjacks?"

Paulie shook her head.

"Griddle cakes? Slapjacks? Drop scones?"

"Drop scones?" Paulie handed him an empty plate and a fork from the table. "Shut up and get your pancakes."

Cam didn't laugh or smile or even turn from the stove except to add three more pancakes to the finished stack. His mind caught the humor and saw it for what it was, but no emotion made it out of the cage of his mind. He felt like his true self was a tiny dot deep within a thick plastic housing in the shape of his body. Nothing that came from that tiny dot—

no humor, no emotion, no feeling at all—could penetrate all that plastic.

Celina was similarly stone-faced.

Cam saw Simon and Paulie glance at each other, then take their filled plates to the table to eat.

They tried to fill the silence with more playful banter. When that didn't work, they asked Celina about the job the previous night. In a clipped tone, she said they would talk about it later, then didn't say any more. After a while, Simon and Paulie stopped trying, fell into eating their food and speaking with each other in low murmurs, their heads bent together like best friends in a middle school cafeteria.

Cam and Celina had cooked all the batter, making a stack of pancakes they would never be able to finish. It stood steaming on the counter while they rinsed and cleaned the pan, the bowls, and the utensils, then sprayed and wiped the counters and the stove. Only when the kitchen was spotless did they make themselves plates of food and sit down to eat.

By then, Simon and Paulie were finished. They sat in silence, watching Cam and Celina for a moment, then excused themselves and went upstairs to get dressed for the day.

Once they left, the only sounds were the clink and tap of silverware on dishes, the scrape of glasses of orange juice being lifted and set down.

Cam didn't look up. He kept his gaze focused on his plate, and nothing else.

He wanted to talk. Desperately. His mind was spinning with things he wanted to say, questions he wanted to ask, accusations he wanted to hurl.

But what he really wanted was for Celina to talk. And he wanted her to start it, to show some hint of remorse or even just a simple understanding of what Cam might be feeling, an acknowledgement that he might feel hurt or, at least, surprised.

Celina had carried that secret with her for months, since they'd met. The topic of her mother had come up many times. Celina had never shown any willingness to explore it.

So, fine, she hadn't wanted to go into detail about her mother before. Cam could respect that. It might have come out over time as they stayed together.

But then they'd started this job, this job that directly involved her mother. Why wouldn't she have said something then? Aside from the personal deceit of hiding her true relationship with the speaker, it was unprofessional. You don't keep information from your crew. Not when it involves something that could jeopardize their safety or affect the potential success of the job. That was rule number one: choose a crew you can trust, then trust them. Give them all the information they need to make an informed decision about whether or not they want to participate. Then, once they're in, give them all the information they need to make and carry out a coherent plan.

Cam wanted Celina to acknowledge that she'd violated that rule, and to admit that it was a mistake.

He wanted her to apologize to him.

He glanced at her without looking up. She was staring down at her plate, just like he was. Her brow was creased in the center, like it got when she was thinking about something, when she was working over the details of a plan or adjusting to new information.

What was she feeling? Was she stressed? If so, was she stressed about how to steal the statue, or was she stressed about the secret she'd kept from Cam?

Simon knew, for fuck's sake. He knew the speaker was Celina's mother. If Simon knew, why couldn't Celina have told Cam?

No matter how he came at it, Cam could only come up with one possible conclusion.

Celina didn't trust him.

After all they'd been through, she still didn't trust him.

He'd opened up to her, told her about his false identity, about his mother in prison. Revealed to her his entire plan to free Paulie, putting the whole plan in jeopardy by doing so. He had trusted her with everything that was important to him. And he'd thought she trusted him back.

But apparently he was wrong.

All this time, she'd been holding out on him. All this time, he'd been putting his beating heart into her hands because he thought he could trust her. And all this time, she'd been lying to him. Withholding information from him.

He was an idiot.

He thought he'd finally found a woman he could spend the rest of his life with, but she turned out to be just another failed relationship.

He stabbed the last few bites of pancake, his fork rapping against his plate, and shoved them in his mouth, then gathered his plate and his glass and stood from the table.

Just as he pushed his chair back, in the corner of his vision, he thought he saw Celina open her mouth to speak. Cam hesitated for a beat.

But she didn't say anything.

Of course she didn't.

Cam washed up his dishes and went upstairs.

Paulie knocked on the jamb of his bedroom door two hours later. Cam was lying on top of his bedspread, hands folded behind his head, staring up at the wide, still blades of the fan on the ceiling, just as he had been doing for the last ninety minutes.

His mind had been playing scene after scene of indignant confrontation, calling out Celina for her betrayal, shouting at her for her callousness. Cam stomping away and leaving Celina wallowing in self-reproach.

Despite the dramatic confrontations, Cam's impassioned speeches, and Celina's tearful remorse, the scenes never ended with Cam feeling any better.

"We're all meeting in the kitchen," said Paulie.

Cam nodded without looking over at her. In the corner of his eye, he saw Simon peek over Paulie's shoulder at him. After a moment, they both left without a word.

When Cam came downstairs, Paulie and Simon were seated at the counter. The counter and the table were spotless, all the remnants from breakfast cleaned and put away.

Their conversation pittered into silence when Cam walked in. He sat beside his mother. She looked at him, then put her arm across his shoulder and leaned her head into him in a sympathetic side-hug.

He didn't respond.

Just like Celina to keep them waiting. Cam supposed it was just in her nature to keep things from other people.

Finally, she came into the kitchen. She didn't bother with any preamble.

"You all saw the feed last night?"

Simon and Paulie nodded. Cam stared at his hands, clasped together on the counter like he was praying for mercy from an unmerciful god. He felt Celina glance at him. His knuckles flashed white as he squeezed his hands together.

"Then you all saw the location of the statue. Third floor study. On a desk, unprotected."

"You're sure?" asked Simon.

Celina glared at him.

"Aren't you?"

"I wasn't there."

"I was," she said. "I'm sure."

"No pressure pads or sensors, no trips that will be triggered if you take the statue out of the room or out of the house?"

"I'm sure," said Celina through gritted teeth.

Simon shrugged. "I'm just asking the question."

"How will we get inside?" asked Paulie.

"Maybe you can just ask nicely," said Cam, not looking up from his hands, his voice low and mean, "and your mother will give you the statue."

Simon and Paulie turned their heads to Cam, then back to Celina.

Celina did not look at him.

"There are three skylights in the study," she said, without acknowledging his comment. "We can come in through one of them."

"With the speaker sleeping in the next room?" Simon asked. "Risky."

"Congress is back in session today," Celina said. "She'll be working late. We can go in before she gets home."

"What about the guards?" asked Paulie.

"Most of them seem to be outside," Celina said. "I only saw one guard inside."

"There may be others that you didn't see."

Celina nodded. "We can use the glasses to check."

"We'll need to do some proper planning this time, Celina," said Simon. "No more dashing around inventing plans at the last minute."

"Guard schedules, security maps," said Paulie, "routines for the speaker and anyone else who might come by."

Cam glanced up from his hands to watch Celina's face darken. She had no patience. She didn't like to wait for anything. It was one of her faults.

That, and a tendency to hide things from the people who cared about her.

Celina didn't say anything, but she pressed her lips together and nodded.

"Simon and I can work on that," said Paulie. She turned toward Cam. "Cam, what do you want to work on?"

Cam stared at his hands for a long moment, then slowly pushed his stool back from the counter and stood.

"Nothing," he said.

He looked at his mother, then at Simon.

Then he dragged his gaze to Celina, let it settle on those green eyes.

He tamped down the flare of heat he felt.

"I'm out."

28

IN THE MASTER bedroom on the third floor, Cam threw all of his clothes onto the bed and began shoving them into his suitcase. It wouldn't take long to pack. They'd only been planning on a short trip to New York to deliver the Picasso. And then Celina had diverted them to this extended stay in D.C.

Had she been planning to come here all along? Was this yet another detail she had been keeping from Cam and Paulie?

It must have been. Simon had appeared out of nowhere just a few days after they'd arrived. Unless he'd dropped everything to hop on a plane from England, Celina must have arranged ahead of time for him to be there.

She'd been planning this whole thing all this time and hadn't bothered to tell Cam.

He jammed a t-shirt into his bag, punching it down into the other clothes.

He was an idiot. Yet again, he'd been taken for a fool by a beautiful woman. When was he ever going to learn?

A soft rap on the door. It cracked open and Paulie stuck her head through, then stepped into the room and closed the door behind her.

"Where are you off to?" she asked.

Cam sighed. He hadn't thought that far ahead, to be honest, and he didn't care. He didn't care where he went, as long as he was with people who wouldn't lie to him.

He thought again about his friends from school. Annie and Motsu were living together in Adams Morgan, not too far from Sarah's townhouse in Georgetown. Jem was in Annapolis, less than an hour away, working for the Maryland Attorney General. Cam had kept tabs on them all, but it had been months since he'd spoken to any of them. The Sam Davis they knew had officially disappeared, but Cam could always resurrect him, make some excuses for Sam's absence. A post-graduation backpacking trip to India to clear his head, something stupid like that.

He could crash with them for a few days. Or he could get a hotel room or an Airbnb. He had plenty of money.

Or he could just go home. He still had the house down in Monterey, the home he and his parents had lived in before his father had died and his mother had gone to prison. Cam didn't spend much time there anymore, just checked in on the cameras every so often to make sure nothing had gone to rot. Paid the landscapers to keep up appearances.

After Paulie got out of prison, they had settled in to Celina's place in San Francisco without a second thought. They hadn't even bothered to visit the Monterey house, even though it was only three hours away.

Cam shook his head. How could he have been such an idiot? As usual, he'd fallen too hard, too fast, and now he was paying the price.

Paulie sat on the edge of the bed. When he reached for a pair of pants to add to the suitcase, she set her hand on his, pulled it into her lap, and held it there with both of her hands.

Her skin was warm and dry. It was starting to get the papery feel of old-person skin.

Cam didn't think of his mother as old, didn't like to think of her that way. But when he looked at her in that moment, she looked older and more tired than he'd ever seen her.

She pushed aside the suitcase and patted the bed beside her, then took his hand in both of hers again.

Dutifully, Cam sat down. He knew what she was going to say. She was going to try to talk him into staying.

"She lied to us, Mom," he said. "How could I stay?"

"Hmm," said Paulie, nodding and stroking the back of Cam's hand. The gesture brought him back to when he was young, when his father was still alive and his family was all together. Happier times. Simpler times.

"That's the number one rule, right?" he asked. "Don't lie to your crew?"

Paulie nodded again.

"That's what you taught me. You and Dad."

"That's true," she said, still stroking his hand.

Why did she seem so calm? She should have been just as incensed as Cam. But she didn't even seem upset.

To be fair, Paulie had never really done upset. Now less than ever. Prison seemed to have that effect on some people. But still, Paulie shouldn't be trying to talk Cam out of this. It was a no-brainer. The crew chief lied. The crew chief sucked. They should both quit the job.

"Why aren't you leaving, too?" Cam asked. "Why are you staying?"

Paulie stopped stroking Cam's hand, but just held it in hers for a long moment. Then she took a deep breath and let it out slowly.

"I don't blame you for being angry," she said. "Celina should have told you the truth."

"Exactly," he said. "She should have told all of us the truth."

Anger flared in him again. He stood and turned back to the suitcase.

Paulie held on to his hand, tugged it gently. When he looked at her, she just raised her eyebrows and patted the bed beside her. Cam swallowed his irritation and sat down again.

"'A good crew chief tells his crew everything they need to know'," said Paulie. "Your father and I taught you that, and it's true."

Cam nodded and started to stand again. Paulie laughed, tugged him back down, and gave him a quick hug from the side.

"So impatient," she said.

Cam frowned. He wasn't impatient. Celina was the impatient one. He was just doing what was right.

"There's no reason to stay here," he said. "I'm not doing this job."

"No reason to stay here?"

"No," he said. "I'm out."

He broke free from Paulie's grip and stood, shoving clothes into his suitcase again.

"The job is one thing," said Paulie. "Your reasons to stay are something else."

Cam hesitated, hand holding a shirt in the air. What the hell did that mean?

"You're talking like Yoda," he said, dropping the shirt into the suitcase.

Paulie laughed.

"What if I was the crew chief on this job?" she said. "What if I'd kept something secret from you? What would you do then?"

"You would never do that."

"But what if I had? Just imagine it." Paulie leaned toward him. "What would you do then?"

Cam couldn't even imagine that kind of betrayal from his mother. They had rules for a reason. She and Cam's father had taught him those rules, again and again. He couldn't even entertain the question. Didn't want to.

"You wouldn't break your own rules," Cam said quietly.

"How do you think we made the rules?" Paulie said. "We made the rules because we made the mistakes the rules are supposed to prevent."

"You lied to your crew?"

"Not intentionally," she said. She tilted her head back and forth in a gesture of equivocation. "Well, yes, intentionally. But not maliciously. We thought we were protecting them."

"By lying to them?"

"By not divulging information that could get them in more trouble if they got caught. We thought that if they only knew what they needed to know—what *we* thought they needed to know—they would be better off."

"And you were wrong?"

"Not the first time. Or the second or the third."

"You did it three times?"

Cam could not believe it. It was as if his mother were telling him she'd been living a double life with a family in Kentucky this whole time.

"We did it a lot more than three times," she said. "We ran our crews like that for years, when we were younger. Before you were born."

Cam couldn't comprehend what he was hearing. The rules his parents had taught him were sacrosanct in his mind. They were like scripture. And now his mom was telling him that she and his father had broken them for years.

"Why did you stop?" he said.

"Because someone got caught. Someone on one of our crews." Paulie stared toward the window, the light soft on her face. "She got caught because she didn't know enough to avoid it. And they killed her because she couldn't tell them what they wanted to know."

She looked down and shook her head.

"After that, we told everyone everything. Always."

She looked at Cam and gave him a weak smile.

"After that, we made the rule."

"So you're saying I should forgive Celina because she doesn't know any better?"

"I'm saying there are always extenuating circumstances. You don't know why Celina did what she did. You haven't talked to her yet, have you?"

Cam shook his head. He could barely look Celina in the eye, let alone talk to her.

"Why should I be the one to talk to her? She's the one who fucked up. She should be apologizing to me."

"Ha," said Paulie. "The love song of the single man."

Cam frowned. More Yoda-speak, more riddles. He shoved a handful of underwear into the suitcase.

"You care about Celina." Paulie put her hand on Cam's wrist, stopping him from packing anything else for the moment. She stared pointedly at him. "You care about Celina," she repeated, softly.

It wasn't a question. It was a statement.

And it was a true statement.

Cam sighed, then nodded.

"Then it doesn't matter who talks first. All that matters is that you talk it through, work it out." She gripped his wrist hard and shook it. "And never forget that you both care about each other. You're both coming from a place of love. That's your foundation. You need to remember that, keep it straight in your mind so you can clear away this argument and get back down to what matters."

Cam dropped the shirt he was holding into the suitcase, then pushed the suitcase aside and slumped onto the bed beside Paulie. His shoulders sagged. His anger dissipated, replaced with a deep fatigue. He remembered then that he hadn't slept for the last thirty-six hours. He was running on caffeine and anger.

"Did you give Celina this same speech?" he asked.

Paulie smiled. "Simon is talking to her."

"Simon?"

"He's a good man," Paulie said, nodding. "A lot of wisdom in that one."

They were both silent for a moment.

In a croaking Yoda voice, Paulie said, "In that one, a lot of wisdom there is."

They both cracked up laughing.

For the first time in hours, Cam felt the weight on his chest lift just a little.

29

"YOU NEED HIM," said Simon, his voice earnest and pleading.

"He doesn't want to be here," said Celina.

For the last twenty minutes, she'd been pacing on the back patio, heels of her boots clacking on the paving stones, while Simon sat in one of the padded lawn chairs, arguing with her. The storm they had been expecting the night before had never materialized. Instead, the weather seemed to be waiting, squatting over the mid-Atlantic, thick and stifling. The winds were gone. In the hollow of the deck, set between the main house and the guest house, the dry leaves that had scraped and scratched across the paving stones the night before were now as still as the dead.

Celina knew she'd fucked up. She should have told Cam about her mother. Should have told Paulie, too.

She didn't know why she hadn't told them. She just hadn't wanted to think about it. Didn't want to see the surprise on their faces, to see them start to re-contextualize everything she'd ever said about her mother, think through all the implications and ramifications of having her birth mother be the Speaker of the U.S. House of Representatives.

It was a big deal. Even if her mother had been a cashier at

the local Walmart, it would have been a big deal if she was the target of the theft. Emotions always ran high on a job just from the nature of sneaking around and breaking laws. Anything external that might heighten those emotions was relevant. The fact that your target is your own fucking mother—let alone a powerful mother that had given you up and publicly denied your existence—was information the crew should know.

And Celina had kept it from them. That was a mistake. A big fucking mistake.

And now Cam was threatening to leave.

Celina paced, her path back and forth mirroring her thoughts. When Cam said he was out, what did he mean? Did he mean he was out of the job?

Or did he mean he wanted out of their relationship?

A hollow pain stabbed sharp in Celina's gut, like someone was jabbing a hot fucking poker into her belly and twisting it around in there.

This was why she hated relationships. She'd only ever felt this way before when she watched the speaker on TV, answering questions about children and why she'd never had one. As she watched her mother deny Celina's existence, lament her inability to have children, and express tearful support for all the women who did and still could have children, Celina felt that same hot poker in her gut.

This, this feeling, was why she never got close to anyone. It was like handing them the poker and asking them to eviscerate her.

So why had she done it with Cam? Why had she given him the fucking poker? Because right now, he was scraping her insides with it.

"He's hurt," said Simon, reclining casually on one of the cushioned wicker patio chairs. "He feels betrayed."

The temperature had plummeted. Where last night it had

been cool, now the air carried the threat of winter. Yet even though she was only wearing a t-shirt and a thin pullover, Celina was sweating. Celina opened the buttons of her pullover to let the air draw away some of the heat she felt. For a moment, she felt relief.

And then she thought of Cam, and the heat came back.

"If he doesn't want to be here, I can't force him to stay," she said.

No matter how forcefully she said it, it still sounded like bullshit.

"You don't need to force him," said Simon. "You just need to talk to him."

"And what would I say, Simon?" Celina stopped in front of his chair and glared down at him. "Sorry I lied to you about this super important detail? Sorry that after all this time together I never told you that my mother was the most powerful fucking woman in the world?"

Simon shook his head. "Americans," he muttered. "She's not the most pow—"

"Sorry I'm such a fucking dumbass that I fucked up this amazing thing we had going, this thing that—"

Celina's voice hitched. Her eyes grew hot and sweaty.

That never fucking happened to her.

Goddamn it. Why the fuck had she let herself fall in love? Love was just an invitation for pain.

She set her hands on her hips and sniffed. She needed to blow her nose.

Fucking hell.

She wiped her nose on the back of her hand, leaving a slimy wet trail across her skin that felt cold in the air as it dried. She resumed her pacing, head down as she stomped back and forth over the patio.

"No," she said. "He said he's out, and I have to respect his wishes."

"Oh, for the love of fucking Jesus," said Simon.

"If he doesn't respect me as crew chief because I'm a fucking idiot, then I have to respect his right to leave. Hell, I should be asking him to leave. For the good of the crew. And the job."

Simon stood and blocked her pacing. Celina tried to step around him, but he stepped with her, then set a hand on each of her shoulders.

"Celina."

His voice was soft and deep. It stopped the train of thought racing in circles in Celina's brain.

She looked up at him. In his eyes, she didn't see recrimination. She didn't see disdain or sarcasm or amusement.

She saw only concern.

"This isn't about the crew," he said softly. "This isn't about the job. There will be other crews and other jobs."

Celina didn't like standing still. A pressure was building in her body. She felt like she would explode if she didn't move, if she didn't let some of the pressure out.

But Simon held her still.

"This is about something far more important," he said.

"More important than the job?"

He nodded.

"This is about you," he said. "And this is about you and Cam."

The pressure kept building inside her. Her skin was swelling, her eyes were bulging, her brain would soon be leaking from her ears.

"You can't let him go without speaking to him."

She tried to avoid Simon's gaze, darting her eyes around the patio in every direction but toward him, trying to ignore what he was saying, trying to ignore the pressure inside her.

Simon put his hands on her cheeks and squared her face to his, forcing her to look at him.

The pressure built and built and built and Celina couldn't stop it. She couldn't relieve it or restrain it any longer. Her eyes bulged until they burst.

Simon's face was a mirror of pain and compassion. He pulled Celina into his chest, let her tears soak his shirt while he smoothed her hair and shushed her softly. That only made her cry harder.

She missed her father. She used to talk to him every single day, about anything and everything.

She missed Cam. She and Cam could talk about anything and everything, too. She'd only been apart from him for a few hours. They'd made breakfast together, though they'd barely said two words to each other. It had been less than a day since he learned the truth, learned about Celina's lies. And yet it felt like Celina hadn't seen him in weeks.

That hot poker scraped her guts again.

What the fuck was she doing? Crying like a fucking two-year-old. Clinging to a man like she couldn't stand on her own two feet.

Poor Simon. She didn't need to be bawling like a fucking baby against his chest. She hated crying. She was a grown-ass woman, for fuck's sake. She needed to pull her shit together and act like it.

She forced her tears to stop, like an iron sluice gate closing in her chest. She pushed herself back, turned away from Simon and wiped her cheeks with her hand. The skin beneath her eyes stung. She could taste the salt from the tears that had run across her mouth. She licked her lips.

"Thank you, Simon," she said, turning back to him. "Sorry about that."

Simon frowned. "You don't need to apologize, Celina. I'm here for you. I hope you know that." He sought her eyes again. "We're family."

Celina nodded. Simon was a good man. Her father had adored him, and Celina did, too. He was like family.

But he wasn't family. Not really.

Since her father died, Celina had no family. No father, no mother.

Just her.

And she had work to do.

30

CELINA KNOCKED on the door to the top-floor bedroom, the bedroom she and Cam had shared until last night. When the door opened, it was Paulie standing there. She pulled Celina into a hug, rocking back and forth and rubbing Celina's back.

Paulie felt warm and small and strong, and she smelled faintly of cinnamon. Her hug was calming, the rocking soothing Celina. She wanted to fall asleep in Paulie's arms and stay there for a while.

The pressure built again behind Celina's eyes, but she forced it back down.

Over Paulie's shoulder, she could see Cam sitting on the edge of the bed, his back toward the door. An open suitcase sat beside him, filled with clothes. More clothes were on the bed.

At least he hadn't finished packing.

Paulie broke their hug, patted Celina's cheek and gave her a long look with so much love in it that Celina's breath hitched in her chest.

No. Pull your shit together, woman.

Paulie glanced at Cam, then back to Celina, then left.

Cam didn't turn.

Celina stepped inside and shut the bedroom door behind her.

The air inside the room was electric, like it always seemed to be when she was near Cam.

She ignored it.

Cam still hadn't turned, hadn't said anything. Celina walked across the room to the glass door that led to the balcony. The sky had grown dark and menacing. Even though it was only two in the afternoon, the room was dark enough to turn on the lights.

Celina was glad they were off.

From the window, she could see the patio below, where she and Simon had been talking. Simon was still there. He turned suddenly and walked toward the main house. After a moment, Celina thought she could see Paulie's head. It looked like Simon walked right into her, but the balcony was blocking Celina's view, playing tricks with her eyes.

And Celina had more important things to think about.

Simon's head disappeared inside just as the first heavy splat of rain smacked against the glass door. Several others stuttered in quick succession, and then the skies seemed to break open. The air that had been squatting and stifling a moment before became a tangled forest of rainfall that Celina could barely see through. It pounded against the balcony, thundering against the wood decking, tinny against the metal chairs. The glass door soon ran with gouts of water that distorted Celina's view, or obscured it entirely.

She pulled in a deep breath and turned toward Cam.

He had stood from the bed. He stared at her, silently.

Her eyes found his, automatically, instinctively. Her skin seemed to spark, all the hair on her arms and neck standing. And she felt that familiar feeling of falling into his limpid brown eyes, that dropping away in the pit of her chest.

She remembered the feeling from a few minutes ago of a

hot poker scraping away at that same pit. She straightened her back and pushed her feelings aside.

Grown-ass woman.

"I owe you an apology," she said.

Cam raised his eyebrows.

"I should have told you the truth about the speaker. About..." She swallowed hard. Her mouth felt like sandpaper. "About my mother."

Cam didn't move, just tilted his head to one side. His gorgeous thick hair fell across one eye. Cam shook it away with a gesture so quick and natural it must have been instinctive.

He was going to need a trim soon.

Again, the dropping away in her chest.

Again, she pushed the feeling to the side.

Focus, woman.

"I put the crew and the job in jeopardy. It was a mistake. I know that now." She stared into his eyes, willing herself not to fall in. "I'm sorry."

Cam stared at her for a long moment, his head still tilted, not saying a word.

Why the fuck wasn't he saying anything? Shit, he's going to leave anyway. She'd broken one of his rules, one of his crew rules. He wouldn't forgive her.

"Okay," he said.

He didn't say anything else.

It took a moment for the word to hit Celina's brain, for her to process the meaning.

"Okay?"

Cam nodded. "Yeah, okay. I accept your apology."

"So, you're staying? You're not leaving the crew?"

"As long as you tell us everything and don't hide any more information from us," Cam nodded, "yes, I'll stay on the crew."

The wind outside howled, great gusts beating the rain

against the glass door in time with Celina's breath, the thunderous pattering rising and falling in volume along with the rise and fall of her chest.

Relief washed over her. The crew was still intact. Cam wasn't leaving. Cam was staying. She hadn't lost him.

Cam turned his back to her, finished putting the clothes in his suitcase, and zipped it shut.

Another gust of wind beat the rain against the glass so hard the glass shuddered and the metal door frame creaked in its track. A clap of thunder broke, sounding like the sky itself was ripping open.

One mississippi.

Barely a moment later, the room flashed white as lightning struck nearby. The storm was right above them.

"What are you doing?" Celina asked.

Cam turned, the handle of the suitcase in his hand.

He raised his eyebrows in question.

"With your suitcase," Celina said. "What are you doing?"

"I'll sleep downstairs," Cam said, "with the rest of the crew."

He pulled the suitcase off the bed and walked to the door without even another glance at Celina. He left the room and closed the door softly behind him.

Celina stared dumbfounded at the closed door, at the empty room.

Another crack of thunder.

She turned toward the balcony.

Another flash of lightning.

In the darkened room, she could see her own face in each lightning strike, reflected in the glass door, distorted by the rain. She looked fragmented, split into pieces. Pale, weak, and vulnerable.

She gripped her hands into fists, pulled them tight until her fingers were bloodless and her hands felt like they were on fire.

If that's how Cam wanted to play this, fine.

Celina could play, too.

She stared into the rain. The rain sluicing down the window shifted. The pieces of her reflection came together. With each successive peal of thunder, each flash of lightning, her face grew more stern, more bold, more determined.

She had no family. She had a crew. And she would use it.

An hour later, she stood in the second-floor hallway, outside the bedroom doors.

"Crew meeting in the office," she bellowed. "Now."

She waited until the doors opened. Paulie and Simon stepped out of one. Celina raised an eyebrow. When Cam came out of his bedroom, Celina stalked down the hall to the second-floor office. The others fell in behind her.

She'd spent the last hour working on a plan to steal the statue. She'd drawn a floor plan of the speaker's house on a whiteboard mounted on the office wall. She picked up a dry-erase marker and spun it in her hand while she paced back and forth in front of the whiteboard, waiting for the others to settle into the chairs Celina had pulled into the room. Simon sat in the middle, with Paulie and Cam on either side.

"We'll go in on a weekday at night," said Celina, "when the speaker is at the Capitol."

"How do we know when that will be?" asked Simon.

"Don't interrupt," said Celina sharply.

Simon rocked back in his chair, looking surprised.

Celina took a beat, then softened her tone.

"Let me lay out the plan. Save your questions until after."

Simon glanced at Paulie beside him, then crossed his arms and gave his attention to Celina.

"There will be guards at the house," Celina continued, "but the contingent should be smaller than if the speaker were at home."

She pointed to Paulie.

"Paulie, tomorrow, you and Cam will scout the house and figure out how many guards stay behind when the speaker leaves in the morning. Set up across the street. Use the glasses. It should be straightforward."

Paulie looked at Cam. They both nodded.

"Watch for their patrol patterns and durations, shift changes, everything. And find their control room, if they have one."

She pointed to her floor plan drawing on the board.

"I checked every room on the second and third floors and most of the first floor. The basement is probably too small, but they could have set up in the attic." She pointed to the floor plan of the attic space that ran above most of the third floor. "Check it all."

She stared at Cam for his agreement. He returned her gaze coolly, professionally, and nodded. Celina felt a twinge in her gut, but pushed the thought away.

"Simon, you'll be doing recon. I need to know if those skylights are protected. I need to know what they're made of, if we can go through them, how hard it will be, how long it will take, how much noise. Everything."

"I can't do all that with a drone," said Simon.

"I didn't say you had to." Celina's voice was clipped, but she managed to hold herself back from saying what she was thinking. That would not have been professional. She was the crew chief, and she had to act like it. "Do what you need to do to get the information."

Simon stared at Celina. She held his stare and didn't waver. But after a moment, he nodded.

"I'll stay here and work on hacking the security system," Celina said. "I've got a few ideas that I want to try."

"So that's the plan?" said Simon, folding his arms over his chest.

His tone was aggressive. He was pissed for some reason and trying to get under Celina's skin.

He could try, but he would fail. Celina was the crew chief. This was her job, and she was a professional. She would listen to any suggestions or objections Simon might bring up, but she would not lose her cool. And she would not put up with any whiny bullshit from the crew. Simon would do his job or he would be out.

"I haven't told you the plan yet," said Celina coolly.

Simon said, "It looks like the plan is to wait until the guards aren't looking, disable the security system, then break in through the skylight and snatch the statue."

"That's one option," said Celina.

"It's shit."

"Why is that, Simon?"

"You already tried hacking the system, and you said it couldn't be done."

"I have some new ideas."

"And going down through the skylight is impractical."

"It's easier than getting through a house full of guards."

"No," Simon said, "it isn't. There was only one guard in the entire house when you were in there."

Celina started to snap back a retort, then stopped herself and thought for a moment.

That was true. When she'd been there, the only guard had been that dumbass standing in the doorway.

"Paulie, check and see how many guards are in the actual house when the speaker leaves."

Paulie nodded.

Celina looked at Simon. She desperately wanted to slide her gaze to Cam, to get some clue as to what he was thinking and feeling. She stopped herself, pushed that impulse down.

"If there aren't many guards inside, we'll go in that way," she said. "Cam can pick the lock, and we'll go in together."

She let herself look at Cam. His arms were folded, one leg crossed over the other. He looked calm and relaxed and completely undisturbed.

That was more than Celina could say. Her heartbeat raced, and a lump formed in her throat. She swallowed hard and tried to ignore it.

"Like we did at the Capitol building," she said. Her voice was raspy. She cleared her throat. Cam nodded, and Celina turned back to the whiteboard. She couldn't look at Cam any longer without having a total meltdown. And she refused to do that in front of the crew.

"How are you going to hack the security system?" said Simon. "Last time, you said it was impenetrable."

"Yes," said Celina. She kept her back to the others until the lump in her throat had gone back down and her pulse had slowed again. When she had collected herself, she turned back toward them.

"But that was before I realized who had built it," she said.

When they were talking over tea, Madeline had commented on Celina's love of art. She'd said she wasn't surprised by it because Celina was her father's daughter. At the time, Celina had made a retort that she was Madeline's daughter, too. But, since then, the comment had kept coming back to her mind. She finally realized why.

"Who built it?" asked Cam.

Madeline had said her father's name. *Of course you like art,* she'd said. *You're Perry's daughter.* But she hadn't said it with the bitterness of an old lover, nor with the coolness of someone who'd made an important decision and come to terms with it long ago. She said it with a smile, with warmth. She said it like she still loved Celina's father. And like she still knew him.

Celina realized then that Celina's father had never stopped being in contact with Madeline. That was how Madeline knew so much about Celina, how she was familiar enough with Celina to ask when she started wearing glasses.

And that's when all the pieces fell into place. She looked at Cam. This time, she didn't force down the feelings, didn't ignore the electricity. She let herself be weightless in his gaze, just for a moment.

"My father," she said.

The gold shielding on the house. The glass in the windows that foiled all digital camera sensors. It was all her father's technology.

Her father had designed Madeline's security system.

And Celina knew how to hack it.

31

Paulie didn't like what she was seeing.

She'd sat with Cam. Simon had talked to Celina. And Celina had gone to Cam. Paulie thought that would be the end of it.

But something had gone wrong. The tension between Cam and Celina was still there, thicker than ever.

Paulie had been sure they would work things out, and they had, to some extent. Cam wasn't threatening to leave anymore.

But now he was sleeping in a separate bedroom. When he and Celina were in the same room together, the same chemistry was there. But both of them were fighting it.

It was really annoying.

Dinner had been awkward. By the time Celina had finished going over the new plan, the storm had passed. Simon cooked delicious chicken breast sandwiches and potatoes on the grill, but Cam and Celina had declined to eat with them. They both made excuses and took their plates with them.

They'd spent a tense and awkward evening watching a movie in the theater room. Cam would watch. When Celina came in, he would leave. Then Celina would get restless, she would leave, and Cam would come back. Then he would get restless and leave, and Celina would wander back in. They couldn't be in the same room together, but neither of them could sit still, either.

They were both so smart, so talented. And they were both so in love with each other. But they were both so damn stubborn.

Cam got it from her. His father, Sam, was a pussycat, but Paulie, when she was younger, had been a real pain in the ass. She'd been lucky that Sam had put up with it until she got older and wiser.

But Celina was no pussycat. She was more like a hungry lioness. And they were both stubborn as mules. Cam got it from her, and it seemed like Celina might have gotten it from her mother, too.

Both of them were suffering, but they both refused to be the first to give in.

After the movie, they'd all gone to their rooms without another word.

Paulie pulled on her pajamas—soft pants and a loose-fitting top—and went into her bathroom to wash her face and brush her teeth. Electric toothbrush buzzing in her mouth, she pulled her hair back and held it with a clip.

She checked herself out in the mirror. The lighting was very forgiving, but still, not half bad for someone who spent the last fifteen years in prison. Paulie's hair looked sleek and healthy. Her skin was clear and relatively unwrinkled. Unlike some women her age, she had no sun damage or age spots. One benefit of only being allowed outside for an hour every day.

Prison life had also left her with a lean, strong body. She turned to the side, smoothed down her shirt over her belly. Her body hadn't changed too much over the years. Her boobs were a little lower, her waist a little more square, but overall, she was fit and healthy. That was what really mattered, more than the shape.

Another benefit of life in an all-woman prison: she knew very well that women came in all shapes and sizes, and they were all beautiful.

Simon appeared in the mirror behind her. She hadn't heard him slip into the bedroom. She looked at his reflection and watched him scan her from top to bottom and back again.

"If you were seeing what I'm seeing," he said, "you'd stop whatever you're doing and come to bed. Immediately."

Paulie smiled. She put down her toothbrush, rinsed her mouth, and walked to him. He was so tall. Her head didn't even reach his chin. She ran her hands over his t-shirt, felt his strong chest underneath the thin fabric. She slid her hands underneath and felt his hot skin, played with the hair on the ridges of his muscular belly.

He groaned and slid his hands over her back. She looked down and saw the front of his pajama bottoms tenting.

"Look who's awake," she said, then glanced up at him with a wicked look.

His eyes were dark with desire.

She met it.

Waking up beside Simon had become familiar enough that Paulie no longer felt any pangs of guilt, but not so familiar that she didn't appreciate it every time. She'd spent so many years alone that the closeness of Simon's body and the openness of his heart were better than the sex itself.

Though the sex was damn good.

Damn.

Good.

Paulie had spent fifteen years in her cell, thinking about Sam. Dreaming about him. Reliving her memories of him. She loved him, still, with every fiber of her being.

But he was gone. And she was still here.

She knew that Sam would want her to be happy. He wouldn't want her to wither, and she wouldn't let herself. She couldn't pack herself in mothballs when there was so much life to be lived. She'd learned to appreciate her life while she was in prison. Now that she was out, the world was an embarrassment of riches.

And Simon was a jewel.

They hadn't sought each other out, hadn't fallen into bed together for a quick tumble. They'd only known each other a few weeks, but they'd spent those weeks in close proximity. While Cam and Celina humped like college kids during spring break, Paulie and Simon had been left alone. They'd talked and laughed late into the night and gotten to know each other. Paulie told him all about Sam, about Cam, about her life in prison. He told her about his father, his childhood, his life as an international playboy.

He was easy to talk to. After only a few days, she felt like she'd known him for years. He was handsome and witty and wise, and she was no slouch herself. Nature had taken its course, and neither one of them had protested as they followed it.

Paulie recognized the guilt she felt as another step in her grieving process, a last step of letting Sam go and moving forward in her life. She didn't know how Cam would feel about it when he found out, but this was her life to live, not Cam's.

And now she was waking most mornings with her head against Simon's warm chest, her body relaxed and fulfilled, the early sun drifting through the window shades to tease her out of bed and invite her into another incredible day.

Life was good for Paulie.

If she could only get her son and her one-day-hopefully daughter-in-law to grow up a little, get over themselves, and make up, life would damn near perfect.

She kissed Simon's bare chest and slid carefully out of bed. She was an early riser, a habit from prison that she didn't feel the need to change. She enjoyed the stillness of the mornings, when everyone else was still asleep. In the summer, she would sit outside, sip her coffee, and listen to the birds and the waves before the noise of the world intruded. Now that the days were shorter, she would wake in the grey early-morning half-light, creep through the sleeping house, and watch the sun stretch across the sky.

She padded downstairs, tying her robe over her pajamas. The lights in the kitchen were blazing. Celina sat at the counter, hunched over a laptop, an empty espresso cup beside her.

Paulie walked behind Celina and kissed her on top of her head. Her hair smelled unwashed. Celina didn't make any sound or take her eyes off her computer. Her fingers flew across the keyboard, lines of computer code flashing over the screen.

Paulie didn't understand any of it, but she understood the bags under Celina's eyes, the hollow darkness in her cheeks. Celina hadn't slept. She was running on coffee, heartache, and stubborn determination.

Paulie held up Celina's empty coffee cup. Celina glanced up from under furrowed brows and nodded slightly before staring back at her laptop again.

Good morning to you, too.

Paulie pulled two double espressos from the coffee maker —another one of life's riches—and set one on the counter in front of Celina. Without looking, Celina picked up the glass, drained it in one gulp, and set it back on the counter with a smack.

Paulie sighed. There would be no progress while Celina was in this mode. And if Cam was anywhere close to Celina's headspace, things would only get worse. They both needed to calm down, get some sleep, calm down some more, and come together with an attitude of openness, love, and trust.

It wasn't going to happen today.

The couches and chairs in the house were not made for humans, so Paulie went outside to the patio. The chair cushions were still soaked from yesterday's rain, but the wide step in front of the door was mostly dry. Paulie sat down to watch the sky lighten as she sipped her coffee.

The paving stones were cold and damp under her bare feet. The coffee was rich and hot on her tongue and her throat. The air smelled fresh and new, the way it can only smell the morning after a big storm.

The howling wind had passed, but a cool, soft breeze caressed Paulie's cheeks. She closed her eyes and tilted her face to the rising sun. She felt the first touch of heat as the sun rose above the horizon.

Life was good. It had its problems, but they just made the ride all the more interesting.

32

Cam and Paulie watched the speaker's house through the window of the house across the street. Cam felt a little weird being there in the daylight. Even though the room looked like a cheap set from a legal drama on TV, the daylight made the setting too intimate. He could see the awards and mementos and pictures of what must have been children and grandchildren, with their dutiful poses and stiff smiles, given pride of place on the bookshelves behind the desk. Picture-ready, should a local magazine ever decide to do a retrospective on the judge's illustrious career.

Picture-ready, stereotypical, and utterly boring. But still, more intimate than Cam liked to be with the owner of a house he had broken into.

They'd been there since well before dawn, watching through their AR glasses, recording the feed. They could see the outlines of all the people inside the house and on the grounds. There were two guards at the gate to the garage in the back, two more in the guardhouse near the pedestrian gate in the front. One guard patrolled the gardens on the east and another patrolled grounds on the west side of the house.

Inside, the speaker was asleep in her bed upstairs. Cam could see only one guard sitting at a table in the kitchen.

Seven guards, total. All from the Capitol police department. They would be armed and trained. Not Navy Seals, but skilled enough to be taken seriously.

Cam and Paulie watched and waited. The speaker rose at 5:30am and left the house at 7am. The interior guard and two of the exterior guards accompanied her, leaving four behind. They repositioned themselves so that two were stationed at the garage gate and the other two at the guardhouse, leaving the grounds on the sides of the house unpatrolled.

"The guard house must have monitors for all the cameras," Cam said to Paulie. He pointed to the laptop that sat between them, showing the feed from Cam's glasses on the screen. "This guard is watching the gate." He pointed to another person's outline on the screen, deeper inside the guardhouse. "But this guard hasn't moved for a while. That's where the surveillance room will be, with all the sensors and monitors."

Paulie nodded.

"The attic and the basement both look clear," she said. "I haven't seen anyone at all in either space."

There would be a surveillance room in the guardhouse, but they didn't know if there was another one in the basement or the attic. So far, it looked like there wasn't, but they would need visual confirmation to be sure.

The front door opened onto the sidewalk. It was the only entrance that wasn't physically guarded, probably to avoid drawing attention to the speaker's home and disturbing the neighborhood. But Cam could see several cameras that would alert the guards if someone got close. And when the speaker was home, the guard inside would be the first line of defense against any intruders.

Cam and Paulie settled in to watch and wait. Reconnaissance was an important part of any job. Before his father died,

Cam and his family would spend weeks on recon, making sure they fully understood the pace, the feel, the rhythms of a place before they hit it.

Celina didn't have that kind of patience. She just wanted the facts so she could get in and out and get the job over with as quickly as possible. She was lucky that she had the talent to make that work for her.

But regardless of how long you spent on it, recon was always boring. It was a whole lot of watching nothing happen. People came and went. They did their jobs, they went home, they came back the next day. Recon was about understanding routines. Not the most exciting work. Important, but not exciting.

The night guards changed shifts at 8am. At 10:30am, Simon showed up in a roofing van. Celina had figured out how to hack the system the Capitol police were using—a separate system from the security on the house—and added a roofing inspection to the day's schedule. The guard at the guard house checked his printout and gave Simon directions to the back gate.

Simon set up his ladders and his gear and climbed to the roof, accompanied by one of the guards. Cam and Paulie watched through Simon's feed as he inspected the shingles, the flashing, the chimneys, the gutters. Cam didn't know where Simon had learned how to do any of this stuff, but he was convincing enough to have Cam fooled.

Simon was methodical and meticulous, working his way around to the skylights. By the time he reached them, the guard had stopped paying attention to Simon and started looking at his phone or staring at the view.

Simon took his time with the skylights, muttering so softly under his breath that even the sound enhancement of the glasses couldn't pick up what he said. When he was finished, he stood and told the guard he needed to see the attic next.

The guard led Simon inside and through the house. As soon as Simon climbed the ladder to the attic and poked his head above the floor, it was clear that no one was using it as a control room. The space was tall and wide, but it was completely unfinished. Plywood covered the floors, but the walls and ceiling were exposed, with nails sticking out in places and spray foam insulation visible between the rafters and the studs. Simon made a show of checking all the insulation, examining the rafters and the ventilation, making notes on a clipboard the whole time.

He talked the guard into taking him to the basement next, giving some story about water drainage and sump pumps. The basement was finished, but the space was small, divided into a laundry room and several food storage rooms. As Celina had expected, there was no space for a surveillance room.

Simon packed up, had the guard sign something, and left. The excitement of the day over, Cam and Paulie settled in for more tedium. The guards patrolled the grounds. Two household staff entered at noon. By their locations and their movements, they seemed to be a chef and a maid.

The guards changed shift again at 4pm. The maid left at 5pm, the chef at 6pm. The speaker returned at 8pm with her three guards, had a late dinner alone in the kitchen, then retired to her study. She didn't climb into bed until 1am, only to get up again at 5:30am.

Not an easy schedule.

Cam and Paulie had taken turns napping on the couch. They waited and watched for a full twenty-four hours so they could get at least one full cycle. It was a Wednesday. There was no guarantee that the routine would be the same on Thursday or any other day of the week. People were creatures of habit, but those habits were sometimes interrupted. There was no way to know if the speaker had been detained at work that day and come home late, or if she'd had a light day and come home early. There was no way to know what her routine was like on the weekends, or if it varied based on the day of the week.

This was why Cam and Paulie liked to take their time with recon. But Cam knew Celina would want to move quickly.

Her impatience was going to get them all caught. Or worse.

They watched the speaker leave on Thursday morning at 7am, her retinue of three guards in tow, just like the day before. Cam debated for a moment, then set up his glasses so he could leave them behind to record everything. It was more useful for them to be there in person to see everything, but this would at least give them a little more observation time. They could review the recording at high speed to verify the movements and get some more data.

It was a risk, leaving the glasses behind. But it seemed a small risk.

Despite the naps, Cam was exhausted as he drove them back to Celina's house in the city. The sun was up and traffic was thick as they fought through the early-morning commute.

"Should have waited another hour or two," said Paulie.

On impulse, Cam swung a hard right at the next intersection. Trying to beat traffic was often a fool's game, especially if you weren't intimately familiar with the drive. But Cam was tired and if he had to sit in traffic much longer, he was going to fall asleep at the wheel.

He sped down a side street to a stop sign. Just before he took a right turn, he glanced in his rear-view and saw another car, a white Toyota, make the same move. Another commuter trying to get ahead. Maybe Cam's impulse had been a good one.

Cam weaved through the back streets of Potomac Yard. Every time he hit traffic, he'd make a turn. Nothing seemed to help. The traffic was thick everywhere. There was no escape.

He stopped at a stop sign to type Celina's address into his

phone. Might as well give up and just get there, traffic or not. He glanced in the mirror to make sure he wasn't holding anyone up.

The white Toyota was there again, just turning onto the street a block behind them.

Cam followed the instructions on his phone, keeping one eye on the Toyota. It kept a safe distance, sometimes disappearing from view for minutes at a time. But just when Cam thought he was being tired and paranoid, it would show up again. He took a few random turns. The Toyota followed.

When he got close to Celina's house, Cam went past it.

"You missed the turn," said Paulie. She'd been napping in the passenger seat for most of the ride.

"I think we're being followed," said Cam.

Paulie checked the side mirror. "Which one?"

"White Toyota Camry."

Cam drove on for a few blocks, then pulled to the curb and stopped.

The Toyota passed them and kept going. Cam stared out his window as it passed, trying to get a view of the driver, but the windows had been tinted too dark to see. Illegal, but not unusual in a Camry. The cops would usually let it go unless something else was wrong.

The Toyota kept going for another two blocks. Cam swung a hard U-turn and sped back to Celina's place.

When he and Paulie came in through the back door, Celina was at the kitchen counter on her laptop, just as she'd been more than twenty-four hours earlier. In fact, she was wearing the exact same clothes. With her tousled hair and her bleary eyes, Cam was fairly sure she hadn't slept at all.

She didn't look up when Cam and Paulie came in. Cam walked past her to the front of the house and peeked out the front window. He looked down the street to the left and saw nothing unusual. He shifted position and looked to the right.

His chest tightened.

"Celina," he called.

He heard the kitchen stool scrape as she pushed back from the counter and came to the window. He knew she was getting closer when the electrical charge in the air grew stronger. He could smell her standing beside him, her usual lavender mixed with the heady scent of her unwashed body. Cam immediately hardened at the combination, his response instinctive, his need more and more raw with each passing day.

He needed her. Not just her body, but her. Celina. He walked around every day feeling like he'd forgotten something important, left behind some thing that he needed. He felt like a part of him was missing.

He swallowed hard and did what he had been doing for days now.

He ignored that feeling. He grit his teeth and moved on.

"What is it?" said Celina. Her voice was low and rasping.

Cam moved to the side so Celina could look out the window. Her body brushed against his. He flinched at the electric shock of her touch. It took everything he had to force down the impulses that rose in him.

"The white Toyota across the street," Cam said.

"What about it?"

Cam let out a long sigh that was about a lot more than just the Toyota.

"I think we have a tail," he said.

33

CELINA OPENED the front door and stormed down the stairs onto the walkway. Cam followed her, slamming the door behind him.

"Fuck you," Celina shouted, pointing a finger at Cam.

"Fuck me?" Cam shouted back. "You're the one who lied."

"You think I wanted to? You think I didn't want to tell you the truth?"

"I think you lied because you're too chickenshit to tell the truth. It's easier for you to lie."

Cam glanced over Celina's shoulder at the street. The front window of the Toyota had rolled down just enough for a camera lens to poke through, pointed at him and Celina.

So it was a photographer. Probably from one of the tabloids. Maybe they'd caught wind of the story of Speaker Kinkaid's long-lost daughter.

"Chickenshit?" Celina continued the ruse. "I'm chickenshit? I'm not the one who wants to sit around all day doing nothing."

Cam glanced down the sidewalk. Simon was approaching the Toyota from the front, hidden by a small crowd of pedestrians. Cam and Celina just had to keep the photographer's attention squarely on them.

"No," Cam said, "you just want to rush into some crazy job with no plan and no information and just see what happens. You're going to get us all killed."

Celina's face turned to stone, her voice fierce. "I'm a professional," she said. "I know what I'm doing."

"Maybe so," Cam replied, "but no one else does."

"You know what you need to know."

"No, we know what you think we need to know. But you're blinded by emotion. You're biased."

"I am not."

"You are. You're trying to hide your secret so no one finds out."

Celina balled her fists, her eyes flashing with anger. Cam couldn't tell if she was acting anymore. He couldn't tell if he was acting anymore. He didn't care.

"But your secret could get someone killed," he said.

"I won't let that happen," said Celina, stepping toward him. "The safety of my crew is the most important thing to me."

"Is it?" Cam said. "Or maybe all you care about is hurting your mother. Punishing her for all the pain she put you through."

"You don't know what you're talking about."

"I know what I see." Cam stepped closer. "And I see a little girl whose mother left her. A little girl who grew up to be a powerful woman."

"Fuck off."

"Who now wants to make her mother pay."

Celina stepped in, pointing a finger at Cam. "Fuck. Off."

Cam wasn't about to back down.

"You know the worst part?" He stepped closer. Their faces were only inches apart now. "Even while you're punishing her, you still want your mommy to tell you she's proud of you."

Celina's anger flared hotter in her eyes, then slackened as Cam's words sank in. She stepped back and looked down at the sidewalk, confusion on her face.

Immediately, Cam felt sick for hurting her. What had started as a ruse had somehow gotten out of control.

He stepped toward her. She stepped back.

Simon came through the gate from the sidewalk, holding a man in an armlock from behind, pushing him toward the front door.

"You two can stop now," he said. "Or at least take it inside before someone calls in a domestic."

Cam looked at Celina as Simon passed between them. She didn't meet his gaze.

Simon pushed the photographer up the steps and called over his shoulder.

"Can one of you at least get the fucking door?"

They sat the photographer down on a stool in the kitchen and zip-tied his hands behind his back. Cam blocked his exit on one side, Simon on the other. Paulie stayed behind the counter, leaning against the fridge.

Celina had the man's camera, flipping through the images on the viewscreen.

"You've been watching us," she said.

Her voice was calm and cold, just like her stare.

But the stare was all for the photographer. She wouldn't look at Cam, even when he was in her direct eye line.

His heart sank. What he'd said on the stoop was true, and he felt better for saying it. But it was too harsh, and now he'd made the whole thing worse.

Cam focused on the situation at hand. He could worry about Celina later.

He could tell from a glance that the photographer wasn't a tabloid photographer. His clothes were too nice. He wore a tan business suit without the tie. His white shirt bulged over a belly earned with too many long stints in a car outside a subject's home, but the cut was custom enough to try to hide it. This guy was a private detective or a high-end paparazzi hired for this gig.

Celina handed the camera to Simon, keeping her gaze fixed on the photographer.

"Who hired you?" Celina asked.

"Some guy, I don't know."

The photographer seemed annoyed, not scared. This was not his first time being caught. But he didn't hesitate to answer Celina, so he clearly didn't have any fear of his employer. Or loyalty toward them.

"He didn't give me a name," the photographer said.

"What did he look like?" Celina asked, slowly circling the photographer on his stool.

"He looked like a political prick," the man said. "Fat guy, bald, cheap suit."

"That describes half of Washington," said Simon, handing the camera to Paulie. She walked over to Cam and held the camera so they could look at the pictures together.

"No shit," said the man.

As they scrolled backward through the images, Cam saw scenes from the last few days, in reverse. He and Celina arguing on the front stoop. He and Paulie leaving the house across the street from the speaker's. Simon pulling away in his roofing van. Zoomed in images of Simon on the roof, as seen from ground level. Simon in his van talking to the gate guard. Cam and Paulie going in to the house across from the speaker's, through the back door. Cam in the backyard of that same house, at night, peering toward the camera.

Cam's stomach dropped. That night, when he'd been so angry at Celina. The glint in the darkness, the twig snapping. That wasn't a raccoon. It was this man, this photographer, taking pictures of Cam.

They scrolled further. Celina coming out of the speaker's home, Celina knocking on the door and going inside, Celina walking toward the door along the sidewalk.

This man had been following them for days.

Cam felt dirty. Violated. What else had this man seen? Had he spied on him and Celina making love? Had he listened in on his conversations with his mother?

He took the camera from Paulie and scrolled quickly back through them, but they looped around. He'd seen them all. No more pictures of them at the D.C. house.

Cam's sick feeling burned into anger. He gave the camera back to Paulie and strode to the man. He grabbed him by the lapels and shook him.

"Who hired you?" he said, seething. He wanted to rip the man's smug little head off, smash the camera over it, stomp it into the ground. "Who the fuck was it?"

"Hey, easy, easy, man! What the fuck? I just told you, I don't have a name. Just some shitty pol's fuckboy."

"Bullshit," said Cam, shaking the man again.

"Cam."

"Give us a name!"

"Cam."

Celina set a hand on his arm. Electricity coursed through his body, shocking him into looking up, into looking at her. She fixed him with those emerald eyes, and the rest of the world fell away.

"It's okay, Cam," she said quietly.

Cam's hands let go, released the man. He fell back onto the stool.

"It's okay," said Celina, pushing Cam's hands down, pushing him gently backward with a hand on his chest.

On his heart.

She stopped, gave Cam a long look. Cam thought he saw the same yearning in her eyes that he felt in his chest, the same emptiness longing desperately to be filled.

But then Celina turned her back to him.

She took the camera from Paulie and removed the memory card. She dropped it on the floor and ground it to pieces under her heel.

The photographer shrugged.

"Lady, it's all in the cloud, anyway. These days, the clients get them as soon as I take them."

"Then I'll smash this, too," she said, holding up the man's camera.

His eyes went wide.

"No, please, lady," he said. "That's my job. My livelihood. I got a family."

Celina's voice was cold. "Maybe you should have thought of that before you intruded on my family."

To his credit, the man didn't back down. "I'm just doing my job, lady. Jesus."

Celina hesitated.

"Cut him loose," she said to Simon.

The photographer stood, rubbing the blood flow back into his hands. Celina shoved the camera hard into his stomach, doubling the man over.

"Get the fuck out of here," she said.

The man tripped over the stool and stumbled away toward the front door.

"If I catch you again," Celina called, "I'll break more than your camera."

The man ran out the door, not bothering to close it behind him. Cam could see him race across the street, nearly getting hit by a car that screeched on its brakes. He got into his Toyota and peeled away from the curb.

"I liked him," said Simon. "Seemed like a genuine fellow."

"Do you know who hired him?" Paulie asked Celina.

"No," she said, "but I have some ideas."

She glanced at Cam, held his gaze for a moment.

Cam frowned. He assumed the photographer had something to do with Celina and her mother, that someone had been watching the speaker, had seen Celina go into her house late in the evening, and had gotten curious.

Celina looked away.

Could there be something else going on?

34

ALL THE NAPS in the world couldn't make up for a lost night of sleep. Once the adrenaline from interrogating the photographer wore off, Cam fell into bed and slept the sleep of the dead.

When he finally opened his eyes, a dull orange glow filled one half of the sky. For a moment, Cam wasn't sure if it was sunset or sunrise, if he'd slept through the day or through the following night, as well.

The clock said 6:30pm.

He'd slept through the day.

He went to the kitchen and found Celina sitting at the counter, hunched over her laptop. Again. Still.

"When's the last time you slept?" he said.

Celina didn't respond.

She looked like she hadn't slept at all, for a long time.

Cam poured himself a small glass of milk and sucked it all down in one gulp. The cold creaminess felt good against his throat.

"Celina," he said, then leaned toward her on the counter.

After a long moment, she glanced up at him, her expression focused and more than a little hostile.

He raised his eyebrows.

She glanced back down.

"I've almost got it," she said, then muttered, "I think."

Simon and Paulie came down. The three of them made dinner while Celina worked. They set a plate of food beside her while they sat and ate at the table, talking quietly. When they got up an hour later to clean the dishes, Celina's plate was untouched.

Unable to pry her from the laptop, Cam and the others went upstairs to watch a movie, leaving Celina to her obsessiveness. Cam felt bad leaving her, but she wasn't communicating with them at all. And when it came to hacking, as good as Cam was, Celina was a hundred times better. If he tried to help her, he'd probably just get in the way.

Halfway through the film, Celina came into the room and stood in front of the screen.

"We're ready," she said.

She stared at them all, letting her cryptic statement hang in the air. Forrest Gump jumped off a shrimp boat on the screen behind her. She left the room.

Cam, Simon, and Paulie looked at each other, paused the movie, and followed Celina into the second-floor office.

As usual, Celina was pacing. Back and forth in front of the whiteboard. In the light from the recessed cans overhead, her face was sallow and sunken. She looked more tired than Cam had ever seen her. When she turned and he could see her eyes, they were sharp and determined. But her body was fatigued, probably to the point of being unhealthy. At some point, no matter how determined she was, it would break.

Celina didn't stop pacing, but once the three of them had sat down, she began to speak.

"I hacked the security system," she said.

"You got through Perry's security?" asked Simon.

Celina didn't reply, didn't look up, just kept pacing, silent for a moment.

Simon glanced left and right at Cam and Paulie, then muttered, "Sorry."

"I've got full access. All the cameras in the house, door and window sensors, everything."

"I thought there weren't—"

Simon cut himself off and held up one hand in apology.

"The cameras are very well hidden," Celina said. "Extremely well hidden. I found feeds from places where I specifically looked for cameras when I was in there and saw nothing." She muttered to herself. "I'm still not sure how he did it."

It was exciting that Celina had finally broken through the security system, but Cam was worried about her mental state. She looked ragged. Unhinged, almost.

The sharp determination he'd seen earlier was more like the wild-eyed focus of a mad genius. Her hair was tousled and a little stiff, like she hadn't showered in days. Which was probably true. She paced and muttered to herself, ignoring the others like she didn't know they were there. She had a whole Beautiful Mind thing going on, and Cam was seriously concerned about her.

"Celina, why don't you clean up and get some sleep?" he said. "We can talk about this in the morning."

"What about the skylights?" she asked, ignoring Cam. "Simon, what did you find on the roof?"

"Can't go in that way," he said, shaking his head. "They're not glass, but they're not acrylic, either. Some kind of material I'm not familiar with, but I tried to dig at it with a small diamond drill."

"What happened?" asked Paulie.

"The drill head shattered."

The clear lens on the skylight was harder than diamond? Cam had never heard of such a thing.

"We'll go in through the front door, then," said Celina, never breaking her pacing stride. "Tonight."

Cam, Simon, and Paulie all spoke at once, all saying a version of the same thing: "Not tonight."

Celina muttered something to herself, but didn't stop pacing.

"Tomorrow night, then," she said.

"Only if you sleep and eat, and you seem like you're back to your normal self by tomorrow afternoon," said Cam.

Celina looked up at him, the first time she'd looked up since they'd walked into the office. Her stare hit Cam with the force of a speeding truck. Thrown off for a moment, Cam took a deep breath and stared back at her.

They battled with their wills for a few seconds, then Celina looked away.

"We'll go in through the front," she said. "I'll loop the feeds. We'll go in while the speaker is still at the Capitol."

"How do we know when that will be?" asked Paulie. "We've only watched them for one day."

"And it was a Wednesday," Cam said. "Tomorrow is Friday. Her routine will probably be different."

Celina shook her head sharply.

"Congress just came back from recess," she said, "and they've got to pass a continuing resolution to avert a shutdown. The Republicans are stalling, but the current funding expires tomorrow at midnight. She'll keep them there all night."

Cam, Paulie, and Simon all looked at each other. It was still a risk. Congress did occasionally act responsibly, but it was a fair bet that they wouldn't. None of them could argue with Celina's logic.

"Let's at least review the surveillance from today to make sure no one else will be in there," said Cam.

"What surveillance?" asked Celina.

"I guess it doesn't matter now that you can access the security system," he said. "You can just review the recordings from the feeds. But I left my glasses set up at the judge's house across the street. We can check the recordings to make sure the chef and the house cleaner won't be in there."

"Fine," said Celina. "Let's check it now."

She started toward the door. Simon was the first to get to her, holding her by one arm.

"Not tonight, love," he said softly. "Tonight, you sleep."

Celina looked at him. She dropped her eyes to Cam's. The sharpness in them dulled as fatigue overtook her. She sagged in Simon's grip.

Cam jumped from his chair to hold her.

"I'll take her up," he said.

Simon released Celina's arm.

Celina let all her weight fall against Cam. He scooped her in his arms and carried her out the office door and up the stairs. She curled into him, her head lolled against his shoulder and her arms tucked against his chest.

Cam reveled in the feel of her warmth against his body, her skin against his skin, her weight on his. Her scent enveloped him. His knees nearly buckled as he carried her, overwhelmed with relief at holding her again.

By the time Cam got upstairs to the bedroom, Celina was already fast asleep. He lay her down, took off her shoes and her pants and her bra, pushing down the urges that arose as he undressed her. She needed sleep.

Cam pulled the covers over her and kissed her gently on her forehead, lingering long on the feel of his lips pressed against her warm skin.

As he pulled away, she moaned in her sleep and reached out to him, looped her arm around the back of his neck and pulled him down to her.

When someone breaks your heart, it feels like your soul has melted. Your body becomes a volcanic crater, your molten soul churning and bursting within, scorching you from the inside. Each moment of your life is another lash of searing pain.

Over time, a thin, brittle, blackened crust forms on the cool exterior, hiding the pain beneath. This is your anger. This is your armor, poor though it is.

When Celina reached out to him subconsciously, the seething cauldron within Cam erupted. His armor melted in an instant, and the crater of his body was seared anew with the pain of his molten soul.

But this time, the pain didn't scorch him. It renewed him. His love had never left, but it surged forward, replacing the brittle armor of his anger with the resilient strength of hope.

He'd just woken up from a full day of sleep, but he slid into bed beside Celina and wrapped her in his arms. He wasn't the least bit tired, but he would lie there as long as she needed him to. As long as she would let him.

The sky was lightening in the windows when Cam's eyes finally drooped shut. When he opened them again, it was mid-afternoon. Celina sat on the edge of the bed, holding a cup of steaming coffee, watching him.

The afternoon light cast a soft glow on her features, backlit them with an angelic shimmer. Celina was no angel, but to Cam, she was the definition of heaven.

And when she smiled at him, the wide, warm, genuine smile he had missed for days and longed to see, the light that spread within him would have made all the angels squint.

"Is that coffee for me?" he asked, pushing himself up against the headboard.

"It's for whoever is awake before it gets cold," she said, handing it to him.

"You're awake, too," he said, then took a sip.

"Good thing I planned ahead, then," she said, reaching for the nightstand, where another steaming cup of coffee sat.

They clinked glasses and sipped, staring into each other's eyes.

As good as the coffee tasted, it was not what Cam wanted in that moment.

Celina looked down at the coffee in her hand, spun the glass around and around, then set it back on the nightstand. She glanced at Cam, opened her mouth to speak, then closed it again and looked down at her hands in her lap, fidgeting with her fingers.

"Cam, I—"

She closed her mouth, shook her head sharply, and blew out an exasperated sigh.

"I fucking suck at this shit," she muttered.

Cam wanted to pull her into his arms, to tell her everything was fine, that she didn't have to worry. He wanted to tell her he knew what she was thinking, knew what she was trying to say, that he forgave her and hoped she could forgive him, too.

But he didn't. He thought he knew what she was going to say—he knew what he hoped she was going to say—but he could be wrong. And even if he was right, he still needed to hear the words.

"This... isn't about the crew," she said. She looked at him. "This isn't about the job, okay? I fucked up there. I admitted it. You accepted my apology. That's done."

She looked down at her hands again, her shoulders lifting and sagging in a heavy sigh.

"This is about us," she said.

Cam set his coffee cup on the nightstand beside Celina's

and waited. Her face was a battleground for her thoughts, first darkening with exasperation, then crowding with determination, then clearing with hope. Cam couldn't tell exactly what she was thinking, but he could see the war raging within her mind.

She dug her fingernails against the skin of her fingertips and scratched at her palm, fidgeting like mad.

Cam slid one hand between hers. She squeezed it hard.

"You've probably pieced this all together by now," she said, staring down at their clasped hands in her lap. "My mother left when I was born, my father raised me. He never kept her a secret. I knew who she was and why she left, though I didn't understand it at the time." She shook her head. "Still don't."

Cam squeezed her hand. She looked up at him, her eyes vivid and searching, then looked back down.

"I watched her on TV and YouTube. Watched all her speeches and interviews. Something happened when I was born and she had to have a hysterectomy. She couldn't have any more kids. She used that, played it into her political story."

Cam remembered. Madeline Kinkaid rose to power as a fervent champion of women's rights, a tragic leader who fought for the right for other women to choose for their own bodies what Kinkaid could not.

"The whole time, she denied my existence," said Celina. "I watched her, over and over, telling the world that she had no children. That she could never have children."

Celina looked at Cam.

"She never wavered, never even blinked when she told that fucking lie. Do you know how that makes me feel?"

Cam shook his head slowly, sadly.

"You're right. I do want to punish her."

She swallowed hard.

"And I do want her approval. You're right about that, too."

She shook her head and gave a bitter laugh.

"I'm a fucking mess."

Cam wanted to pull her into his arms, to kiss away her pain. He wanted to tell her everything was okay, tell her that he loved her enough to make up for her mother's stupidity a hundred times over. But all of that would only make him feel better, not Celina.

"When I was sitting on her couch," Celina continued, "she said she figured I'd come to ask if she loved me. If she'd ever loved me." Her voice fell into a rasping whisper. "She was right. I do want to know."

She looked at Cam, her eyes so wide and so fragile that Cam's stomach dropped and his chest grew tight.

"But I'm afraid to ask," Celina said.

She pulled her index finger along the bottom of one eye, flung away a single tear, and laughed in a mocking tone.

"Mommy issues," she said. "What a fucking joke."

Cam leaned forward on the bed, reached out and took her hand in both of his.

"Best case," he said, "she's loved you this whole time and regretted her choice her whole life."

"Worst case," Celina replied, "she doesn't give a shit and never has."

"Okay," said Cam, nodding slowly. "Okay, say that was true. What would that change?"

Celina looked up at him, her brow furrowed. She was searching his eyes with her own, but Cam sensed that she was searching inside herself.

"Nothing," she said softly, then nodded. Her voice grew stronger. "It wouldn't change a thing."

Cam nodded back.

Celina let out a long breath. She curled up on the bed, tucking her head against his chest like she had when he'd carried her upstairs the night before. Cam kissed her head, stroked her hair gently, and held her.

He watched the soft afternoon light streaming through the windows, Celina's warmth against his chest, her scent bringing him some long-needed peace of his own.

"Wouldn't change a thing," he whispered.

35

CELINA LAY in Cam's arms on the bed for a long time.

She'd never done that with anyone, before Cam. Ever. She'd never lain in bed with a guy without wanting to fuck him or waiting until she could leave after fucking him.

She would lie with Cam all the time after sex, of course. They slept together every night. That was a new experience for Celina, but one she'd gotten used to. One she actually loved.

But this was a whole other thing. No sex at all. Just a bunch of emotional baggage, the kind of shit that would send most people—Celina included—running for the hills. The kind of shit that Celina always thought of as bullshit. Just get over it and get on with it.

But she hadn't been able to get over this one.

Until now.

For the first time in her life, the darkness hanging over her seemed a little less dark.

Cam was right. So what if Madeline Kinkaid didn't love her? It's not like she was ever a part of Celina's life, anyway. Celina's father had been there. He'd given all the love he had to her, and it was more than enough.

And now she had Cam.

She'd almost fucked that one up. When he packed up his suitcase and left the bedroom, she lost her shit. Couldn't eat, couldn't sleep, couldn't concentrate. She didn't shower, didn't even brush her fucking teeth. She kept herself upright by guzzling enough coffee to give a horse a heart attack. And if the heart attack didn't kill the fucking horse, Celina's coffee breath would have finished the job.

It had only been three days since Cam left, but it felt like forever. Now that she was back in his arms, she never wanted to leave again.

They lay there for an hour, at least, maybe two, in total silence. With her head against his chest, all Celina could hear was the sound of Cam's heart beating and his breath rushing in and pushing out of his lungs.

And that's all she wanted to hear. For that time, her world shrank to just her heart and his heart, her breath and his breath.

Jesus, when did she become such a fucking romantic sap?

The shadows in the room were getting long, the light golden, when Celina sat up. Cam was still leaning up against the headboard. Celina straddled him. His head came up to her breasts. She took his head in her hands, his stubble scratchy against her palms. The way he looked up at her, his eyes all dreamy and dark, made her core flush with heat.

But she didn't want this to be about sex.

She leaned down and kissed him.

Soft, so soft.

At first.

Then harder and deeper.

His hands went under her shirt and across her back, his fingertips raking over her skin, sending lightning bolts racing through her body.

She'd only meant to kiss him, but her body had other ideas.

His seemed to agree.

The room was pitch black by the time they finished, panting and sweaty, the pillows scattered around the room, the bedspread half on the floor. They lay there for a few minutes, catching their breath.

Celina rolled onto her side next to Cam, kissed his neck and ran her hands over his bare chest, then down his chest, and further. He swelled to meet her hand, and their bodies took control again.

She could have gone on like that all fucking night, like they'd done so many times before.

But that night, they had work to do.

With a groan, they dragged themselves out of bed and into the shower.

It was a long shower.

A long, hot shower.

They finally managed to haul themselves down to the kitchen, into a more public place where they might actually be able to keep their hands off each other. When Celina came down the stairs, pulling Cam by the hand behind her, Paulie and Simon were sitting at the table, their backs toward her. Simon's hand was on the back of Paulie's chair, and it looked like Paulie was feeding something to Simon. He bit it and chewed and they both giggled before they heard Celina and turned toward the stairs.

"It's about bloody time," said Simon, seeing Celina and Cam holding hands.

"Fuck off, Simon," said Celina, but she couldn't keep the grin from spreading across her face.

Paulie stood and gave first Celina, then Cam, a broad smile, a tight hug, and a kiss on the cheek.

"Have you two..." Celina pointed a finger at a plate of

grapes on the table and raised her eyebrows at Paulie and Simon. "Have you two already eaten?"

They both looked a little embarrassed, like Celina had caught them messing around. As if she didn't already know they were knocking boots on the regular. And why the fuck shouldn't they? They were both hot as shit, both single, both willing and able. They should be fucking. More power to them.

But it was a trip to see them blushing like two kids she'd caught under the bleachers.

Celina turned toward Cam with a grin. He was frowning, looking confused.

He didn't fucking know yet.

Celina glanced at Paulie, who shrugged.

Celina didn't want to keep any secrets from Cam any more, but this one was on Paulie. She'd talk to Paulie later, tell her if she didn't tell Cam soon, Celina would. He deserved to know the truth. Celina had learned that lesson the hard way.

Simon cleared his throat. "Just a snack," he said, "but I'm hungry for dinner."

"I'll start it," said Cam, his voice hesitant, his brow furrowed as he turned into the kitchen.

"I'll help you, mate." Simon hustled into the kitchen after Cam.

"I," said Celina, sitting down at the counter in front of her laptop, "will pull up the feed from Cam's glasses."

Within minutes, the sizzle of a hot pan and the smell of sauteing onions filled the kitchen. Celina checked the tunnel she'd built into Madeline's security system, just to make sure it hadn't been compromised. She glanced through the camera feeds, arrayed twenty at a time in a grid on her laptop screen, and saw no one inside the house. The usual deployment of guards manned the garage gate and the guard house, with two guards in each.

Scanning quickly through the feeds, Celina almost missed two more guards that were patrolling the grounds. Unlike the other guards in their Capitol police uniforms, these two were dressed all in black and blended in with the shadows cast by the exterior lights.

That was new. When the speaker was home, there were six guards outside. But when she was away, there were usually only four.

Usually. But like Cam had said, they'd only watched the house for one full day. Maybe that day, with the contingent of four outdoor guards, was the anomaly. Maybe the two extra ninjas in the garden were the norm.

Cam was right. They should take more time to surveil the house. But Celina was confident that the speaker would be away for most of the night. And she and Cam could get past these guards in their sleep, even with the extra two thrown in.

Still, since they had the extra footage from Cam's glasses, they might as well look through it. Procrastination in the guise of surveillance was bullshit, but more information was always a good thing. She switched to another program to tap into the feed from the glasses.

While she waited for it to load, she watched Cam and Simon at the stove. Their backs were toward her. They talked and laughed while Cam stir-fried veggies in a large pan and Simon cooked some noodles in a pot.

Celina smiled to herself. The hiss and billow of steam, the smell of garlic and onion in the air, the heat from the stove filling the room. All of it combined to give her a feeling of coziness and belonging she hadn't felt in days.

She let her eyes draw slowly down Cam's lithe, muscular shape, getting all sorts of other wonderful feelings. She sighed, content and happy, and returned her attention to her laptop.

The feed from Cam's glasses was black.

That was weird.

"Cam," she said, "did you turn off your glasses by accident?"

"No," he replied over his shoulder. "I made sure it was still transmitting and recording before we left."

"Well, it's off now," Celina said.

She flipped to a different screen to access the recordings from the glasses.

"Maybe the battery ran out," Cam offered.

"Maybe," said Celina, but she doubted it. The glasses Cam wore were originally Nestech hardware, but Celina had overhauled them herself. The batteries should easily last a week, and they'd been fully charged when Cam and Paulie went scouting just two days earlier.

She found the recording and started it from the beginning. Cam's face filled the screen as he set up the glasses, then pulled away, revealing a view of the speaker's house. The house itself was empty. Celina could see the shadowy outlines of the four guards at the two entryways.

The only unguarded entrance was the front door, which opened onto the public sidewalk. But once she'd hacked into the security system, Celina had seen that it was well-guarded, nonetheless, with two cameras, three locks, and a battery of sensors monitoring the door and the sidewalk in front of it.

Celina set the playback on the recording to double-speed and let it run, a clock spinning in the corner of the window so they could see the timestamp of the video.

Paulie sat in the seat beside her. While they watched, no one entered the house.

Celina increased the playback speed. Still nothing happened, except foot patrols of the grounds every half-hour and a shift change for the guards at 4pm.

Celina increased the playback speed again. At this speed, the outlines of the guards in the guard house bounced around like balls in a pinball machine.

Then something flashed on the screen and the recording went dark.

"What happened?" asked Paulie.

Celina had no idea. She stopped the playback, jumped back an hour, and let it run again at normal speed.

The image was back to the speaker's house. The guards moved here and there. One of them left the guard house for a patrol.

The view from the camera shook, then tilted upward, then inverted.

A face filled the screen, upside-down. A broad-faced man with a goatee that didn't quite hide his double-chin. He tilted his head from side to side, frowning in concentration as he examined the glasses.

And then the screen went black.

Fuck.

36

THEY ALL HUDDLED around the laptop on the kitchen counter. The stir-fry was done. Simon had added the noodles to the vegetables and Cam had cooked them all together, then dumped the mixture into a large, colorful serving bowl. It steamed on the counter in front of them, ignored for the moment.

"Who is it?" asked Paulie.

After replaying the end of the video for Cam and Simon, Celina had paused it on the upside-down image of the man with the goatee, then rotated the image one hundred eighty degrees so they could look at him right-side up.

"No clue," said Simon.

Cam shook his head.

Celina didn't recognize him either, but she recognized the type. Stocky, older, just a little out of shape. But there was a hardness in his eyes and an efficient focus to the way he investigated the glasses that suggested strength and brutal efficiency.

Ex-military, possibly a retired colonel or even a one-star general. Someone who was used to giving orders. And not necessarily in the US military. He looked vaguely Middle

266

Eastern in his skin color and his features. Could be El-Sa'ka from Egypt or Sayeret Matkal from Israel or even Pakistani SSG.

In other words, he looked like someone who would not be fucking around.

But what the fuck was he doing in the house of a former US appellate justice? It didn't make any sense. The judge hadn't been there for weeks, and wouldn't be back for months. It was common knowledge, easy to find out. If they were looking for the judge, they were completely incompetent.

And the man on Celina's laptop screen did not look incompetent to her.

"Can you track the glasses?" asked Simon.

Celina was already on it. She pulled up a map showing the location of the glasses, a small blue dot moving along Maryland Avenue in downtown Washington, not far from the mall and Celina's house.

"Should we go after them?" asked Cam.

He was looking at Celina. So were the others.

Celina took a deep breath.

"Yes," she said, "but not right now. We already have one job to do, so let's keep our focus on that. We go ahead tonight, as planned. We can go after the glasses tomorrow."

They discussed the plan while they ate. Celina would hack back into the security system, loop the cameras, and disable the sensors. Cam would pick the locks on the front door and the two of them would go inside for the statue. Paulie and Simon would be across the street at the judge's house, with Simon on the drone for surveillance and Paulie monitoring the various camera feeds and the general situation, watching and waiting to alert everyone if and when the plan went wrong.

By the time they finished dinner and set up at the judge's house, it was almost 9pm. Celina set up her laptop beside

Simon's in the judge's office, on the wide windowsill facing the speaker's house across the street.

The office had seen a lot of traffic in the last week. Celina wondered idly if Chief Justice Wilkins had any clue how many times his home had been breached. His security company would have a bitch of a lawsuit on their hands if he did.

Simon was in the backyard with Cam, setting up the drone. Celina could see the feed come to life on the laptop beside her, showing Simon and Cam bent over the drone, peering into the camera, then looking up and shrinking quickly as the drone shot into the air.

Celina opened her own laptop and flipped to the window for her tunnel into the speaker's security system. She spent a few minutes configuring the loops on the cameras. Fortunately, nothing had moved in the house for hours, so the loops were easy to set up. The guards wouldn't see a thing when Cam and Celina broke in.

Paulie, on the other hand, would be able to monitor their movements through her own glasses, through the feed from Celina's glasses, and through the real-time feeds from the cameras both inside the house and on the grounds outside. In addition to that, Simon would get the bird's-eye view from the drone so he could spot any unusual movements on the grounds and in the surrounding area. Since Cam's glasses were currently being worn by some Egyptian ex-special forces goon on a sightseeing tour of Washington, he'd go in alfresco and follow Celina's lead.

Once the loops were set up, Celina spent a few minutes reconfiguring the failsafe triggers on the sensors and the door locks. They'd been set up to send push notifications not just when the sensors were tripped, but also when they were disabled. Celina changed that setting so that she could turn everything off without the guards being alerted.

Simon and Cam came into the room.

"Drone is in the air in a monitoring pattern," said Simon. He sat in the chair beside Celina and fiddled with his laptop, bringing up several windows monitoring the drone's functions and position. He expanded the camera feed to show several different views.

"Added a few more cameras this time," he said to Celina when he noticed her watching him. "Now I can see a 360-view around the drone."

Celina nodded and turned back to her own work. After a few more minutes, she tapped a button and the sensors on the front door of the speaker's house went dark. She checked the camera feeds. The guards showed no reaction, no clue that their system had been hacked and they were about to look very, very stupid.

"Okay," she said, "we're ready."

She got up from her chair. Cam and Paulie were standing in the center of the room.

"You sure you don't want to take my glasses?" Paulie said to Cam.

"You need them more than I do," he said. "You need to keep an eye on everything. I've got Celina."

He looked at Celina and she couldn't keep the grin off of her face. Real professional.

"She'll let me know if anyone is coming," said Cam.

He had a broad smile on his face, too. At least they were unprofessional together.

"Alright," said Paulie. She gave Cam a kiss on the cheek, then gave one to Celina, as well. "Be safe, you two."

She sat down in the chair, and she and Simon situated themselves with all the feeds coming into their glasses and the two laptops.

"You ready?" said Celina.

"Ready as I'll ever be," Cam replied.

Celina felt the usual adrenaline as she and Cam went

down the stairs, out the back door, and around the side of the house. Every time she started a job, her senses came alive, like she was transforming into a more primal form of herself, a super-predator form. Musicians and performers sometimes talked about how their time on stage was so exciting and vivid that real-life seemed dull by comparison. Celina felt the same way. Nothing could compare to the thrill of a job.

Well, it used to be nothing. She and Cam stood in the shadows across from the speaker's house, watching the street for any movement. Now, her life had new thrills in it, every bit as exciting as a job. She might even be willing to give up her criminal hobby, settle down and see what more a life with Cam could offer.

Jesus, she really was turning into a romantic sap. What the fuck was Cam doing to her?

The night was very dark. Thick clouds had moved in, obscuring the moonlight. A streetlight on each corner provided the only illumination, thick shadows draping over the street between them, pierced only by two bright lights on either side of the speaker's front door.

Celina took a long minute, watching carefully, but didn't see anything moving on the street. Nothing at all. It was a sleepy Friday night in Alexandria. She took Cam's hand and gave it a quick squeeze.

If she was a romantic sap now, Celina didn't care. Three days without Cam had nearly killed her. Now that she had him back, she was never going to fuck that up again.

He squeezed her hand back, flashed her a smile that made Celina's pulse quicken, then nodded.

Celina let go of his hand, took one last look at the street, then moved with Cam out of the shadows.

37

PAULIE USED to love her work. She and her husband Sam had made a great team, and they'd spent decades robbing first local banks, then federal banks, before lifting their sights to art galleries and private art collections. They had plenty of money by then, and were doing the work more for the love of it than for any financial gain. They both loved art, and so many works of art were owned by arrogant assholes who cared more about the prestige of a piece than about the piece itself. Stealing the art back from them was a greater good.

When she'd been in prison, she couldn't wait to get out and get back into the work again. So much boredom, with nothing to plan, nothing to think through, nothing to look forward to except her weekly visits from Cam. She was a lot older than she'd been the last time she'd run a job, but she still loved the thrill of it.

Only now, she had a different perspective.

She lost Sam, one of the two most important people in her world. The thought that one of them could die had never occurred to Paulie before. Not really. They were non-violent criminals. They never carried weapons, and they were meticulous in their planning, taking great pains to ensure that no one would get hurt, including them.

But the possibility was always there. A nervous guard or a trigger-happy cop or a private citizen with a concealed carry permit and delusions of vigilante glory. Lots of things could go wrong on even the simplest job.

Or even when you weren't on a job at all. Fate had taught Paulie that lesson in the cruelest of ways.

As she watched Cam and Celina cross the street, she didn't feel the thrill of the job. She felt concern. Why risk so much for so little? They were breaking into the home of a powerful politician, a home surrounded by armed and trained guards, all to steal a statue basically for its sentimental value.

Fifteen years ago, Paulie wouldn't have questioned it. Hell, fifteen minutes ago, the question hadn't occurred to her.

But now, seeing her son and the woman she had come to think of as her daughter walk into harm's way, the question was screaming in her mind.

But it was too late now. The job was underway, and Paulie needed to do her part.

She focused on her laptop screen, peering at the array of camera feeds before her. The interior feeds showed no movement, as expected. Paulie focused on the exterior feeds. She glanced up through the window. Her glasses showed her the outlines of the two guards in the guardhouse, the two in the back at the garage gate, and the two new guards Celina had spotted on either side of the house, in the gardens.

Those guards were strange. Paulie's glasses highlighted any weapons a person carried. The Capitol police carried Glock handguns. The two new guards carried M4A1 high-powered automatic rifles. Also, they didn't patrol like the others. In fact, the other guards had still maintained their perimeter patrols, even with these new guards in place. Why would they bother if they already had guards stationed in the gardens?

Even stranger, the last time the guards had patrolled the grounds, just before Cam and Celina had left, the two new guards had moved away from them, pushing themselves into the shadows against the wall that surrounded the property, almost as if they were hiding from the patrols.

Maybe they were from different departments. The speaker was in the middle of contentious negotiations to avoid a government shutdown. Maybe something had happened that had increased the security risk to the speaker, and the Secret Service or someone had beefed up security without informing the Capitol police. Wouldn't be the first time two government agencies failed to communicate with each other. And it wouldn't be the first time political tensions had escalated to the point that death threats and security concerns for an elected official had reached a dangerous level.

Still, something about those two new guards tickled the back of Paulie's brain. She kept an eye on them. Right now, they were in place in the garden, unmoving, like the other guards. From their perspective, all was well on a dull, quiet night.

Celina and Cam reached the front door. Celina turned her back toward it, surveying the street while Cam bent behind her and picked the locks. Within a minute, he had them all open. They slipped inside and closed the door behind them.

Paulie checked the internal camera feeds. She could see Celina and Cam in the foyer, then watched them move into the room where Celina had sat for tea with her mother.

She checked the position of the guards. The four Capitol police guards hadn't moved from the garage gate and the guard house. The two new guards in the gardens had shifted position, moving away from the perimeter walls and into the gardens themselves. One appeared to be running a patrol toward the garage gate, the other toward the guard house. She checked the external cameras, but the guards were sticking to the shadows.

"How does it look to you?" Paulie asked Simon, sitting beside her.

"Quiet," he replied.

Paulie could tell from Simon's voice that he was nervous, too. A quiet job sometimes meant a good job, well-planned and well-executed. But more often than not, it meant the shit was about to hit the fan.

Paulie just wanted to know where the shit was coming from before it did. Even a little advance warning could make the difference between a successful job and a total failure.

But all remained quiet as she watched Cam and Celina slink through the house up to the speaker's study on the third floor. No alarms, no more movement from the guards, nothing at all as Celina took the statue, wrapped it in a small towel and slipped it into a leather shoulder bag, and turned with Cam to go back downstairs and out of the house.

Paulie watched the one of the new guards meet up with the Capitol police at the garage gate, the other with those at the guard house. And maybe all the tension Paulie had been feeling was just nerves. She'd been out of it for a long time and she was rusty. Her instincts might be off.

Maybe this would be one of those rare jobs that went off without a hitch. Celina worked a lot more quickly, a lot more loosely than Paulie would. But technology made things a lot simpler than they used to be. Security guards relied on sensors and cameras and computers now, sitting on their butts watching monitors all night instead of patrolling like they used to. Celina was a master of controlling technology.

Maybe all the planning Paulie was used to just wasn't necessary any more. Times had changed. Paulie just needed to adapt.

Celina's voice came through Paulie's earpiece. "Heading back," she said.

"Roger," replied Paulie.

They'd only been inside the house for three minutes.

Paulie let out a long breath, then looked at Simon and smiled. He smiled back, his handsome profile lit by the glow of the laptop screen.

Then all their screens went blank.

38

CAM ACTUALLY FELT a little relieved when all the lights went out.

At first.

They had been halfway down the stairs between the third floor and the second floor. The statue was snug in Celina's shoulder bag. They'd seen no one and heard no one. They'd slipped into the house and all the way up to the speaker's study, and were on their way out. Quick and easy.

Way too easy.

Every plan goes wrong at some point. It was one of the lessons Cam's parents had drilled into him over the years, one of the lessons Cam had seen proven time and time again. It was practically a law of nature, at this point.

And until the lights went out, Celina's plan had gone perfectly.

With each passing moment of perfection, Cam had become more and more nervous, waiting for the other shoe to drop.

So when the lights went out, he felt a moment of relief.

And then all hell broke loose.

"What?" hissed Celina, behind Cam on the stairs.

She was speaking to the others through her glasses. He felt her squeeze past him and tug at his arm.

"Come on, Cam," she said. "We have to move. Now."

He heard her go down the stairs ahead of him. From the rhythm of her footfalls receding into the distance, she was taking them two or three at a time.

But she had the benefit of her glasses. She could see in the dark.

Cam could not.

And it was very dark.

"Celina," he whispered.

He got no response, and he couldn't hear her footsteps any more.

He held one hand against the wall to guide him to the bottom of the stairs, then turned right. The stairwell to the first floor should be ahead on his left.

"Celina," he whispered again, keeping one hand on the wainscoting as he groped his way down the hall.

"I'm here, Cam," she said, then grabbed his hand and tugged him forward.

Cam heard a loud bang somewhere below them as he followed Celina.

"Shit," said Celina. "Yeah, I see them."

She was talking to Paulie and Simon. Cam immediately regretted not taking his mother up on her offer to give her glasses to him.

"Fuck," said Celina. "Roger that."

Her voice had changed. Before, it had been clipped, but vibrant. Now, it was cold and hard. All business.

Something had gone wrong.

Cam kept his muscles relaxed and his feet light. Celina was moving fast, and he had to keep up, even though he couldn't see a goddamn thing. He couldn't even see Celina's hand holding his in the darkness. She was pulling him toward the stairs. The last thing Cam wanted was to fall headfirst down them because he was dragging his feet.

"Stairs," said Celina in that cold, hard tone.

She pulled him hard to the left. Cam barely had time to shift his weight and throw his hand to the stairwell wall for balance before he was going down after Celina. His descent was more of a controlled fall than anything.

He heard two quick sounds. Short, sharp pops. Something sharp hit Cam in the cheek near his eye. He turned away instinctively, still descending the stairs.

He ran into Celina's back.

She pushed his shoulder to turn him to the side, then squeezed past him on the stairs and grabbed his hand again, pulling him back up the stairs.

Cam knew enough to keep his mouth shut. He followed Celina, doing his best to stay relaxed, even though his mind was anything but.

He only knew of one thing that would make that popping sound, then throw shards at Cam's face. One thing that would make Celina stop and turn back when the front door was just a short distance away.

Someone was shooting at them.

39

Cam stumbled as Celina pulled him up the stairs. He reached out one hand and caught himself.

Celina did not stop pulling.

She whipped to the left at the top of the steps and jerked Cam behind her into the hallway.

"What about the other one?" Celina whispered into the earpiece of her glasses. Her voice was quiet, but harsh and clipped. "Roger," she said in response to whatever Paulie and Simon had told her.

She stopped and shoved Cam through a doorway into one of the second-floor bedrooms. She followed him in and shut the door behind them.

It was so dark Cam could barely see. His eyes should have adjusted to the darkness by now. The bedroom had large windows. There should have been light coming in from the street. But there was nothing. Two feet in front of him, Celina was only a faint outline. She stood behind the door, a shadow in the shadows. Waiting.

Cam's eyes weren't the only things struggling to adjust. His mind was confused and scrambling. He had no information. He couldn't see, couldn't communicate with the others. He had no idea what their tactical situation was. Without his glasses to give him focus, he struggled to fight down his instinct to panic.

He forced himself to breathe and focus. He'd done this for years before he'd stolen the Nestech glasses. He could do this without them. He took deep breaths and focused on what he knew.

Someone was shooting at them, but Cam had no idea who or why. The guards outside would have no way to know Cam and Celina were there. They didn't make routine patrols inside the house, so they wouldn't have stumbled on them. Celina was too good for the security system to have detected her hacking. And the guards wouldn't have come in shooting. They would have announced themselves.

Unless the speaker had come home from the Capitol earlier than expected. If she was on the premises, the guards might shoot first and ask questions later.

And why had the lights gone out? Cam glanced toward the bedroom windows. No light from outside meant the whole block was out. Could be bad timing. Or the power could have been deliberately cut.

Were the people shooting at them good guys or bad guys?

Good guys were easy to beat. They had rules to follow. Rules that could be exploited.

Bad guys were not so easy.

With one hand, Celina pushed Cam backward and to the side, clearing him out of the doorway. A moment later, the bedroom door slammed against the wall. A rustling sound. Something banged against Cam's shoulder, knocking him to the side. A heavy thump. The sound of metal slapping against flesh. Then a dull thud. Another thud. Again and again. A cracking sound. The dull thuds took on a wet, squishy tone, then stopped.

Silence.

And the smell of blood.

Cam couldn't see, but he could smell Celina's scent mix with the smell of blood as she came closer to him. He heard her breath, fast and hard. She pulled in a long, slow breath and blew it out. Then another.

"You okay?" she asked, her voice a jagged whisper.

"Yeah. You?"

She took his hand. It was warm and wet.

"Watch your step," she said.

She pulled him back toward the doorway. Cam nearly stumbled as his foot kicked against the leg of the man Celina had taken down.

Bad guys. Definitely bad guys.

40

Celina pulled Cam behind her down the second-floor hallway. In her glasses, she could see the outline of the other attacker on the floor below them. He would have heard the shots from his partner, then would have lost communication with him after Celina knocked him out.

Knocked him out or killed him. She didn't care which, but she knew Cam did. Cam didn't like violence. Paulie had raised him to be opposed to it. Cam had mentioned in the past that two of his prior girlfriends had been killers, that he'd left them because of it.

Celina had never killed anyone, but she knew she could. She had the skills. She had no particular desire to kill anyone, but if it came down to her life or theirs, she knew she wouldn't hesitate.

Not that long ago, she'd wanted to kill Vernon Stratham, the man who ordered the hit that killed her father. And she'd had the chance to do it.

But Cam had stopped her.

In her glasses, she could still see the outline of the man in the bedroom. That meant he was still alive. She hoped he stayed that way. Not for his sake, but for hers.

She didn't want to lose Cam again.

The hand pulling Cam was slick with the man's blood, getting sticky as it dried. She'd surprised the man and taken him down in the doorway, but he'd still managed to pull his pistol as he fell. His instincts were good. He was well trained.

But not as well trained as Celina. She'd gotten his gun from him before he could get off a shot, then beaten him with it until he stopped fighting.

She still had the pistol in her hand, a Jericho 9mm. Israeli special forces. Guess that explained where they came from. Still didn't explain why.

She tugged Cam down the hallway toward the back stairs, stepping as lightly on the wood floors as she could. Thankfully, Cam was doing the same. And he was running blind in the dark, with no clue what was happening.

And no time for Celina to explain.

They had to get out.

"Where are the regular guards?" said Celina. She spoke quietly, under her breath. The microphone on her glasses would detect the sound and amplify it.

"All four confirmed dead," Paulie responded.

Celina pressed her lips together. "Roger," she said.

The guards at the garage gate and in the guardhouse were dead. Whoever was in the house with them was not taking prisoners.

Celina watched the outline of the other attacker move below them as she jogged down the hallway with Cam. He moved with them toward the back stairs. Celina stopped, caught Cam and turned him, and headed back toward the main stairs. She didn't care how they got down, just as long as they were away from the man with the gun when they did.

But the attacker shifted when Celina shifted, moving toward the main stairs right after she did.

Celina stopped.

The attacker stopped.

She pushed Cam against the wall in the middle of the second-floor hallway.

"Wait here," she whispered.

"No, Celi—"

But she was already running away from him. She knew she was leaving him vulnerable, alone in the dark with no vision and no communication. But it was a calculated risk. Cam was smart and skilled. He could handle himself.

And Celina had to figure out whether or not the attacker downstairs would follow her.

He did.

She ran toward the back stairs and the attacker's outline shadowed her perfectly.

There was no way he could hear her running. She was moving too quietly. That meant he had tech, a sound amplifier or heat signature goggles.

Or something like her glasses.

She had assumed the tech wasn't widespread yet, but Cam had stolen his glasses from Christopher Nestrom years ago. And if Nestech had the glasses, everyone did. Thomas Crowell was CEO there now, and he only cared about money. They would have sold the tech to the highest bidder. The U.S. military usually fit that description. Israeli special forces wouldn't be far behind.

Celina had to assume the attacker downstairs could see her as well as she could see him.

And that meant he could see Cam, too.

And if his glasses were like hers, he could see that she was armed and Cam was not. That was an advantage for Celina.

Celina slipped off the bag with the statue, ran back to Cam, and put it over his head.

"What are you doing?" he hissed.

"Take this," she said. "Go down the hall to the back stairs. They'll take you straight to the front door."

"What are you talking about?" asked Cam.

"Celina, no," said Simon in her earpiece.

"Shut up, Simon," Celina whispered. To Cam, she said, "This guy can see us. He's got glasses like ours. And he can see that I've got a gun."

Cam shook his head. "He'll follow you."

"I want him to."

Celina put her hands on Cam's cheeks.

"I'll lead him away," she said. "You go down the back stairs and out the front door. Once you're safe, I'll find a way to get out."

"You'll need help."

"Then get me some," Celina said.

"I'm coming in," said Simon in her earpiece.

"No, Simon," said Celina. "You'll just be in the way."

She looked at Cam, staring back at her, blank-eyed in the dark, unable to see her right in front of him. She kissed him, soft and lingering.

"Go," she whispered, and pushed him down the hall.

Before he could catch himself and turn back to her, she was running the other way.

41

CAM HEARD the soft padding of Celina's sneakers against the wood floor. She'd shoved him away. By the time he caught himself, the sound was gone. He could hear only silence, could see only darkness.

He put his hand out to feel the wall. It was the only marker he had, the only thing that told him he wasn't floating in a dark, empty void.

He wanted to run after Celina, to stay with her. To help her.

But he wasn't helping her. He was slowing her down, putting her in danger. Every moment she had to spare a thought for him, stumbling in the dark behind her, was a moment that the man downstairs could gain advantage.

Cam choked back the panic, the fear, the worry in his mind.

Celina wanted him to get out. She'd used herself as a decoy so he could get out.

He could do as she asked, run outside and across the street, get Paulie's or Simon's glasses, then come back to help Celina.

But by the time he got back, it would all be over. One way or another.

He wasn't about to leave Celina in here all alone. He had to find a way to help.

Celina said the man downstairs had glasses. Cam hadn't seen or heard of the tech being on the market, but Nestech could be selling privately to militaries and arms dealers around the world.

If the man downstairs had the tech, the man lying dead or unconscious in the bedroom probably had it, too.

Cam groped his way down the hallway back to the bedroom, then staccato-stepped in until his feet kicked against the man's legs.

The man groaned.

A spike of fear cored Cam. Instinctively, he fell on top of the man and punched him twice in the head, then once more.

The groaning stopped.

Cam's hand came away hot and wet. It felt like it was on fire.

He felt for the man's neck, checked his pulse. Still strong. He wasn't dead, just knocked out.

Cam felt the man's face, found a pair of glasses there and put them on, hoping the beatings hadn't damaged them.

Instantly, the darkness around him went away, replaced by a crystal clear view of the bed, the windows, a dresser, a sitting area, the man on the floor.

A rifle lay to the man's side, slung by a strap from his shoulder. He wore a military-style bulletproof vest. His face was blacked out with grease paint.

Working quickly, Cam set the rifle to one side, removed the vest, and slid it on himself. He pulled the straps as tight as he could make them. The fit was a little big, but it would have to do.

He found a pair of handcuffs on the man's belt and cuffed him to the leg of the bed frame. The frame was sturdy. Probably not heavy enough if the man came to, but it would slow him down.

And Cam didn't have time for anything else. He could see in his glasses that Celina was creeping down the main stairs. The man on the first floor was waiting for her. He looked like he was setting up for an angle.

Cam kicked the rifle into the corner. He didn't know how to use it, but he didn't want the unconscious soldier to find it too easily. He had to get downstairs and figure out a way to help Celina.

Cam was halfway to the back stairs when he heard the first shot.

Celina's outline in his glasses flickered.

Cam's heart stopped.

Cam leaned on the handrails and swung himself down the back stairs, his feet barely touching the steps.

His mind had detached from his body. His movements felt like they belonged to someone else, like he was watching them from a distance.

Celina's outline flickered on again, down the hall from the stairs.

It wasn't moving.

And she didn't have her gun. It was back on the steps.

The outline of the man with approached her slowly.

Cam hit the landing at a dead run. Through the foyer, through the tea room, down the hallway.

He saw the man turn toward him, surprise on his face.

He saw the man lift his rifle.

Cam flung his body at the man.

He saw a white flash.

Then darkness.

42

Celina jerked backward. Instinct.

Instead of catching her between the eyes, the bullet grazed her left temple. Close enough to knock her glasses off her head.

She fell. Stair treads jammed into her spine. She heard the glasses clattering across the bare wood of the first-floor hallway.

Her temple seared with pain. Hot blood dripped into her eye and down her cheek.

As soon as her glasses came off, the world went immediately dark. A bloom of panic, then Celina forced herself to focus. Cam had dealt with the dark. She could, too.

Hopefully, Cam was safely across the street by now.

If the glasses were still functioning, there was a chance the asshole with the rifle would be following their signal down the hallway.

Celina pushed herself into a crouch against the wall of the stairs a few steps from the bottom. She couldn't see him, but she hoped she'd be able to hear him or feel him before he noticed her.

Celina still had the Jericho she'd lifted off Asshole Number

One upstairs. The skateboard grip was tight and scratchy against her palm.

She'd done a press check after she knocked the asshole out, so she knew she had a round in the chamber. Normally, she'd do another one, just to be sure. But she couldn't see shit in the dark. She'd have to hold the grip with one hand, pull the slide back with the other and try to feel for the round with her finger. Awkward. And the sound of the slide snapping back would be deafening in the silence if her hand slipped. She didn't want to give her position away. She'd have to trust her memory.

Her eyes were useless in the pitch dark, so she closed them. She slowed her breathing, extended her senses, listening and feeling for Asshole Number Two.

A floorboard squeak. Not even. Just the start of one, caught mid-squeak, to her right.

He was good.

Celina was better.

She raised the pistol. Aimed at where she hoped his center of mass would be. Steadied her breathing. Waited for him to pass in front of the stairs.

Two more seconds.

One more second.

The lights came on, blinding after so long in the dark.

A shot. To Celina's right.

Two bodies, falling past her from right to left.

As Celina blinked in the bright light, they looked like an old-fashioned movie flickering.

A heavy thump as the bodies landed against the bottom stair.

One body stayed where it landed.

The other body rolled across the hallway.

Celina squinted against the light.

Asshole Number One was twitching on the stairs, glassy eyes staring upward.

Celina's vision adjusted.

She looked across the hallway at the other body.

Her heart stopped.

Cam.

The other body was Cam.

43

People rushed in. Men in suits.

Celina didn't give a fuck about them.

She didn't give a fuck about their shouting. Didn't give a fuck about their guns pointed at her.

It was like they were behind heavy glass, muffled and separate.

They tried to pull her off of Cam's body. She wouldn't let go.

Why the fuck was he there? He was supposed to be across the street.

He was supposed to be safe.

Blood ran into her eyes. Both eyes. It stung, ran hot across her cheeks.

"Ma'am."

She wiped one side.

It wasn't blood. She was fucking crying.

"Ma'am."

A hand under her arm. She shook it off.

She didn't cry. She never cried.

"Ma'am, I need you to step away."

Again, a hand under her arm. Again, she shook it off.

She touched her hands to Cam's cheeks. With one shaking hand, she felt for a pulse.

It was there.

He was alive.

Celina sagged against Cam's chest, her cheek over his heart.

Over something hard.

An arm across her shoulder.

"Celina."

A vest. A hard vest.

Celina sat back on her knees.

Cam was wearing Kevlar.

"Celina, honey, come with me."

The speaker's voice.

Where the fuck did Cam get Kevlar?

And... glasses?

"Come with me, Celina."

"Fuck off," she said over her shoulder.

"Celina."

The speaker's voice.

Her mother's voice.

"Come with me."

It meant nothing to Celina.

"I'm not leaving him."

"At least stand up, then, Celina, so the doctors can look at him."

Celina looked around her.

Most of the guns were back in their holsters. She heard boots thumping upstairs. A woman holding a small green bag was bouncing from foot to foot beside the speaker, trying to see around Celina to get a look at Cam.

She stood, let her mother pull her to one side. Two men in suits with guns surrounded Cam. As Celina backed away, one of them bent and felt Cam's body to make sure he was unarmed, then waved for the medic with the green bag. She slid to her knees beside Cam, started removing his vest.

The vest had a shiny, shallow dent in it.

Celina's mother tried to pull her toward the front door. Celina resisted.

She looked at the asshole on the stairs. His head was on the edge of the bottom tread, his eyes staring up at the ceiling. A pool of blood lay beneath his head. A tiny river of blood dripped off the tread into a larger pool on the floor.

Dead.

Cam's back arched. He sucked in a deep breath. His eyes were wide and white and searching.

"Celina," he said.

"Cam."

Celina pushed through the suits, shoved aside the medic.

"I'm here, Cam."

She took his head in her hands and kissed him. He kissed her back, put one hand against her cheek. His hand was freezing. Her cheeks were hot and stinging again.

"Why are you here?" she said. "You were supposed to leave."

"No." He shook his head, a tiny shake, then closed his eyes like it hurt. "Won't leave you."

She lay his head down gently and let the medic push back in. Celina kneeled beside Cam until they brought in a stretcher and lifted Cam onto it.

Celina followed the stretcher, holding Cam's hand, followed it through a tangle of people in suits and uniforms looking pissed off and serious. Her mother followed, two of the suits surrounding her, holding their hands to their earpieces and looking at everything but the speaker as they walked out the front door.

The stretcher clacked down the stairs onto the sidewalk. Cop cars and chunky blacked-out Cadillac Escalades and two ambulances filled the street. Red and blue and white spinners cast bruised shadows on the buildings and the brick and the pavement. The streetlights were back on. Lights were on in some of the windows. Celina saw Paulie and Simon standing in half-shadow across the street and nodded to them. Paulie saw and sagged against Simon's chest in relief. He held her.

Cam's stretcher went into one ambulance. Celina let Madeline lead her into the other one, a few feet across from it by the curb.

Celina sat on the bumper, the bay of Cam's ambulance in clear view before her. Two EMTs were working on him.

"Don't let that ambulance leave without me," she shouted at no one, but loud enough for everyone to hear.

One of the suits looked at Madeline, who nodded. The suit pressed his earpiece and turned away.

Another EMT put one of those tin foil blankets around her shoulders, then shined a pen light in both eyes, checked her vitals, cleaned and covered the wound on her temple.

"She'll need tests," said the EMT to Madeline. "It looks like a bullet wound, a graze on her temple."

That's exactly what it fucking was.

"There's no sign of concussion, but she'll need an MRI to make sure there's no internal damage."

"Thank you," said Madeline.

"How is Cam?" said Celina.

The EMT looked at Madeline as he unwrapped the blood pressure cuff from Celina's arm.

Madeline nodded.

Celina ground her teeth, irritated that everyone looked to her mother for permission to answer Celina's questions.

"I'll see what I can find out," he said, then walked across to the other ambulance. Celina saw him confer with one of the EMTs that had been working on Cam. They both glanced back at Celina.

Madeline sat on the bumper beside her.

"He's going to be fine," she said.

Celina didn't say anything. Madeline Kinkaid may control everyone there, but she wasn't a doctor and she wasn't all-powerful. Celina didn't give a shit about Madeline's empty assurances. She wanted the truth, from someone who knew.

The EMT came back.

"The vest caught the bullet. He has a large contusion on his chest. Might have a broken rib. The X-rays will confirm." He paused. Celina looked back at him blankly. "He's going to be fine."

All the tension that had been holding Celina upright drained from her then.

She slumped against her mother. Not because she was her mother, but because she was there.

Madeline put her arm around Celina, leaned her head against hers, rubbed her shoulder softly and slowly.

Celina closed her eyes, briefly, and let herself be a daughter in her mother's arms.

Briefly.

She pulled herself upright, stood, and shucked off the fire blanket.

"I'm going with him," she said, and strode across to the other ambulance.

Behind her, she heard Madeline say to the EMT, "It's alright. You couldn't stop her if you tried."

Even fucking politicians were right some of the time.

44

CAM HAD FELT WORSE pain in his life. But he didn't feel good.

Three cracked ribs, a nasty red and yellow bruise that covered half his chest, and a broken middle finger on his right hand. And his body felt like a tidy giant had used it as a dishrag.

The bruise and the cracked ribs were from the rifle shot. The Kevlar vest saved his life, but the shot came at close range, with enough force to do some damage.

The doctors figured the broken finger came from the stairs, when Cam tackled the shooter and landed on it. That's probably when he banged his head, too. He was unconscious for a few minutes. Mild concussion, but no lasting harm.

The shooter was not so lucky. His head had hit the stairs in just the wrong way, cracking it like an egg. Dead in seconds.

That bruise would stay with Cam long after the bones had healed.

He hissed as Celina helped him out of the passenger seat of the car and up the steps to the back door. The pain was mostly just a dull ache. They'd given him some pain meds that helped. But every so often, if he moved the wrong way, he'd feel a sharp twinge that would take his breath away for a second.

Could have been a hell of a lot worse.

"Couch, kitchen, or bedroom?" asked Celina.

Cam looked around. He didn't want to sit at the kitchen counter, but the couches on the first floor were all hard as rocks. He could go upstairs to the theater room or to the bedroom, but he wasn't ready to navigate the stairs just yet.

He settled for the counter, easing himself into one of the high chairs. It wasn't exactly comfortable, but it was good enough for the moment.

Paulie and Simon came in just behind them, Simon carrying two handfuls of rustling grocery bags, Paulie carrying a large plastic bag with Cam's personal items from the hospital. Paulie set the bag on the chair next to Cam, gave him a tender kiss on the forehead, and sat on the stool on the other side while Celina and Simon put away the groceries and started making lunch.

Cam had been in the hospital for about a day and a half, getting a battery of scans and tests. Celina got a similar treatment.

The doctors were friendly, efficient, and clearly some of the best in their field. The hospital was unlike anything Cam had seen before. It wasn't a large institutional complex with people of all types streaming in and out of the emergency room. It was a small building that looked more like something a tech startup would use. All sleek metal and glass. There were only a few rooms, and it seemed like Celina and Cam were the only patients.

A gunshot had been involved, so Cam had expected to be interviewed by some kind of law enforcement. Local police, at least. Maybe Capitol police or Secret Service, since the incident took place at the speaker's house. Standard procedure in gunshot cases, from what Cam knew.

But no one came. The only people Cam saw were his doctors and Celina.

Paulie and Simon stayed away to keep their profiles low, but they were there when Cam and Celina were released, groceries already loaded in the car.

Back at the house, Cam felt a little better, but he wanted to go home. Real home. Back to California, where the couches were made for sitting and the sounds outside were crashing waves, not honking car horns.

Celina slid double espressos to Cam and to Paulie.

"Do you want to stay here until you're feeling better?" Celina asked. "Or would you rather head home?"

"Home," said Cam immediately, then took a long sip of the coffee, draining half of the glass in one swallow.

"Okay," said Celina. "We can leave in the morning."

"Can we leave tonight?"

Celina tilted her head at Cam, then smiled.

"How about wheels up at seven?"

Cam nodded. "Perfect." He drained the rest of his coffee.

Celina took the empty glass and fixed him another.

The shoulder bag was shoved in the bag of Cam's personal items. He opened it and pulled out the statue, still tightly rolled in a towel.

All that trouble for a piece of stone.

But it wasn't just a piece of stone. It was a priceless work of art. And a piece of Celina's family history.

Still, was it worth all the trouble? It wasn't worth dying for, but no one here had died. And if it was important to Celina, it was important to Cam.

Cam unrolled the towel carefully, preparing himself for the worst. After tackling an assassin into a stairway and rolling on the floor, Cam expected to find the statue in pieces.

It wasn't.

It was intact, and stunningly beautiful.

The limestone was cool and smooth and heavy in Cam's hand. He held it by the back of its slender neck. The neck rose to an elongated head, its features serene and regal. A woman's pursed mouth. A long, slender, elegant nose. Her eyes closed, her hair billowing behind her, as if she faced bravely into a maelstrom, prepared to meet her fate.

The piece immediately pulled Cam in. He marveled at the craftsmanship, the artistry. It told a story, left Cam wondering what the woman was thinking. Was she meditating? Was she angry?

Great art pulls us out of our own lives and into the world of the artist, makes us ask questions that lead us through the artist's world and back to our own again, seeing it with new eyes, new questions. Hopefully giving us new answers that enrich our futures. This statue did all of those things.

Tête. The French word for head. Such a simple title for the piece, and yet that simple title contained an infinity of thought and feeling. It was a perfect name for such a bare, transcendent sculpture.

Cam set the statue carefully in the center of the kitchen counter. He and Paulie stared at it. Celina turned with Cam's coffee, set it before him, then walked around the counter and stood beside him to look. Simon, too, came to Paulie's side to admire the piece.

They were all standing there, lost in their own thoughts, when they heard a key turn in the lock on the front door.

45

When Madeline walked through the front door, a large Louis Vuitton purse hung from her crooked elbow, Celina felt like she'd been pulled into an alternate timeline. The whole world seemed to have tilted two degrees to the side. The same, but just a little bit off.

Madeline pulled the keys from the door, walked in, and flipped the door shut behind her like she'd just come back from a quick trip to the post office.

No one said a word. No one moved.

Celina tried to speak, but could not form words. She'd never seen her mother come home before. The experience was so out of kilter with her entire life that she was struck completely dumb.

And being speechless was not a common experience for her.

Madeline strolled in, dropped her keys on the counter, set her purse on the floor, and looked at the statue.

"That's it?" she said. She looked at them all in turn, then settled her eyes on Celina. "That's why you broke into my house?"

Celina felt her cheeks burn under her mother's gaze. A

spurt of anger erupted within her and broke her stunned silence.

"It doesn't belong to you," she said in a low voice. Her teeth slowly clenched harder and harder until she felt like they would splinter in her mouth.

Madeline's voice softened. Her face was kind. "I know that, Celina," she said softly. "It never did. Perry asked me to hold on to it. For you. He said that one day you'd come for it."

She looked at the statue and sighed.

"I don't think he expected it to be like this," she said.

Celina fought back the feelings that surged in her. Cam caught her eye, but she shook her head quickly and looked away, down at the counter.

If she looked at Cam, she would start to feel things. She didn't want that right now. She didn't want to cry. She didn't want to think about her father. Not then. Not with her in the room.

She balled her hands into fists, digging her nails into her palms until she felt the pain and had to harden herself against it.

"How did you know we were here?" she asked.

The speaker raised her eyebrows. "Are you kidding?" she laughed. "I've known you were here since you arrived."

"Bullshit," said Celina. "I swept the house before we got here. Disabled the security, the cameras. Everything."

Madeline nodded, smiling. "Perry always said you were brilliant, Celina," she said. "He was right." She leaned her elbows on the counter, her hands clasped before her. "But he also said you hadn't learned patience quite yet."

She made a knowing face toward Paulie, who smiled faintly in return. Madeline pointed toward the corners of the ceiling, pointed along the backsplash above the stove.

"More cameras," she said. "Very well hidden. And a secondary security system. All Perry's design, of course."

Celina's cheeks burned again. She'd been fooled by the cameras at the speaker's house in Alexandria. It never occurred to her to check the D.C. house for the same setup.

Her father's design.

"Dad set this up for you?"

Celina frowned. She'd checked the records. The speaker had only bought this house ten years ago, eighteen years after she'd abandoned Celina's father with a newborn baby girl to raise by himself.

"We stayed close," Madeline nodded. "Very close. We talked almost every week. Even saw each other in person a couple times a year."

That off-kilter feeling came back to Celina. Her world now felt like a ship sinking at sea, listing to one side, paintings swinging on the walls, furniture sliding across the floor, books falling from the shelves, glasses slipping from tables and shattering on the deck.

"Then why didn't you..."

She couldn't get the words out. They caught in her throat, choked her into silence.

"I wanted to, Celina," Madeline said. "Many, many times. But I couldn't."

Celina balled her fists tighter, digging deeper into her palms.

"Couldn't," she said, "or wouldn't?"

Madeline smiled that kind smile again.

Celina didn't want her kindness. She wanted Madeline to be a bitch. An evil woman. A heartless devil who abandoned her only child and denied her existence to the world.

Sometimes wolves came in sheep's clothing. Celina wanted to kill the wolf.

"The answer is yes," Madeline said.

"The answer to what?" said Celina through gritted teeth.

"To your question. The question you came all this way to ask."

"I didn't come here to ask a question."

"Yes," said Madeline, nodding slowly, sadly, "you did."

Celina opened her mouth with another retort, then closed it and swallowed hard, her mouth suddenly dry.

The question Madeline had brought up over tea. Did she regret her decision. Did she ever love Celina at all.

Celina did want to know that answer. Madeline was right. And Celina hated her all the more for it.

"And the answer," Madeline said, "has always been yes."

She walked around the counter behind Paulie and Cam. Celina wanted to push her away, to hit her, maybe, or run away from her.

But she didn't. She stood there and watched as her mother put her hands on her shoulders.

Madeline was short, at least two inches shorter than Celina. Had she been this short when Celina had visited her house? She'd seemed taller then.

"I might not have been a mother to you," she said, "but you've always been a daughter to me."

They were words Celina had spent her whole life wishing she could hear. They made a part of her melt and shake with relief.

But they made another part of her furious. Words were cheap, especially from a politician.

"That's not what you've said on television," she said. She pushed one of the speaker's hands off her shoulder.

Madeline looked stricken, then pulled back her other hand and bowed her head for a moment. When she lifted it again, she'd regained her speakerly poise.

"I left you and your father because I knew I could make a difference. In the world. I knew that I was hurting you, but I had a choice. I could stay with you and Perry and make one little girl's life better, or I could leave you both and improve the lives of millions of women." She shrugged. "It wasn't an easy choice, Celina, but it was a simple one. I knew your father would raise you well. And I was right."

"You abandoned me," Celina said, her voice loud and clear and strong for the first time since the speaker had walked in. "That was bad enough. But then you denied my existence, over and over and over."

Madeline's face hardened. "I still believe in the choice I made. It was a sacrifice for the greater good."

"I was the sacrifice," Celina said. "There was nothing good about it."

She turned away and let out a deep breath. When she turned back, arms folded across her chest, her voice was firm but calm.

"We'll be out of here by this evening," she said, staring coolly at the speaker. "You won't see us again."

Madeline regarded Celina for a long moment, then took a deep breath and nodded slowly. She glanced around at Cam, Paulie, and Simon, who had been waiting quietly, trying to be invisible, then walked back to collect her purse and her keys.

"Oh," she said, reaching into her purse. "I believe this belongs to you."

She set Celina's glasses on the counter. They were broken on the side where the bullet had struck.

"Who were those men?" asked Cam.

The speaker looked at him and tilted her head to one side. Celina recognized herself in the movement and burned inside.

The speaker appraised Cam for a moment, then gave him a wan smile.

"Israeli Sayeret," she said. "Ex-Sayeret. We don't know yet why they were there." She glanced at Celina. "Or who they were after." She looked back at Cam. "But we know one thing. They weren't the ones in charge."

She slid her purse into the crook of her elbow and walked away. She stopped in front of the door.

"You know where to find me, Celina," she said. "I hope we speak again soon."

She opened the door, but stopped before leaving. Cars drove and honked on the street outside.

"And next time you want something from me," she nodded toward the statue on the counter, "all you have to do is ask."

Celina wished she could rush over and slam the door, but the speaker closed it with only a soft click.

46

Paulie observed Celina carefully in the moments after her mother left. Cam stood from his stool, wincing with pain, and went to her.

Celina was frozen in place. Her face was pale, her hands balled into fists, pressed white with strain. Paulie didn't know which way she would go. Would she open up and let all her pain come out, or would she retreat behind that iron will of hers again?

Cam approached her slowly, pulled Celina's eyes to his, and waited for her to decide which way she needed to go. Paulie knew her son was a good man, but in that moment, she knew that he had become a great one.

He'd earned Celina's trust.

Celina buried her face in Cam's chest and stayed there for a long time, her quiet, shaking sobs the only sounds in the kitchen. Cam held her, rubbed her back and kissed the top of her head and let her pour out all that hurt she'd been carrying for so long.

Paulie met Simon's eyes, then stood and went to him, nestling herself under his arm. Simon kissed her head. She tilted her face to him, and Simon bent to kiss her on the lips.

When Paulie looked back, Cam was watching them. He frowned for a moment, then turned his attention back to Celina.

Paulie had to talk to him. She thought he must already know about her and Simon, or at least a part of him did. But he didn't seem to have accepted it yet. She needed to help him do that.

Later.

For now, he needed to focus on Celina.

Madeline Kinkaid was a real piece of work. She clearly loved her daughter, but she had this crazy sense of self-importance that made her actually believe that it was somehow noble for her to turn her back on her own family so she could advance her political agenda. Maybe it took that kind of crazy for someone to become a politician these days. Maybe it took someone that self-centered, someone who believed that much that their way of thinking was the only right way of thinking.

For Paulie, it was just plain crazy. You never turn your back on your family. Not your real family, the people that love and support you, blood-relatives or not. Paulie had never been close with her parents, not like she was with Cam. But still, they never turned their backs on her, even when they didn't approve of her criminal lifestyle. And she had never turned her back on them.

After a little while, Celina brushed back her tears, sniffling and swearing and apologizing for being such a boob. They reassured her that it was okay, that it didn't make her weak or foolish. By the time they ate lunch and packed, it was late afternoon. They headed for the airport.

When they all got out of the car on the tarmac, the sun had slipped below the horizon. The sky was a palette of dusky blues and oranges behind the bright white lights of the airport. Cam grabbed some bags and headed toward the stairs for Celina's jet.

The others stayed behind. Cam stopped, confused, and came back toward them. Paulie could see his steps growing slower as he approached and realization overtook him.

Celina gave Simon and Paulie long, warm hugs and kisses and said her goodbyes, then put a hand on Cam's shoulder for a moment before walking off to wait for him at the bottom of the stairs.

Paulie went to him, Simon trailing a few steps behind. She stood an arm's length away, looked him over, and sighed. He was a good-looking boy, a wonderful boy. A wonderful man.

"I'm so proud of you," she said.

Cam frowned, but not in confusion this time. He knew, and Paulie could see that he had finally admitted it to himself. His was the kind of frown that comes when you know something is true, but wish it wasn't. He glanced at Simon, then back to Paulie.

"How long will you be gone?" he asked.

Paulie looked back at Simon, who stepped up to join them. She took his hand.

"I don't know, love," she said. "Simon is going to show me some of his favorite places in the world. Paris, Morocco, Venice."

"There's a chaiwala in Mumbai that I haven't spoken to in years," said Simon. "He makes wonderful chai."

"You'd go all the way to India for a cup of tea?" asked Cam.

"It's very good tea," replied Simon with a grin.

Cam stared at him, blank-faced, for a moment, then glanced back at Paulie.

This was the moment. This was the moment when he would decide how he wanted to feel about this change. He'd spent fifteen years without her while she was in prison. He'd only had her back for a few months, and now she was leaving again. She wouldn't blame him for being hurt or angry.

And if he demanded it, she would stay. You never turn your back on your family.

Cam put his head back and laughed.

Paulie let go of the breath she'd been holding and squeezed Simon's hand tight. She smiled so wide she didn't think it would ever come off her face.

Cam shook Simon's hand, then Simon pulled him in for a hug. Cam grunted at the squeeze on his broken ribs, but laughed. He looked at Simon for a long moment, one of those man things where they're saying things with their eyes like *you take good care of my mother* or *if you hurt her, I'll hunt you down* or that kind of masculine bullshit.

But it was tender bullshit. Paulie knew Simon cared for Cam, and she could see now that Cam cared for Simon, too.

And then he turned to Paulie.

"Let me know what you two are up to," Paulie said, nodding toward Celina in the distance.

"Every week," Cam replied.

"I want to hear all about your exploits."

Cam laughed and glanced at Simon. "I want to hear about yours. I think they might be more interesting."

Paulie put her hands on Cam's shoulders. So big. So strong. He'd only been eighteen years old when she'd gone to jail. A strapping youngster. Now he was a full-grown man. Her chest pinched at the thought of leaving him again.

He seemed to see it in her eyes.

"It's okay, mom," he said. "Go live your life. Make up for the time you lost."

Paulie's smile was shaky. She nodded.

"Be good to each other," she said, glancing again at Celina.

"We will," said Cam. "I promise."

Paulie looked into his eyes, those deep, clear brown eyes. His father's eyes. She stood on her tiptoes and pulled him in for a fierce hug.

"I love you, son," she whispered.

"I love you, too, Mom."

She and Simon watched and waved as Cam and Celina boarded the plane. They watched and waved as the plane taxied to the runway. They didn't leave until the plane was a memory of a distant speck in the evening sky.

"And now, my dear," said Simon, wrapping his arms around Paulie, "let us begin our great adventure together."

He bent and kissed Paulie, long and deep.

Paulie had had one great love in her life, her husband, Sam. He'd given her another, her son, Cam.

And now she might have found a third in Simon.

How could one woman be so lucky?

Paulie Hauk didn't know. But if she'd learned anything in prison, it was this: be grateful for what good life brings.

And enjoy it while you can.

47

CAM SAT on a lounge chair on the deck, bundled in a warm blanket and a thick sweatshirt with the hood pulled up, watching the blue-grey waves curl and crash and shatter, wash in pieces onto the brown sand, then pull back in a web of foamy white to form and crash and shatter again.

The sky was blue, a hard, monotonic blue, but the air was cold enough to numb the end of Cam's nose. The weather never got cold enough to snow in San Francisco. This was the worst it ever got.

And Cam liked it. He liked to be bundled up and feel the salty wind sting his cheeks, hear the ice-cold waves crash and swirl, see the blue of the sky shift from shade to shade as the lazy days wound by.

So far, Celina was tolerating his lassitude. His ribs had finally healed, his bruises faded to a pale yellow now, barely visible unless you knew what to look for. She occupied herself with projects around the house, shifting furniture, rearranging artwork, cataloguing her books. Cam knew it was hard for her to be so sedentary for so long.

She spent a lot of time in the gun range she'd built in the basement a few years back. It was completely soundproofed, but Cam would sometimes sit in the observation room and watch her, the sound of her shots a soft popping through the thick, bulletproof glass.

He'd even let her give him a couple of lessons. He was surprised to find that he didn't hate it, shooting. It was loud and scary. He was always worried about shooting off his own finger or a backfire on the gun that would blow his head off or, worse, injure Celina. But she laughed and told him he was an idiot and showed him, again and again, the proper way to handle a gun safely, the way to maintain a gun so it functioned properly every time. Once he got used to it, he started to enjoy the challenge of hitting the targets, so long as they were made of paper or clay and not living flesh.

He still thought about the man he'd killed. He saw the man's eyes staring at him at night, in the dark, while he lay next to Celina's warm, sleeping body. He heard the drip of the man's blood as it fell from the wooden step to the pool on the floor below.

It was an accidental death. Cam knew that. And he had acted in self-defense. He knew that, too. The man would have killed him or Celina or both if Cam hadn't killed him first. No jury in the world would convict Cam for what he'd done.

And no jury would have to. No law enforcement personnel had ever contacted him. Celina learned that her mother had swept the whole affair under the bureaucratic rug, made it disappear, officially.

But it wouldn't disappear for Cam. Not yet.

He'd killed a man. Justified or not, he'd ended a man's life. Cam would carry the weight of that life with him for the rest of his.

He heard the glass door of the deck slide open behind him. Celina appeared beside him with two steaming mugs in her hands.

They'd spent Thanksgiving alone, just the two of them, but

Cam hadn't felt lonely, aside from missing his mother. He had a file full of postcards his mother had sent from all the places she and Simon had visited so far. Tangier, Casablanca, Marrakesh, Cairo, Alexandria, Jerusalem, Amman, Dubai. Her last was a photo of Simon with an arm around his chaiwala in Mumbai.

"You look cold," said Celina. "Thought you could use some warming up."

She handed him one of the mugs, then set hers on the deck and snuggled in beside him on the lounge chair, wrapping one leg over his, pressing her body against his side, and nuzzling her face against his neck.

"I brought some hot cocoa, too," she whispered, then flicked his earlobe with her tongue.

Cam's body responded instantly.

He smiled. Would he ever stop wanting this woman? Needing her?

He hoped not.

They both set down their mugs and turned into each other's arms.

There was more than one way to stay warm in winter.

48

Celina was going nuts with the waiting. She'd cleaned and rearranged and torn down and rebuilt everything she could find in the house, waiting for Cam to heal, giving him time to rest and recuperate.

She would do anything for him. If he told her he never wanted to set foot outside the house again, Celina would seal the doors and arrange for drone deliveries on the roof.

But she hoped he wouldn't say that. She was not a homebody. She needed to be active.

Of course, there was one activity inside the home that she could never get enough of. Not with Cam. And they'd done a lot of that in the six weeks since they'd come home from D.C.

But it had been six weeks. Thanksgiving had come and gone. Christmas was two weeks away. They'd been sedentary for a long time, and Celina was getting antsy.

But she didn't say a word to Cam. If it came to it, she would, but he was still healing. So Celina worked on her marksmanship in the gun range and focused on little jobs around the house. Tête held pride of place in her art gallery now. She'd built a new installation and set it on a pedestal under a spotlight against one wall. She looked at it every day and thought of her father.

And her mother.

She still couldn't figure out why her father would have stayed in such close contact with Madeline all those years. She knew he still loved her, but how could he stay in touch with her after what she'd done to them? Were they lovers? Even after she married the senator, did they sleep together? Did they sneak around, use false names for their rendezvous? Or were they just friends? That might be even stranger for Celina.

It was a puzzle she just could not piece together. She wished her father were still alive to explain it to her. And she refused to call her mother for answers. Madeline texted every week. Celina deleted every one, deleted the number from her phone every time. Madeline still never spoke in public of having a daughter, but that story had been told so many times that the reporters had mostly stopped asking about it.

Someday she'd run for president. Celina was fairly sure about that. She would be worried that the truth would come out and ruin her political chances. Madeline Kinkaid was not the type to overlook a risk that obvious. But she also wasn't the type to leave it to chance. She would have a plan in place to deal with that situation already. Celina wondered if that plan involved her.

Probably. Fucking politicians.

Celina stood at her stove and stirred the chocolate melting in the double boiler, then checked the milk steaming in the pot beside it. Cam was out on the deck, where he spent most of his time lately. Celina figured she'd bring him a hot drink and a hot piece of ass and get him moving again. She savored the thought as she stirred.

She set the spoon down and flipped open the laptop on the counter beside her. She couldn't believe that the tracking on Cam's stolen glasses was still active, couldn't believe the fucking idiots who'd stolen them hadn't been able to figure out how to disable it yet.

But, as usual, their stupidity was Celina's advantage. And she'd already learned who was behind their theft, and probably behind the Israeli attackers, too.

Attorney General William Jenkins.

He was an old protégé of Celina's father, current front-runner for the presidency, and already the presumed winner, even though the election was still eleven months away.

In the tracking program on her phone and her laptop, Celina had watched the glasses bounce around D.C. for a few days until they settled in a location that was very familiar to her, the Office of the Attorney General in the Department of Justice building in downtown Washington. Celina and Cam had spent quite a bit of time there earlier that year. Celina still had her backdoor into their security system. She opened the camera feeds and saw the glasses on Jenkins' desk. He had been dumb enough—or arrogant enough—to let them stay there for far too long.

But since that morning, they had been on the move again, headed out of the city. They must have been on a plane, because they arrived in New York far too quickly for any other mode of transport. Now, the tracking dot on Celina's laptop screen was moving at a normal automotive pace, first through the city, then into the suburbs, and now into the outlying towns. She zoomed in as it turned off the main road, watched the dot wind through the countryside into a very wealthy part of southeastern New York.

She knew where it was going.

Of course it was. She should have thought of it before.

Christopher Nestrom and Perry Maxwell, Celina's father, had been close friends. Both eccentric tech geniuses. Both billionaires. Both disillusioned with the state of the world.

And both had died suddenly. Perry's death had been ruled

a heart attack, but Celina knew the truth. He'd been murdered in a hit ordered by Jenkins' campaign finance chairperson, Vernon Stratham. Nestrom's death had also been ruled to be of natural causes. A massive seizure. Had Nestrom's death been foul play? Was Jenkins involved in that death, too, somehow?

Celina didn't know, but she knew Cam's glasses were on their way to Nestrom's home, now owned by his daughter, Kat. As luck would have it, Kat was a friend of Celina's. Well, an acquaintance, at least.

Celina snapped the laptop shut, checked the double boiler, and poured the melted chocolate into the steaming milk and whisked them together.

She'd give Kat a call soon. Time for two old friends to catch up. It was the holiday season, after all.

But that could wait. For now, she had more important things to think about. More important people to check in on.

She poured the steaming cocoa into two large mugs and carried them toward the deck. She was going crazy with the waiting, but when she did things like this, bringing cocoa to Cam on the deck or sitting on the couch in front of the fire with him or coming downstairs in the morning to find him making breakfast, she could see the appeal of a quiet life at home.

And as she snugged her body up against Cam's on the lounge chair on the deck, felt him firm against the leg she'd thrown over his waist, nuzzled his neck, pulled in a long, warm breath redolent with his intoxicating scent, and felt her own body grow hot in response, she could see the appeal even more.

Oh, yes, she thought as she slid up to straddle Cam's waist. She could definitely see the appeal.

Celina could tell that this was going to be a very fucking merry Christmas.

ACKNOWLEDGMENTS

As always, my love and thanks to Holly. Without your support, my love, none of this would be possible.

ABOUT THE AUTHOR

Kevin Robert Aldrich lives in California and is the author of several mystery and romance novels:

If you love a twisting, pulse-pounding mystery, you'll love the Cameron Hauk series: Eyes in the Dark, Key Witness, Scale of Justice, and Tête A Tête.

If you love heart-pounding romantic suspense, you'll love Bare Trap and Flames of Freedom.

If you like vampires, witches, and forbidden love, get a copy of Spellbound now.

And if you love powerful contemporary romance, try Racing Hearts and Ollie & Alli today.

NEWSLETTER SIGN-UP

To learn more about Kevin Robert Aldrich and stay up-to-date with all of his stories and novels, please visit his website:

www.kevinrobertaldrich.com

To be automatically notified of every new release, sign up for the Kevin Robert Aldrich newsletter at the website above.